The Gilgamesh Well

Cover artwork by Nycolas Pedro

Copyright © 2023 Connor Maples
All rights reserved

Prologue

[Entry 1: 2/6/2038]

    This morning, a great calamity befell the world. We cannot begin to explain the cause of this devastation. I'll spare the emotions for later once the damage has been fully assessed.

    At approximately 7:15am, golden spouts of cataclysmic matter erupted from the Earth on the central Atlantic coast of the United States. This light, for lack of a better word, forged a perfect circle six hundred miles in diameter, catching eight million unaware souls in its blast.

    It is unknown what the fallout will be. This is now the single most significant breach of national security in the country's history.

    We shall watch what unfolds with anxious eyes.

[Entry 2: 2/11/2038]

    I have volunteered to lead a select research unit to study the light. Initial expeditions have proven ineffective. Those who reached inside have remained unharmed, though unable to see through its radiance. We have no measurements of depth. Probes cannot detect solid ground within the charted circumference.

    Despite these foundational failures, we have uncovered one promising revelation. The first anomalous property of this light has been observed. While measuring energy output, voltmeters projected power beyond the instrumental parameters. We may be able to harness it.

    The investigation will continue.

[Entry 3: 2/15/2038]

    I devoted my life to science and learned under the greatest minds, yet what has been discovered in these recent days dwarfs the combined work of all human efforts. The Well, as we now call it, is the single greatest happening in the natural world. Put frankly, this can only be the power of God. But... I'm getting ahead of myself.

    A second miraculous property was observed today. While testing The Well's effects on matter, we exposed a chunk of slate to the light. When we retracted the sample, its entire chemical composition changed to that of pure gold. What we now possess will disrupt the entire economic structure of the world.

    This is a power that must be controlled at all costs.

[Entry 4: 2/26/2038]

    Our experiments have progressed tirelessly. A third miracle has been documented. In a flippant gesture of curiosity, a colleague's assistant decided to expose her hand to The Well's light after cutting it. When retrieved, the injury was healed. The skin was also noticeably smoother. We will run a genetic study of the affected area.

    I do not have the words to describe this marvel. The Well is the future of humanity. Theoretically, it could be the key to immortality. So why then, did the people die?

    I will solve this mystery.

[Entry 5: 3/13/2038]

    Pure excitement has caused me to neglect my journal. The discoveries have proceeded exponentially. We are already harnessing The Well's light on a massive scale, able to transport energy through standard conductors with no limitations, no interference, and across great distances. If I cannot deduce an explanation, I fear it may never be fully understood.

    The others have accepted the futility of researching The Well's origins. Mutually, we agreed to look toward the future. I believe this is the best course of action. I only hope this newfound power does not bring more tragedy in its wake.

[Entry 6: 3/16/2038]

    Everything has changed. We are no longer researchers, but pioneers of an uncertain future. A governing authority has been formed to maintain the new civilization that is being built along The Well's border. They call it the Guiding City. Due to the miraculous nature of the light, technology is advancing rapidly.

    Today, we received notices recommending we resign. We still have a choice, but our future will be determined by this authoritative force. They signed our letters with the name Aureate. That must be what they're branding themselves. Gilding their own names, putting themselves on a similar pedestal as The Well. I find it abhorrent.

[Entry 7: 3/20/2038]

    The situation in the Guiding City has turned volatile. According to whispers among the scientists, the light has been detected in the strangest place *imaginable. Babies. Every child born in the immediate area bears a bioluminescent mark on their head. We speculate a joint communion between the children and The Well as they appear to be drawn to it. Yes, this attributes a form of sentience to The Well, however, we cannot rule out any possibility.*

A horrid measure has taken place to collect these children. The Aureate has elected numerous task forces to seek them out and bring them to newly constructed housing within the Guiding City. The children are being stolen from their parents.

My wife, Maria, is in her final months of pregnancy. I fear my child will bear the mark. If this is science, I will have no part.

[Entry 8: 4/30/2038]

These marked children are called Clerics, and my child is one of them.

Research has determined that these children are born of pregnant women who were in view of the light during the initial blast. After nine months, there will never be more like them.

I was prepared for this possibility and have taken measures to get my family out of the Guiding City. We will flee to the southern slums, in the ruins of Old Baltimore. It will not be a pleasant life. The world's economy has its eyes on The Well and pilgrims from all stretches of the globe are flocking to the Guiding City. This has created anarchy outside the walls.

I write this with a somber heart. The Guiding City is every bit a haven for the future as I imagined it would be. Everything is gold. It is quickly becoming a jungle of prismatic structures, offering a simple life to its inhabitants, but I have chosen my family instead.

This is my final entry, but my journey to understand The Well is only beginning.

Chapter 1
Arrival
[1/15/2059]

"Don't test me! *I* decide how things work around here, not you!"

Kale was thrown across the damp room, skidding into muddied ground. The boss' two giant bodyguards grunted and dusted off their knuckles.

"Listen to me! You don't understand. It's the opportunity of a lifetime!" Kale pleaded, his bloodied face was bright and his eyes glowed as he smiled at the thought of boundless gold beyond the walls. He extended his hands out beside him and his umber jacket fell apart. "Think about it! We can finally crawl out of this hole and break into the city. Look!" He held up a reflective rectangle. Gilded trim lined its edges, reflecting the color of his skin in the low light. The occupants of the room recoiled at the sight of the access card. "I nicked it off a guard outside a brothel, a one-way ticket inside. If we can just slip in and find a way into the armory-"

A massive fist stifled Kale's words and his nose met dirt once again. His vision became cloudy and black bangs covered his eyes.

"You must think I'm stupid... Those access cards have trackers! Once that ignorant guard realizes it's gone, he'll send an army!" The boss rose from his makeshift throne, a chair of rusted steel and tangled copper. The light of the flickering bulb bounced along his shaved head like a third eye. He stomped over to the tattered boy lying face down in front of him and knelt. "Did you forget about the sentinels? They can flatten our station in one step! Now, since you acted without orders, you've given them a reason to do it! This is the last time I'll deal with you, Kale."

A hand grabbed his hair and turned his face upward to view the superior.

The boss stood and turned a gaze over his shoulder at the pitiful boy beneath him. "Don't think for a second that because you're my son I'll show you any pity. Get out, chuck that access card in a sewer somewhere, and never step foot in my cove again."

Kale whispered as he pulled himself from the earth. Blood ran from his nose and he coughed. "I can do it. I can get into the city and steal their technology. They can't keep everything to themselves. I'll make The Vultures rich!"

"No," the boss growled, "no more chances."

A fat hand rose from his father and the two henchmen stepped forward. Each of them stole an arm as Kale kicked and struggled.

With a hearty swing, Kale was flung into the murky street of bustling immigrants. Angry voices flooded his ears as he struggled to find his equilibrium. He turned back at the entrance to his gang's hideout; an old noodle shop flickered a neon red sign of ancient oriental lettering that he couldn't read. The stench of iron littered his nose and he cursed at the frigid wind.

All his life he'd been a useful member of The Vultures, a syndicate of tricksters that capitalized on the confusion of the many melding cultures. Under the extraordinary leadership of his father, they and their numerous companions swindled ill-fated foreigners into buying stolen scrap at a much higher price than Pre-Waking transactions. It was heavily illegal, he knew, and morally wrong, but since The Well's opening, officers rarely wore their badges.

He rose to his feet and brushed the dirt from his jeans.

Everything's gone... I'm homeless...

Such was the way of the wicked world outside the Guiding City. The unfortunate pilgrims could only fight against nature and one another with the fleeting dream of one day obtaining an access voucher.

There was rain in the slums that day, and when it rained the mud would run. He could feel sludge sloshing in his boots and it chilled his toes. Kale hated the feeling but was all too familiar with its discomfort. In the twenty years since The Well's opening, the slums had only grown more grotesque. Between the vomit in the streets, the stench of the packed populace, and walls of litter lined along buildings, it was a wonder anyone could survive more than a few days. But he was accustomed to the mire. It was his home and though he knew of the old world, the times of plenty and granted abundance long gone, Kale was genetically predisposed to adaptation.

A sea fog had begun to roll in from the east and he ruffled his hair into shape. The long black bangs blocked his vision if unattended. Calluses ran deep through his hands, tattered by years of hauling heavy scrap metals. Kale's face was strong, battered by conflict, but he still felt inadequate and untested by the world, especially after losing the boss's favor. He ran his finger along a scar that passed through his right eyebrow, a reminder of how swiftly a dishonest deal can go south. The art of deals, in a time of individual survival among the pilgrims, typically took the form of lies and when The Vultures made a deal, their sheer numbers guaranteed success… most of the time.

A strong shoulder struck him from behind and he buckled over. Strings of curses in Spanish followed and he looked to see a perturbed man flipping him off. Beneath the ruins of the slums, he would never find lodging, not for free at least.

Why would he kick me out? All I've done is work to help him… But… What now? Am I supposed to just wander around? I'll end up getting mugged and killed or freeze to death in this rain… I have to go see her. She'll tell me what to do.

There was an ally, someone he could still count on. High above The Vulture's cove in the steeple of an old world mosque, was the nest of their matriarch.

While the boss held power over the action of their gang, wisdom resided with the Den Mother. Kale would be granted an audience, he was sure of it. She'd always found a fascination in him, though he wasn't entirely sure why.

The trek to the Den Mother was not a difficult one; Kale knew the route by heart. Three blocks beyond the main cove was a ruined park where the city's tallest church fell into itself. High and terrible architecture blocked out the fragments of the sky where the sun managed to peek through. The ruined brick structures twisted and poked like malevolent thorns all around. Without organization, none had ever bothered to clear the rubble, however, it proved to be an adequate border for the old woman's residence. For many years, he'd snuck to her warm embrace, but anyone unfamiliar with her wisdom would've mistaken her for a mythic witch.

Kale knew better.

Out of the hundreds of lackeys making up the flock, none could slither through shadows quite like Kale. It was his singular pride, the ability to disappear into obscurity. Even while desperately avoiding the gaze of other peons around the area, he cursed as he slipped in and out of dank streets. He bit his tongue when the innate reaction to call to his comrades was felt in his throat.

Only a remnant of the church still stood. Before The Waking, it was an impressive feat of construction. Golden domes capped ornamental stones, perfectly rounded and staggered into winding towers, however now, a single rise remained. The Vultures weren't religious by any means, but such a fortress could not be overlooked when the world fell to chaos.

The room was dark, hanging a mist that wrapped around his ankles. There were cracks in the robust ceiling, filtering in the outside humidity and allowing emerald rays of light to trickle down. When The Waking destroyed common civilization, most people rationally clung to necessities such as food and water, but the Den Mother found a particular fondness in tapestries that she'd stolen from the local art museum. Decorative vistas sewn into rugs hung along the walls. Old tales of heroes past, and portraits of beautiful women stared him down as he entered her room. The door was opened, almost as if she expected a visitor and when Kale took the final step, a strained voice spoke slowly. "Ah, it's been quite some time since you came to see me."

Hawkish, azure eyes pierced him as he leaned carefully forward, brandishing an awkward smile at her introduction. Her hair was finely braided, white as snow, around her neck and feeble arms clutched a dark blanket that covered her knees.

"Sorry to intrude," Kale meagerly conjured through a dry throat, "I wanted to talk to you."

"What did you do?" She snapped back at him. Kale's follies were no mystery among the gang. Being the son of the boss meant he couldn't keep secrets.

His smile faded when he reached her. The black mud on his face cracked with a frown. "I messed up. They kicked me out."

The Den Mother spread her hands apart. "Come."

As was customary when imparting secrets, he knelt before her and placed his head on her lap. It was warm. The spindly hands of the crone coiled around him, comforting the darkest disappointments.

"I… I don't know what to do."

"So," The age-dried lips wheezed forth the words, "the old man finally snapped."

"I guess…"

"And what did you do this time?"

"Nothing…" He paused. "I stole a guard's access card. I thought he'd be proud. I know he said guards are off-limits, but It was too much of an opportunity! We could use it to get in."

"That's dangerous, Kale. You're playing with fire."

"I know, but…"

"That arrogance always got you in trouble."

"I get it. I know. I'm just trying to get him to recognize me. He hasn't given me a new rank in years."

"The Guiding City is a fire that burns everything. If you get too close to that flame, it'll devour you."

Kale didn't respond.

A hand stroked his hair. "Leave it behind."

He stared upwards at her. "What do you mean?"

"Oh, Kale. You were never cut out for this business. It's far too brash for someone with your curiosity."

"B-But they're my family. What else am I supposed to do?"

She sighed at him, releasing the disconsolate youth from her embrace. "You'll figure it out. You've got your wings. A bird has to leave its nest eventually. Heaven knows your chance of survival isn't any better here."

Perhaps, in the back of his mind, he figured she could wave her hand and make everything okay. Reality, however, was inescapable.

Her eyes crawled to his, causing the outer world to grow colorless. "You know the rules, Kale. Either you escape now or they'll kill you. That's all I can tell you." Her hands left him, cloaked her body in the blanket, and slowly, she fell back into a rested posture.

He couldn't speak.

"The rules are absolute."

"But…"

Before Kale could muster another excuse, the woman reached forward with quickened swiftness, snatching his wrist. Her fingers bore a chill so deep it was as if their skin froze together. She pulled him in, inches from her. Her eyes were so immensely deep.

"So without another word, go. Please… Don't let me see you here again."

He stared desperately at her face, afraid of the ultimatum he'd been presented with. "I… I'll miss you."

The Den Mother smiled. "And I you."

Pale-faced and confused, he exited the room, casting a parting glance back.

For several hours, the beaten thug strode aimlessly down sidewalks and explored shadowy alleys of the slums. Nameless faces in similar squalor stared back from the corners. Homelessness was rampant and he was no stranger to its toils, though indirectly.

As he walked beneath dilapidated concrete structures, past Baltimore's old Museum of Art which had become a deprived hive for squatters, hands hung from windows nearby yelling threats and begging for money. Even though he attempted to tune out the raspy calls, a terrible sound pierced his ears. He heard a cry. It was high and vulnerable; a child's.

Kale looked down between the darkness of his hair to see a young girl sobbing beneath an awning of an empty shop. She wore a dirt-stained dress and buried her face in her hands. Her golden hair was matted and soaked from the rain. Azure shoes stuck out in front and though everything about her was dirty, the shoes remained polished and reflective.

Kale raised his hands atop his head and frowned. "You alright?"

What a stupid question. Of course she's not...

The girl sniffled and looked up at him. Her eyes were bright green and full of longing. Her face, soft and pure, glowed red from intense crying. After giving him a once-over, she quickly resumed the wailing.

Ouch. Guess I can't blame her for being afraid of a man covered in blood and dirt.

He knelt down beside her and his gray boots wrinkled. "Can you tell me what's wrong? My name's Kale, what's yours?"

The girl looked up once again, her gaze bore periorbital puffiness. "I'm lost... I don't know where my sister is..." Her head returned to her lap and she continued to sob.

Kale forced himself to smile at her and wiped away the blood from his nose. "Lost, huh? I'm lost too."

The words caught her attention slightly, though she barely managed to speak. "You're lost too?"

Kale nodded.

After catching her breath, the girl sniffed and found a semblance of composure. "I-I'm Phoebe. My sister... I need to find her."

Maybe whoever she belongs to can help me find a place to stay...

Kale did his best to appear less threatening, "Since we're both lost, would you like me to help you?"

A glimmer shone in her eyes beneath the anxious reservations. "You can help me?"

He kept his smile while she talked and offered her a hand. "Sure, Phoebe. Where does your sister live?"

"I don't know how to get there, but it's by the city wall. When I look out the window, I can see the Jötunn."

Kale's eyebrows furrowed, "Jötunn? What's that?"

Phoebe reluctantly took his hand and stood beside him, barely rising to his waist. "The big robots. The ones that guard the Guiding City." Her lip quivered, deep in worry.

The sentinels of the Guiding City, or the 'Jötunn' as the girl called them, were not something Kale thought pleasantly of. He'd seen firsthand the destruction they could cause. Fueled by the limitless energy of The Well, the technology that bound their form far outdated any Pre-Waking automatons. They stood as tall as buildings, ran with surgical precision, and could decimate whole cities with ease. Anyone that dared to provoke the wrath of the sentinels met a swift end. They were the reason the Guiding City could not be so lightly sieged. They were the reason The Vultures could never reach the height of their ambitions.

Once, the gang tried to sneak through a city gate, using mnewly developed software that could imitate staff identifications. Even through the cover of night, a sentinel spotted their trespass. Yellow-plated armor covered the infinite wires and pistons that allowed it such power. Its face stared at them with six lenses of eyes, whirring gears of teeth, and a golden helm resembling the legionaries of Rome. With a single swipe, it crushed the boss's two best agents, Marco and Adonis, reminding them that the peak performance of mankind stood useless against The Well's magic.

That's the last thing I want to see…

"Alright then, maybe if we find where you're from, it'll help me figure out where I'm going." He lightly grasped the outside of her hand which was cold and shaking.

The sentinels stood beside the main entrances of the Guiding City, two to each gate. Each city entrance was evenly placed exactly seven miles apart for the entirety of its border.

I doubt they left her that far… Should be an easy find if she can remember what the place looks like… I wonder how she got separated… Even so, should I help her? People might think I'm a kidnapper…

"Phoebe, what were you doing when you got lost?" Kale asked as they shifted through crowds of foreigners.

She held onto his arm tightly, "Sister and I were out to get supplies for Richmond."

"Is Richmond part of your family?" he asked curiously, offering her crinkled eyes.

"No", she coughed, "he's a scientist."

"A scientist... In the slums? What does he work on?"

"H-He..."

She was struggling to maintain composure, falling back into a saddened state.

"It's okay... Let's keep looking for your sister."

Scientist? I need to prod more... Do they have a place to stay?

He knelt down beside her. "I'll get you to your sister. Can you be tough until we get there?"

Between harsh sniffs and a recoil as he drew closer, she spoke, "Okay..."

Her posture withdrew, quickly shifting back and forth away from the passing vagrants. He placed a hand on her shoulder softly, reassuring his trust. It appeared to work, he thought.

"You said Richmond's a scientist?" He attempted to distract her mind.

Maybe I can get one question in before she cries again...

"H-He works on the golden star."

"Star?" The word piqued his interest.

"It's really bright."

A golden star? A scientist? It sounds like some technology... That means they have electricity... Maybe they're rich!

Kale did his best to pester her further, careful not to be overbearing. "Can you tell me more about the star?"

A pain became written on her face as she tried thinking about something other than her sister. "I... He says it's what lets us have power... Like a pretty golden light... B-But it's special..." Her breaths became fragmented, leading to another string of tears.

"Special?" His thoughts ran a mile a minute.

Is it a generator? Electricity? But it's golden? Could he have made a conductor for The Well's energy? If so, that's some risky business. If the city ever found out who knows what they'd do. One of those is worth a fortune... If I could get my hands on that... Maybe the boss would...

She stepped in mud and began to cry more, but he noticed that her bright blue shoes remained untarnished.

After several more minutes of walking, the sun had begun to set, casting orange rays through the thin fog.

The towering ruined buildings caused a feeling of unease to grow in Kale's spine when the sunlight began to dissipate. Something like a sixth sense triggered the hairs on his neck to stand on end. It wasn't the meandering crowd of potential thieves, that was normal, but still, a shiver caused his gaze to dart fiercely.

Something's off...

Many faces among the crowds around them began to turn upward. A sinister sound of bending metal pierced the air and he followed their eyes, about three stories to see a wall twisting towards the road. Dust filtered through the air down onto their shoulders. Everyone collectively knew it was about to fall.

"Hey! Look out!" He yelled and dashed forward, pulling Phoebe by the arm which prompted a sharp scream from the girl.

BOOM!

Several tons of brick exploded onto the busy street, and people began to run with screams in tow. The fallen wreckage had created a large plume of dust that rose to his shoulders.

All eyes began to converge on the area, but from the haze, something came forth.

A fist knocked Kale to the ground.

His hand let go of the girl.

With a sudden ripping pain in his cheek, he looked around frantically. "What the-" he couldn't fully see the attacker.

"Sorry to do this," a deep voice grunted as a foot pierced his side, "It's just orders."

A cough ripped from his lungs.

Another kick came from his right and he rolled to avoid it. He could hear Phoebe, scared and yelling nearby.

I need to protect her! I can't let my only chance get away!

When he looked back up he could see his opponents. Two cloaked men in ragged attire marched forward. Cloths were wrapped to conceal their faces and each wore a black jacket over leather.

Kale backed away, scanning his surroundings for an opportune weapon.

"Hey! Who are you?" His voice was loaded with panicked anger.

The men laughed in unison.

"Ya' don't need to worry about that," one growled.

A whimper came from behind him and he looked to see Phoebe cowering at an alley's edge.

I can grab her and run or stand and fight. But… These guys look tough…

To his left, an old drug shop's window was busted to shards and as the men closed in, his hands found a particularly jagged fragment of wicked glass. He wound the unimpressive tool between his fingers, hiding it from view. "Look, I'm broke! Whatever you want, I don't have it."

The men sneered and one rushed forward with a punch. Kale slipped beneath the strike and jabbed the glass upward, stabbing it deep into the attacker's side. The flesh and cloth broke apart and he sent his full weight into the object.

A sharp, pained scream erupted through the air and the other assailant recoiled in confusion.

"PHOEBE!" Kale yelled, turning on his heels, "We gotta run!"

His hands looped beneath her arms and he threw her over his shoulder. She cried out with the motion, but he didn't care. They simply had to escape.

For as long as his adrenaline could sustain, he ran towards the walls of the Guiding City, breaking through clumps of people along the sidewalks. A few times, his feet slipped on rainwater and he almost dropped the girl, but as they gained speed his balance became regulated. She was deathly afraid, he could tell by her silence.

After several minutes, he sat her down when they found the cover of another crowd of pilgrims.

"You okay?" He asked between staggered breaths. Bending over to her height.

"I-I…" Her bottom lip quivered and water began to build in her eyes. "I think so."

"I don't know who those guys were but they're gone now." His attempt to reassure her helped a little. Her hands shook in front of her uneasily. "We'll get you home soon, okay?"

She couldn't manage words but replied with a strong-willed nod.

Who were they? Do they know that I'm a Vulture? Do they think I'm a kidnapper? Or… were they after Phoebe?

Kale shuddered and ushered the little girl to walk again. Kidnapping was a rampant issue in the slums. The conflux of numerous languages made finding missing children nearly impossible and with no established law enforcement, there wasn't much hope.

As darkness loomed with the setting sun, Kale walked the girl to a nearby parking complex, at least the remnants of one. Concrete walls were collapsed around, but a roof overhead would provide shelter from the trickling rainfall.

"Let's go here. We can stay until the sun comes up, then we'll find your sister." He silently scoffed at the idea of spending the night out among the busy streets, especially near a gate where the mass of pilgrims congregated. "Listen, It's going to be cold tonight. I'll try to get a small fire, but here." He slipped his jacket off his shoulders and softly wrapped it around her.

The green eyes inspected the new article of warmth and her mouth opened to speak, "T-Thanks…"

He smiled in reply.

Darkness grew greater and deeper and he toiled around the expanse searching for various flammable items that might provide a modicum of warmth. An abandoned pallet lay in a far corner of the lot, but bits of dust and concrete powder covered its surface. It would work, but not ideally. Phoebe watched in a corner as he worked to form a reasonable pyre. He'd always carried a lighter, for various reasons, and held the flame beneath the tattered wood for several minutes before it ignited. Gas lighters were exceedingly rare, but The Vultures had collected a hearty supply after The Waking.

As the flame grew to a quaint illumination, Phoebe's eyes glazed over and her head began to bob as she nodded in and out of sleep.

"Go ahead and sleep," Kale reassured her, "I'll watch for us."

"Okay…" Her voice was labored. "Is that a fire?"

The question was odd. "You've never seen a fire?"

"He tells me about them. In books…" The words rolled like molasses as she began to fall asleep.

Kale furrowed his brow.

How would she not know what a fire is? It's the only way to survive out here… and we don't have any books…

He wondered why, even reluctantly, she agreed to go with a dirty and greasy gangster. Surely, if she'd been raised in the slums, she would've formed a deep caution about those who inhabited the streets.

Could she be a citizen of the city?

He stared at her for a moment. Her appearance didn't give off the air of a pompous elite but was also far too clean to be that of a pilgrim. Somehow she was ignorant of the world in the slums. He couldn't decipher the reason why. There were too many uncertainties. The answers would have to wait.
As the night crept on, Kale daydreamed about his father and comrades that he could no longer call family while warming his hands against the flame.

How could they abandon me? I didn't deserve to be kicked out! I'll make it up to them. I'll find my way into the city. If I accomplish that, he'll have no choice but to accept me back into the flock.

A determination brewed in his stomach and his jaw stuck out at the thought, keeping him awake to prod away any greedy hands of pilgrims seeking to steal their warmth.

When the sun rose the next morning, Kale gently nudged Phoebe awake to begin their trek. She didn't protest but sleepily muttered the name 'Astrid' until her recognition of the surroundings returned. "Did you find my sister?"
"Not yet." Bags had begun forming beneath his eyes. "We need to start walking. I'm sure your home isn't too far."
A spray of salty mist collapsed into the slums with the morning Atlantic tide rolling in. The air was chill, but warm sunbeams blessed their shoulders as they began to walk. Crowds had slightly grown as more and more people made their way towards the Guiding City and an hour of undisturbed journey allowed them to cover several miles.
"Come on," he whispered to her as her posture began to slouch in fatigue, "we're almost to the gate."
The giant walls of the Guiding City began to bob behind the ruined buildings in their view. Such massive amounts of gold made Kale drool in thought. He couldn't imagine what riches lay behind the impregnable borders. He drew in his jacket.
Phoebe interrupted the thoughts.

"There! Over there! That's where I live!" her golden hair bounced around and she let go of his hand, running through the crowd.

"Hang on! Don't go too far." He could barely see her between the shifting people wandering the street.

"It's over here, just around the corner!" She called him to the other side beneath a half-fallen building and he made his way over. He jogged across the street, meeting up with her. "We stay in an old hotel."

"A hotel?"

He didn't believe the words until he saw it.

Situated behind ruined structures and along a winding sidewalk was a construct that shouldn't have existed. The girl wasn't lying. It was an old-world hotel, practically untouched by the collapse. Kale admired the upkeep on the entrance. Four stories of ornate steel still preserved the magic of pre-Waking society. The roof curled over the many windows that each reflected the radiance of The Well. It was beautiful.

"Wow, it's a miracle you guys managed to find one. Most were snatched up by squatters immediately."

A tan awning where cars used to drive through presented itself like comforting hands, welcoming Phoebe as she ran to the door. He gulped to hide his mystified expression.

How did I not know about this place? We should've robbed it a long time ago! It's a wonder that people aren't clawing like zombies to get in here...

Her fingers tapped rapidly on a black keypad. The gesture was met with a ringing to which a man's voice called from a speaker at the bottom. "Yes? Who's there?"

"It's me! It's me! I found my way back!" Phoebe begged impatiently to be let in. "I brought someone too!"

"PHOEBE!!"

A voice called from behind. He turned around to see a woman standing at the street's edge. She looked like the spitting image of Phoebe but much older. On her head was perfectly brushed golden hair, emerald eyes, and enough makeup to cover a canvas. She wore a dusted black suit with a tie to match her eyes. Given the dilapidated nature of their surroundings, the hotel and the woman made Kale feel as though he'd interrupted a professional corporate meeting.

"Oh god, I've been looking all day!" She ran to the little girl's side, squeezing her deep into her chest.

Kale awkwardly stood beside them. He kicked away bits of dirt from his boots to make himself more presentable, hoping his bloodied face didn't scare away the potential hosts.

As the girl's tearfully cried at their reunion, Kale's movement caused the double doors in front of them to begin sliding apart with an eclectic hiss.

They really do have power!

He looked at the woman who'd suddenly appeared. Tears rained down her face. "Phoebe! I can't believe I let that happen! You're never getting out of my sight again!" Her voice was soft, but something about it felt commanding. Jumping slightly when she saw him standing next to them, she promptly straightened her posture and cleared her throat. "W-Who are you?"

Kale ran a hand through his matted hair and smiled. "I found her crying a ways back. I couldn't leave her out there. She asked me to help her find her sister."

She eyed him from head to toe and frowned. The sight of a muddied, bloody, and rough-spun thug couldn't have made an ideal first impression.

"Well," she said matter-of-factly, "Thank you." Immediately, her attention fell back to her sister.

I have to get in!

"I didn't know hotels like this were still around." He gave an expression of disbelief as his eyes followed the many floors.

The words appeared to annoy the woman, whose body language, obvious enough for anyone to read, told him to go away. "Surprisingly, we've been able to keep it standing."

A tinge of slight embarrassment traced his senses, "I'm a pilgrim. I could tell she didn't belong out there. It's been a rough day for her."

"It's been rough for all of us, but… well… Since you helped her, would you like to come in? I'm sure our host will want to thank you." She extended and retracted her hand in an ushering although he could tell the motion was extremely forced.

"Yes!" He jumped instinctively at the invitation but noticed the muck falling from his jacket. "But- I'm full of mud."

Irritation was written in her crooked brows. "That's okay. I'm sure he won't care too much."

I'm embarrassing myself.

As they walked into the hotel, Kale's eyes were graced by a crimson carpet under dimly lit fountain lights. The aesthetic reminded him of picturesque old casinos his mother had told him about. He felt guilty stepping on such a relic with his tarnished boots. A small front desk was to their left. It was topped with black and white granite and a gilded chandelier hung prominently in the center of the room. An ornate spiral staircase wound its way up to his right and Kale stopped questioning how such a place existed in the slums. "You must be Astrid. I'm Kale," he said, trying to break the tension in the air, "forgot to mention it."

"Yes," Astrid said, eyes darting down to his muddy boots, "did Phoebe tell you about me?"

"A little. She was scared that you'd be worried about her."

"She never thinks about herself, always concerned with others." Astrid ran a hand over her younger sister's head, to which Phoebe smiled.

"He protected me from the people out there," Phoebe said, looking up at her sister. "Maybe we should let him stay. He said he was lost too."

You're a saint, Phoebe!

A pause followed. The older girl let loose a quick protest but corrected her expression in hopes that he didn't hear. "Do you have somewhere you stay, Kale?" Astrid asked. She had a reluctant look and her green eyes wandered everywhere except to meet his gaze. She tugged at the bottom of her suit coat.

"About that... The place I was staying at just went under. Currently, I don't." He couldn't tell her the truth about being kicked out of a crime syndicate. His mouth curled up into a half smile. Everything was going too perfectly. "Phoebe told me you stay with a man named Richmond, is that your host?"

"Richmond?" Something clicked in Astrid's mind. "Right. He's probably messing around with some contraption. Phoebe, come with me, let's get you some clean clothes. Geez, I'm so glad you're safe..." Quickly, Astrid turned and jogged up the spiral staircase, pulling Phoebe by the hand. He scanned her as she walked away. On the surface, she looked perfectly put together, like an ideal working woman, but he could tell by her actions that something was off. Apart from her words, subtle signs communicated that she wanted anything but to speak to him. Her suit was tight to her body and she looked uncomfortable. He wondered why she wore it in the slums. Surely, such an appearance would make her an easy target for thieves. Even if the hotel was straight out of his fantasies, the world outside showed the true nature of their situation, a dogged misfortune.

Kale brushed dried mud off of his jacket. He wished he could've put on a better appearance for them, but all of his possessions were gone. The Vultures would never let him back in to collect his old clothes or memorabilia, of which he had little. They'd peck at all his scraps.

The thought about the golden star lingered. If this man, Richmond, really had gotten ahold of the Guiding City's technology, then it could be the key to The Vulture's success. He fumbled around in his pocket, feeling the access card he'd swiped, but the sound of nearing steps forced him to quickly wipe as much blood and dirt from his face as possible. Ruffling around with his hair, he stood straight as he saw shadows round the corner above.

At that moment a new voice broke his thoughts. "Hello, I'm told your name is Kale?"

He looked up to see the face of the most unrealistic man he'd ever had the pleasure of viewing. Richmond was a walking Greek sculpture. He was tall with an athletic frame, cloaked in a white lab coat that flowed over a suit similar to Astrid's, though his was the color of freshly bloomed marigolds. His face was perfectly angular and he looked to be in his forties, but pearly white hair fell around his head. If angels existed, this man was one of them. Such a powerful presence entered the air with his arrival.

Kale found it difficult to form a sentence. "Y-Yes, I helped Phoebe find her way home. You've got quite the place here!" He waved around in the lobby.

"Indeed, it's my family's heirloom, a marvel that it still stands, though. I was never interested in such a business... I wanted to extend my thanks to you. After Astrid told me Phoebe was lost, I didn't know what to do. With so many people in the slums, I thought-" he pulled Phoebe close, placing his hands on her shoulders. "Anyway, tell me about yourself, Kale." Richmond spoke in poetry, with a uniquely faint northern European accent, like every word carried a weight of higher knowledge too great to understand.

Lie... I have to lie...

"Me? I'm really a nobody. My parents and I were stranded after The Waking. We struggled our entire lives just bouncing around wherever we could find shelter. They both died of disease in my teenage years and since then, I've been a bit of a vagabond." Kale did his utmost to appeal to their generosity.

Richmond found a spot in front of him and leaned gracefully against the wall. He opened his eyes and pierced Kale with an interrogating gaze. The host's eyes were identical to his hair, pale and unnatural like the gates of Heaven. Kale felt as though he knew his deepest secrets at that moment.

"I see," Richmond replied in a sweet, yet powerful tone, "The life of a pilgrim is always a struggle, but you decided to help another. The least I can do is offer you a warm bed. Would you like to stay?"

The least?! People sleep in dirt out there and he's offering me a bed this quickly?

"I-," Kale turned his eyes down humbly, "I'd really like that."

"Well then, it would be our pleasure to welcome you. This place is *Le Lien*, I hope you find it hospitable. Come, let me show you to your room." Richmond rose from the wall and motioned for him to follow.

Phoebe jumped up and down in new red pajamas and ran up to him.

"I'm glad you get to stay!" She seemed like a new person in the company of her sister.

"I'm glad too," Kale said kindly.

As he and the host climbed the steps, his fingers ran along the cold steel railing which twisted in perfect craftsmanship.

Kale started, "When she told me you were staying in a hotel, I couldn't believe it. It'd be perfect for any pilgrim... Surprising that no one is trying to break in."

Richmond chuckled, "Funnily enough, I think the appearance deters them more than it attracts. A place like this so unmistakably infelicitous in the slums, makes them feel as though they don't belong. Of course, we do have the occasional visitor as any walled structure would, but we have our ways of deterring them."

He figured he shouldn't ask about the deterrents, but remembered a far more important question. "Phoebe told me you're a scientist. What do you do around here?"

The host laughed once more. "Did she now? Interesting. That mouth of hers... Yes, you could call me a scientist, though 'engineer' would suit my line of work more appropriately. My projects involve creating power sources. I want the slums to be the bustling city of Baltimore once again."

"I see. I noticed the electricity." Kale roused courage for the question that followed. "She said something about a star. Is that one of your projects?"

The press was met with a pause of silence.

"She mentioned that also… Very well. Kale, you're a pilgrim. I imagine you don't have much out there in the slums?" Richmond's cheerful expression became stern as he turned and furrowed his brows.

Maybe I should've kept my mouth shut...

Kale shuddered. "Correct. Why?"
"I'm a man of trades. I can't simply show you this technology for nothing in return."
"I guess I might have something I can offer…"

What's he talking about?

"Then, I'll show you my secrets, but it will not be without consequence. Do you wish to continue with your query?" The seraphic man crossed his arms and his lab coat fell around him like folded wings.
"Sure, but what would you want from me?"
Richmond squinted his eyes. "That… will be determined afterwards."

He really is terrifying. It's as if at any moment he'll snap… But I can't stop now. If it really is a receptacle for The Well's power, I have to steal it and bring it to The Vultures. They'd have no choice but to let me back in!

"It's a secret?" Kale jested in reply.
"It's really quite amazing." Richmond leaned in.
The premeditated thief donned a tone of concern. "But there's a consequence?"
"Let's not say consequence. A barter."
Kale snickered and closed his eyes to appear unphased, but his legs trembled. "I don't see why not. After all, I have nothing to go back to."
"Very well. Your room," Richmond pointed down a long hall they'd just stepped into. Vermillion carpet stretched to the end where a shining window peeked outside, "is the third door on the left. Don't forget it. Now, I'll show you my star. Follow." He turned to walk back from the direction which they'd come but placed a hand on Kale's dirty shoulder in passing. "You're interesting, Kale. You don't strike me as an average slum-dweller. The fact that you asked about my creations before even seeing your room, well… I'm flattered. I'd like to learn more about who you really are." His tone fluctuated in interrogation.
Kale couldn't respond but followed him down the spiral staircase.

"I keep my projects down below. Phoebe's prying eyes are difficult enough to manage, but since she and Astrid stay on the third floor, it's best if I occupy the basement." Richmond returned to the cheerful voice of greeting. "How old are you, Kale?"

He cleared a lump from his throat and found his voice, "Twenty-four. I'm old enough to remember The Waking. Thankfully, my family and I were outside the blast, but we could still see it. That golden light is burned in my memory."

"I see. Too old to be a cleric then?"

Kale had been told about the clerics but never had the experience of meeting one firsthand. Rare as they were, The Aureate snatched them up as soon as their abilities were discovered. "Yes. Have you ever met one?"

Richmond smiled, "One. It was long ago. It's interesting, don't you think, that they're not allowed to be among the populace? When I met her, she was as normal as any elementary girl. It's sad really, living with such a stigma, a product of the worst tragedy in mankind's history."

"Right..."

The two continued to a metal door that hid in the corner of the lobby. A keypad similar to the one on the entrance was next to a large handle. He tapped a code that Kale swiftly eyed before turning his gaze away. 5507.

"Memorized it already, have you?" Richmond inquired with a toothy smile.

Sweat fell down his back. "Honestly, I wasn't looking. It's none of my business."

A white eyebrow rose. "But my most prized secret is?"

Crap! I can't outsmart this man. He's on another level!

"Something Phoebe was so passionate about piqued my curiosity plenty. That's all it is. You chose to show me, after all." Kale placed his hands on his head and ruffled his dark curls.

"No, you chose to be shown."

"Is it too late to ask what those consequences are?" Kale hesitantly pleaded.

"Oh, nothing too terrible, I can assure you of that."

What am I getting myself into...

Richmond turned the handle with a creak and a shadowy staircase loomed before them. A golden aura slithered around the exit at the bottom.

24

"In here."

Each step down the staircase felt like he was trespassing on the holiest of grounds. A bloodied, filthy, ex-gang member didn't deserve to stand in Richmond's presence and now, by simply being, he was desecrating a perfect mind.

As they reached the bottom, he saw it. Sanctified in the center of a garden of wires, it blessed the room with golden light. The star resembled a crystal cylinder, bearing a core that shone brightly as God himself. Kale felt his sensorium scream. He shouldn't have been there. Possession of such an object warranted death from the Guiding City, yet there it was. He could immediately tell that his theories about the star were correct. It was a converter, a receptacle for The Well's infinite light, giving power to the hotel, and stealing from the city.

"I take it you can deduce what my star is?" Richmond asked as he ran a finger along its glass.

Kale frowned, dropping his facade. "It runs off The Well's light, doesn't it."

"Yes." A pride filled Richmond's words. "This is the key. This is how we can liberate the slums and restore balance."

"You do realize you'll be killed if anybody finds out. The sentinels will flatten this place."

"You sure know a lot for a slum-dweller."

Kale flinched, "I just like to learn a bit... That's all."

"I'm well aware of the situation, which is why that knowledge will never leave this building." His quarts eyes rose and penetrated Kale's view. "I will now tell you the consequences of viewing my work. You will become my servant. You will do as I say and be where I tell you at all times."

Servant? Servant for what?

The air grew frigid and Kale peeled his gaze. "And if I refuse?"

"You won't. You can't and you never will. Do not think for a moment I have not had eyes watching you from the second you entered *Le Lien*. Astrid, Phoebe, and others you've yet to meet are under my command. I protect them, offer them understanding, and fill their stomachs. It's a better life than anything you've had before as I can tell from your appearance and the fabricated story you told me."

Fabricated story? How could he know? Wait... The card! I forgot to throw it out! Does he work for the city? Can he track it?

25

Kale opened his mouth to protest but found himself unable to speak.

"Kale, my vision for this world is order. I now have the technology to bring about a great change, to inspire the people of the slums to action. A revolution will soon occur," he threw his hands aside and the golden light of the star illuminated his form. At that moment, he truly looked as pure as divinity. "Together, we will bring about the fall of the Guiding City and accelerate humanity on a global scale. I will become the exegete of salvation, first of creation, savior, and I will topple this world, O' vassal mine."

Chapter 2
Jötunn

It was the first time he'd been cleaned up since his childhood. The feeling of a hot shower cured any chagrins of inadequacy and grime. He felt the water stroke his skin like tender hands and a pained nostalgia filled his mind. Richmond had offered him a suit, black as night, but with a yellow tie. Kale groaned at it. While it wasn't his style by any means, he guessed he could appreciate the high-class feeling a little, a particularly rare opportunity for a slumdweller.

He's really dedicated to good appearances, isn't he?

The Guiding City guard's access card sat next to him on the dresser's top. He couldn't bring himself to part with it. Even if Richmond had technology equal to that of the city in his possession, the card remained the only guaranteed way inside. It was a key, after all, one far too valuable to simply be thrown away. The sentinels hadn't moved from the gates as long as he'd been alive, but still, the threat caused him to sweat.

Would a whole sentinel go after one card?

He studied himself in the mirror. The shower had washed away the blood, dirt, and swelling, and it was rare that he got the chance to see his face. Kale's eyes were azure like the sea. His scars told a story, one that Richmond seemed to have already read through simple observation. The years of struggle had helped him develop a muscular build; carrying ancient scrap metal and weapons across the slums did well to form his body. The brand of The Vultures was tattooed on his chest, a bird swooping down to snatch bones. He didn't necessarily like the artwork, but he couldn't help feeling a familial presence when looking at it.

Ranks among The Vultures were assigned by merit. Those who swindled the best deals were rewarded accordingly. Kale managed well in the past, but constantly found himself unlucky and on the receiving end of a knife. He assumed he only lasted so long in the gang due to nepotism.

The boss, Kale's father, was Arabian; a real estate mogul in the past life, he no longer allowed his son to call him by name, only boss. The tender soul of his mother, Dianne, was American, living out her dreams of being a cosmetologist. She used to tell him stories of the athenaeum worlds beyond the walls and that one day, he'd be a part of it all, but the noxious corruption of the slums brought about her death.

He was born four years before The Waking and The Waking was his first memory; gold, only gold, and seismic activity. He couldn't remember where they were or what they were doing, but he could feel it. When the light sprung forth, a blast shook the Earth and every building for miles was leveled. He couldn't breathe, but he didn't remember being afraid. The air was dust, yet the light still shone.

Staring back were the eyes of determination. He now had a goal. There had to be a way to outsmart Richmond and steal the star. Such an invention could liberate them all. If The Vultures got ahold of that technology, they could build weapons and arm themselves to the teeth. There were plenty of engineers within their ranks, ones smart enough to develop a means by which to bring down the sentinels. It could be done.

Richmond, however, stood in the way.

After their meeting, before he was allowed to escape to the room, Kale had been fitted for a suit by an old man named Buchannon. He was Richmond's family tailor before and after The Waking and had more suits than people to fill them. The bald and hunched tailor insisted he could have the suit finished by morning and swiftly ordered Kale to clean himself up. He was sent away with a loose tuxedo, but one that was relatively his size. Apparently, two others lived in the hotel, but he hadn't seen them. After being examined by the tailor, he spoke with Phoebe who wanted to show him the room but was snatched away by Astrid. Kale eyed the walls for cameras. There was an abundance of classical paintings lining the surface, but the black lenses of spying devices were nowhere to be found.

The host intimidated him beyond belief. There was no way he could know who Kale was unless he had inside information about The Vultures. Unlikely as it may have been, he had no choice but to play his game for now. Servitude to Richmond didn't seem like a bad deal. He would receive a comforting dwelling, companions, and fresh food every day; far more than The Vultures could offer in their squalor.

Now I've done it. How in the world am I going to get around Richmond? If he actually is watching my every move then I have no choice but to play along for now. It'll take a long time, but I have to gain all of their trust one by one. Phoebe trusts me. That's one down. Buchannon doesn't seem interested in conversation; I doubt he's Richmond's informant. Astrid... She looks to be close to Richmond, but something is off about her. It's like she doesn't want to be looked at, makes me feel like she's hiding something that should be painfully obvious. So far, they're the only ones I've met. I've already gotten my foot in the door by saving her sister. I'll start with her.

He grinned. It would be a tough job, but if it meant a future for The Vultures then it would be worth it.

After fastening his suit, donning his reflective shoes, tucking the access card into the pocket of his jacket, and slicking back his hair, he exited the room to explore the lobby more.

As Kale stepped gracefully down the spiral staircase, he spotted his target lounging on a couch beneath the chandelier. Astrid was still in her extra-formal clothes, though newly clean, and looked incredibly uncomfortable.

It's like everything I need is falling straight into my hands...

"I don't think we really got to meet earlier," Kale called as he completed the final step.

Astrid jumped. Her head turned in his direction and for a split second, their eyes met. She looked desperately afraid, but cleared her throat and darted her eyes away. "No, I don't think we did."

"He gave me a suit. Haven't seen one of these in a long time."

She glanced away, hiding her eyes subconsciously. "You look better than before."

He let out a disingenuous chuckle. "Same for you."

An awkward silence followed as Kale found a seat across from where she sat. The light of the chandelier cast an illusion over her. She looked perfect, like a well-to-do stateswoman and Kale felt as though he must respect her. She was relatively skinny. Her golden hair was braided down her back and makeup was still blanketed on her face.

It was getting late, he assumed Phoebe had already been put to bed. "So," he attempted to break the ice, "Richmond seems like a nice guy. How'd you meet?"

Astrid responded normally, but continued to avert his eyes, "It was a long time ago, before Phoebe was born. My mother was an immigrant from Scandinavia; Finland to be exact. She worked in research, a nearby department as him. But that was before The Wak-" she suddenly stopped. "Anyways, it was a chance encounter, but he helped us get through the hard times, so to answer your question, yes, he is a kind man."

The way she talked confused him. The sentences were sharp and quick, but he continued to pry. "When he talked to me, he used words I've never heard before. It makes it hard to hold a conversation."

She brought a hand to her chin and looked up, "that's just the way he is. He says it's to keep himself smart, but I think he just likes to show off."

"It's hard for people to be smart these days. You have books?"

"Richmond collects."

He could tell an aversion to their conversation was building. Perhaps it was shyness, or a disposition to slumdwellers, but he was determined to break her boundaries.

I need to get deeper...

"Is your mother still around?"

"My Mother..." She turned and looked at him. Reclining an arm over the back of the leather couch, her entire composure changed. She became frighteningly serious. "That's... not something I want to talk about."

It caught him off guard. "Sorry, I understand." he attempted a laugh, but Astrid's face was cold. Her brows frowned and the dark eyeshadow made him feel small. "I get it."

They sat in silence for a moment and Astrid crossed her hands over her lap. "No, I'm sorry, I didn't mean to be rude." He could see a tinge of red beneath her makeup. She was blushing.

I don't understand this girl at all...

Kale began to rise from his spot, straightening the black slacks he wore, "It's late... been a long time since I had the opportunity to sleep in a bed. I'm pretty excited about it."

"Oh, don't go!" Astrid reached a hand out but quickly shot it back to her lap.

Kale's face wrinkled in confusion, but slowly he sat back down.

"I'm sorry. I don't really know how to talk to people." She was clearly embarrassed, looking straight down at her feet that crossed inward. "I only ever talk to Richmond and Phoebe so it's nice to meet someone new."

"Then, you have questions?" He would have to be informal with her, kind enough to make her comfortable, but relatable at the same time.

"You said you lived in the slums," she started, "what was it like out there, day in and day out?"

Kale's dark hair reflected the dim lights and his eyes wandered along the girl opposite him, "It's tough. Life's a struggle every day. There aren't many ways to make money out there so my family and I lived off the rare kindness of others with more. The dust was the worst part. My mom was asthmatic to begin with, so the transition from a clean and healthy society to what we have now eventually led to her death. She educated me though. Between the days of coughing and struggle she would teach me about the way things used to be. We thought about going west where things are more stable, but my father thought he could get us into the city. Clearly that didn't happen," he looked up. Astrid had her hands covering her mouth and was staring directly at him. He recoiled a bit and turned away slightly, "Sorry if that was too much."

She didn't budge, "No! Not at all! I couldn't imagine it was that hard for you. I hate to hear that."

He couldn't control the edge of his lips that rose in a grin. His half-truth was enough to get her guard down.

"It wasn't all bad," he continued, "there were good days every now and then. I'd make friends with some pilgrim kids even though we couldn't understand one another and we'd play games with scrap metal or a ball if we were lucky. That's really all there is to my life. There's nothing special to note."

Astrid replied as she lowered her hands to her lap once more, "it's kinda the same for me. I've been here as long as I can remember. Phoebe is my world, though. I try to make the slums outside a distant enigma for her, but she loves to explore. The little bits of the city we can see are enough to keep her imagination alive. Richmond tries to teach us about the old world whenever he can. He was a PhD student before The Waking happened."

Kale let out a chuckle and smiled at her, "I think I'm on his bad side already. I asked too many questions."

To his surprise, she smiled back. "Don't worry! It's really hard to make him angry. The only time I've ever seen him upset was when Phoebe knocked over one of his inventions and broke it. I wasn't there to see it happen, but he had her by the hair!" she laughed in a cute manner, bringing her hand over her mouth like royalty.

A few more questions…

"Why does everyone wear suits here? No offense, but you look really uncomfortable."

31

She turned away, "You noticed? I guess it's like a form of respect. He wants to honor this place and the work of his family so he makes sure we all dress to the occasion. The suit they made me is a little tight as you can tell," she tugged on the sides of her jacket, only able to pull it a centimeter at most, "but I don't have the heart to tell them."

I better leave it at that. She's given me enough to work with.

"Well, I'm tired from everything that's happened today." He stood up again and adjusted his tie. "If you ever want to practice conversation, feel free to ask."

She smiled at him, "Thank you, I enjoyed it."

He began the climb back up the staircase.

Astrid was interesting. She claimed to be bad at conversation, but all of her words flowed naturally. It was her atypical actions that threw him awry. It almost came off as a facade, improper. She was hiding something, feigning ignorance and he thought in the moment he asked about her mother, the real identity emerged.

We're both playing the same game then… This ought to be interesting.

The room he'd been assigned had a standard layout: a bed in the center, one nightstand, two chairs, a bathroom, and a television but no signal to receive. When he removed his coat and unbuttoned his shirt, he noticed a note folded in half on his bed. He snatched up the note and unfolded it.

'8:00 am, at the star. I know you know the code.' -Richmond

The last thing he wanted to do was talk to Richmond again. The act of playing as a tortured saint exhausted him. He already missed the authenticity of The Vultures. No one had to pretend, they simply were.

As Kale tactfully removed the many pieces of his suit, he stood at his window and looked out. Golden streaks of The Well's light launched through the clouds above and the edges of the Guiding City rose in his view. The pellucid skyscrapers peeked above the golden wall and his eyes focused on something closer, a yellow head, sticking out over the entrance gate to his right. It was far away, yet still managed to intimidate him. It was the head of a sentinel, the mechanical devil that plagued his memories. He was still scared of them even as an adult. The expressionless face of the automaton stared back in his thoughts and he shivered.

The pillow felt indescribably soft that night and his body sank into the mattress. When he stayed in the company of his father, he was only offered a pallet of hay. Mattresses, among most things in the slums, were swiftly picked by pilgrims after The Waking and it had been years since he last felt one. A tear almost fell. As he pulled the heavy covers over himself, he caught a whiff of laundry detergent. It crept through every nerve in his body and joy filled his heart. He could get used to the comfort, even if he knew it would only be temporary.

Night was no longer dark around the city. The Well produced light equal to that of the sun and while the atmosphere took the form of ink, sight was not inhibited. Kale found solitude in the dark. He enjoyed the cloak of shadows more than light's blasphemous exposure.

When he woke the next morning, only unattainable strands of his dream remained and it took a moment to recognize where he was. A sudden knocking ripped his attention from his waking thoughts.

"Kale, Richmond wants to see you." It was Astrid.

He spoke between groggy groans, "tell him I'll be there shortly."

"He wants you down there now. He was very serious," he could sense hesitation in her voice.

"Well, I have to get dressed, don't I?"

"Oh… Okay, I'll tell him." Her footsteps scurried away down the hall.

I wonder why he wants to meet down there. Surely he wouldn't want me scouting out his work if he really did have suspicions…

As Kale rose from his bed and prepared himself to play the part once again, he exited into the hall.

There was a chill in the air that morning.

"KALE!" Phoebe's voice rang out.

"Phoebe get back he-" he heard Astrid fumble around at the end of the hall.

The little girl's blue shoes shone in the light and she ran to meet him. "Did you enjoy your first night here? This place is really cool! Astrid told me you two talked a lot. I'm sorry I was asleep."

She's so different now… I guess it's good that I could help.

Smiling, he knelt down to reach her eye level. He placed a hand on her soft head and ruffled her hair. "When you're growing, you need your sleep. Don't be sorry."

Sighing, Astrid walked to meet them, "You'd better get going, he doesn't like to be kept waiting." Her voice was hoarse as if she'd just woken, but her makeup appeared flawless like an actress. Still in her skin-tight suit, she took Phoebe by the hand. "Don't keep him any longer, he has somewhere to be."

"But I want to talk some more," she protested.

Kale let out a carefree laugh and rose to his feet. "We'll talk more later," he reassured her, "I still need a full tour of this place."

Phoebe hopped on her toes, "I can do that! I can show you!"

"Perfect."

As he found his way to the spiral staircase, the scent of fresh breakfast entered his nose. He could pinpoint eggs, bacon, and blueberry muffins within the aroma. As his tongue began to salivate, he almost abandoned his mission and swore servitude. Aside from the filth that the inexperienced cooks of The Vultures prepared, he hadn't had a meal so sweet since early childhood. The smell alone was enough to expel the horrid memories.

They're really doing their best to bribe me...

Approaching the keypad on the door to Richmond's lab, Kale glanced over his shoulder to make sure no one saw. He appeared to be the only one in the lobby. Three fingers traced the numbers 5507 to which a clicking followed. He grasped the metal handle and turned.

It opened.

Maybe this was a test... I shouldn't...

"Come on down, Kale." Richmond's commanding voice echoed from below.

Too late...

He felt the access card in his pocket.

I have to make sure he doesn't find it.

34

He descended the dark staircase, following the golden light. Richmond was fast at work on a new piece of technology at a desk on the right side of the wiry room. Energy flowed from the star in the center, enough to illuminate all surroundings.

Without looking up, Richmond spoke lowly, "I believe it's due time to drop our acts. Allow us to speak to one another honestly and openly. Kale, you can start by telling me who you really are."

Kale stoically frowned and crossed his arms over his chest. "What's not to believe about what I told you yesterday? Everything I said is true."

"Is a half-truth so different from a lie?" Richmond turned around to make eye contact. Power exuded from his stern face.

What? How does he know that... Does he recognize me? I don't think I've ever made a deal with him...

"I guess not, but what's that have to do with me?"
"There's more to you than meets the eye."

I can't escape it...

"Maybe..."
A pale hand waved downward. "So then, by all means, complete your truth."

He stood there, uncertain. Was there such a lie that could slip through the mind of the genius standing before him?

What would he think if I told him? It's not like he'd kick me out with the knowledge I have. That would be a death wish. I'd tell the boss and we'd raid this place tomorrow. Maybe I should escape and-

The scientist's voice cut the air, "Kale, I reason that you're an intelligent man. You stand before me, playing a fool, lying to my face, seeking pity, yet I have insight. The slithering of your manipulations ends here. Tell me the truth and I'll spare your life."

Spare my life? What does he mean by that!? Who are the other guests of this hotel that I haven't met? Assassins? Officers? How much power does this man have? Or... could this all be a ruse to intimidate me into spilling my secrets? This is all so strange. Though, if he could make this technology, what else could he come up with? Is this a setup to crack down on The Vultures? I'm screwed...*

He couldn't afford to lie any further, at least not to Richmond.

"Fine," Kale raised his hands and snickered, but a flare filled his eyes, "you got me. I'll tell you."

Richmond eyed him suspiciously. "Continue."

"I'm the son of a local gang head. You may have heard of The Vultures."

Kale expected the revelation to shock the host, but Richmond was unfazed.

"Indeed." His head nodded. "So then, why were you so interested in my star?"

He's not surprised?

"What? Why wouldn't I be?"

Maybe I can get away with a few more half-truths...

The question in return was met with a contest. "Any pilgrim would slink away when I mentioned consequences and accept their room. You seem to believe in your own judgment, so why did that not stop you?"

After a long exhale, he answered.

"It's like you said, based on what Phoebe told me I had an idea of what it could be. The slums have never seen something like that before, so I wanted to." The words, inadequate as they may have been, were all he could muster.

"Curiosity? You take me for a fool. You wanted to steal it, didn't you? Your arrogance made you gloss over the consequences so that you could confirm your prize. At least tell me how you planned to do it."

No matter what I say, I don't have a choice anymore...

"You're right. I wanted to steal it, but I didn't have a plan."

Richmond's chin turned upward. "And what of the gang? Do they know your location?"

Wait... This could work to my advantage! If I convince him I'm not with them anymore... It IS true after all.

36

"No. I'm alone. I was kicked out a few days ago. I don't know why, but I swear that's the truth." Kale slumped but kept an eye on the host.

Richmond smirked and let loose a chuckle. "Well... That's a relief isn't it?"

He thinks I'm stupid! I can't stand this guy! But this works well for me. He'll likely think this little intervention is enough to scare me, but I won't stop.

"It wasn't a thought-out plan, just a passing opportunity I guess." Kale shrugged, "now I don't have a reason to go through with it. I think that warm bed was enough to stop me."

"I certainly hope so." A crooked smile grew. "Since we're in the mood to be honest, I should tell you that this hotel is outfitted with a multitude of security measures of my design. I won't be so foolish as to reveal my cards, but trust that when I said you will never refuse my commands, I spoke the truth. So, this act and game ends here, Kale." Richmond took three steps closer to him and placed a hand on the star. "This is the key to our salvation. Had you succeeded in manipulating me, stealing my star, and withholding it from benefiting the world, I could only compare you to the devil himself."

Kale's expression was cold. Even though the eyes that stared were determined, he shivered at Richmond's threats. A bead of sweat trickled down his forehead. He knew the other man would notice immediately, so he turned and wiped it away.

"Then," Richmond replied quietly with a smile, "shall we have breakfast? I'm beginning to tire of these mind games. If the warm bed wasn't enough to buy your loyalty, I hope a freshly cooked feast will do the trick."

The offer ticked a nerve. "I don't want your bribes."

"Indeed. Though, if I were you, Kale, I would accept them. You are now my subject either way, so you have two choices: you can humbly partake of my generosity or I can have you tossed from the roof for threatening me the way you have."

Kale gulped.

Richmond leaned in. "Do you know why I hate animals?"

What's he talking about now?

"No. I don't know anything about you." The reply wore a smart-aleck tone.

"They're fickle-minded, not looking beyond satisfaction and momentary pleasure. An animal does not question its own existence. A beast does not consider the life of its prey. Life outside of human consciousness looks not to the greater world, only the tiny fractal environment of their day-to-day endeavours."

"Why're you telling me this?" An irritation spread between the thug's brows.

"Because if you were to steal my work, my ambition, my dream for the greater world, I would become such an animal, a beast, and I would have no qualms about ending your life."

The air froze.

"Now," he smothered Kale with an arm around his back, "breakfast."

As they climbed the staircase back to the lobby, the wires lining the walls began to rattle.

The lights above flickered.

A sound of breaking glass came from the kitchen and Richmond took off up the staircase before him. Something was happening, something that demanded the scientist's attention over the thief.

He's left. I could line my pockets with all his gadgets... But I wonder what's happening...

With a groan of complaint, Kale followed.

When he entered the lobby, Richmond stood in the center looking up. His pale hair fell across his head and he was frowning, eyes wide in confusion.

"What's going on?" Kale called to him.

The scientist didn't respond.

The disturbance grew greater. Paintings fell from the walls and the chandelier swung on its hinge.

"What's happening? An earthquake?" Astrid yelled from the top of the spiral staircase. Her face was contorted in fright.

"Astrid!" Richmond yelled, "Where's Phoebe?"

"She's in our room. I… What should we do?"

He hissed under his breath, "Hurry! Bring her dow-"

The words were cut short by a scene out of Kale's nightmares.

A colossal hand of flaxen steel and wires broke through the wall in front of them. Clouds of glass and shrapnel threw them backwards.

To their right, the ceiling collapsed, blocking the staircase down to Richmond's lab. Tangled steel rods stuck from the wall like claws.

Astrid screamed.

Through the dust, he could make out her figure, holding dearly to the railing. It was a twelve-foot drop to the lobby floor.

Kale shouted, "Help her! She's gonna fall!"

The smoke and dust had collected slightly above the ground and he couldn't see the others. As physics refused to cooperate, he found his footing. A loud creaking of steel ripped through his ears and he stomped to a spot beneath Astrid.

I have to catch her!

The hand slashed through the hotel once more, tearing the entire wall away. He could see clearly to the outside and the light of The Well shone brightly in the morning sky. Kale froze. Six deadly lenses stared at him. The unforgettable face of a sentinel leered down.

With a scream above him, Astrid fell.

He quickly jumped backwards and tried to catch her, but his hands grazed her side. He heard a crunch and she cried out. Cold crawled through his veins and he dropped beside her.

His voice cracked, "Are you okay!?"

She couldn't respond and looked at him in fear. Her hands reached for her foot which faced an improper direction.

As the cries of machinery deafened him once more, the sentinel began to kneel. Paralyzed by fear, he trembled as its giant hand reached for him. He tried to scoot away, but the nerves of his body had completely turned to ice. The mechanical hand stopped inches from him, stealing his view and from the palm, a hatch of metal opened. An even smaller hand grew from it. Pistons extended the miniature appendage further, coming to his chest. He whimpered in fear. He couldn't run.

It grabbed his coat and retracted in a whir of mechanics. He was swiftly yanked into the air and looked down to see Astrid aghast. Tears ran down her face and her mascara was leaking across her cheeks. Growling, he tried to fight the machine, but its metal was strong and its grip was immovable. He heard a tear. The seams of the coat began to give way as he rose.

After about ten feet, the coat ripped in half, sending him to the ground. Pain erupted throughout his body. He turned his eyes to the sentinel once more which had become busy, surreptitiously bending and folding his jacket until access to the pockets was granted. From the pocket, the massive machine pulled an orange and gold card.

A deep voice over a loudspeaker consumed his hearing, "*Stealing from the Guiding City is no small crime. Violation: 5th ordinance. Punishment: capital.*"

Kale rose to his knees and his arms fell beside him. His white button shirt was stained brown.

Something dripped onto his head.

A finger rose to inspect it.

Blood.

He looked up. Unable to speak, his lips quivered.

Hanging from the steel rods above that once held *Le Lien*'s walls together was a leg. It was upside down and the rod penetrated above the kneecap. The leg had been ripped apart at the thigh, but the most horrific part of what he saw came from the foot. A perfect, polished, and reflective blue shoe covered it at the end.

Kale's eyes traced along the sentinel's arm to its left hand, which opened and dropped something to the ground. With a horrific chill creeping through his senses, he recognized a head of blonde hair and the face of Phoebe staring back at him, lifeless.

The robot turned its head to them once more. Something grew from its shoulder.

BANG!

Kale felt a touch.

He looked down at his body. The shirt had grown red and he felt chills. More blood, his blood, poured from his stomach and the world began to grow dark.

His thoughts ended with the sounds of Astrid screaming and in the tiniest sliver of sight, he watched the sentinel walk away.

Chapter 3
Integration

[Cardiovascular activity stabilized. Cognitive function remains abnormal.]
[It refuses to bind at the cellular level. What's your recommendation?]
[We keep trying until it does.]
[If the body continues to reject it, he'll die.]
[He's died four times already. We can afford to be more experimental.]
[Yes Sir.]

Darkness.

[Sir, integration is continuing as expected, he may see improvement.]
[Indeed. That's good. Though, I wonder if his current biological capabilities can sustain the physical induction if he were to recover successfully.]
[We won't know that until the time comes.]
[Do bone density and muscular potential match accordingly with its weight?]
[Yes.]
[Well that's a positive. What about nerve attachments? Has it rejected them?]
[No sir. They're recognizing the artificial mechanisms.]
[Sensation?]
[Brain activity is regulating to quotidian levels.]
[Good.]

Light.

"How the hell did it find us? Those things haven't moved in years!"
"I don't know. It was after him."
"I need to calm down... I don't suspect he lured it here on purpose. After all, it did kill him. How's your leg?"
"I can move it. It doesn't hurt too much anymore."

"That's good, and your mind?"

"I... I can't believe it. I don't know what to do. I don't want to live anymore... Not without her."

"Have funeral preparations been made? I wanted you to decide how her life is honored."

"I've tried, but... I just can't... Every time I see her face I... There's no purpose to my life anymore."

"Stop that. You matter to us. You belong. Even though she's gone, your life still holds value. Besides, I have a plan."

Pain.

[Existential values climbing. He's going into shock.]
[I thought the integration was continuing smoothly, what changed?]
[He appears to be remembering.]
[That's the last thing we need. Continue to administer antientheogens.]
[His veins are in no state to take on additional fluids. I'm afraid I can't.]
[Can it be ingested?]
[Sir, I... It can.]
[Do it. He doesn't deserve sympathy.]
[Yes Sir.]
[This is my fault. I was careless. My own arrogance has never failed, and yet... I need a cigarette.]
[You smoke, sir?]
[Only in times of extreme distress... I should've searched him...]
[It's too late now.]

Guilt.

[The neural networks have fully stabilized. Integration is successful.]
[Good. What's our time frame until consciousness is restored?]
[It could be days, weeks, or months. I don't have a way to pinpoint the exact time.]
[I need at least a week. If he wakes up, subdue him. Keep him down until I give the order.]
[Constant interference could lead to permanent cognitive damage. Are you sure about this?]
[My word is final. I need time.]

[Yes sir.]
[One more thing.]
[Yes?]
[Long-term functionality... Will it sustain harsh expeditions?]
[I suspect it will. What do you mean by expeditions?]
[Let's not discuss this now. Theoretically, he can still hear.]

It was blurry at first, but after some time he could distinguish the lights above. It was difficult to accomplish and if he tried to perceive other surroundings, they would disappear. He had no temporal sense, no feeling except weight in his lower abdomen, and only a faint taste of citrus on the tongue. He couldn't remember where he was.

How did I get here? Who were those voices? I don't understand.

A ringing.

[Sir, if I may, ethically are you okay with this?]
[You are far from the arbiter of morality, Pierce. I don't need a lecture.]
[Yes sir.]
[I gave the order three days ago. Why hasn't he woken?]
[The strain of such tremendous anesthesia requires extensive recovery. Perhaps it was too much.]
[With him, there is no such thing as too much. Her blood is on his hands, yet to be washed.]
[Regardless, I swore the oath.]
[The Hippocratic oath was lost the day they built that city. You stand before me pure. Any detestable acts you may find here are mine alone.]
[Yes Sir.]

He had begun to distinguish them. Richmond's voice continued in his thoughts, repeating conversation over and over again. But the other voice was new. He must not have met them yet. Faintly, the memories of transpired events rippled through his network. Visions of yellow, crimson, and Astrid's screaming face replayed themselves and he felt fear. It hurt. A dizziness resounded in his head.

"Someone," attempting to speak, he noticed that thought conjured his voice in his head, but no sound manifested physically, "please help me."

It felt like hours that he spent screaming into the void, begging for a hand to find him. "HELP! HELP ME! SOMEONE PLEASE!" The feeling was difficult to describe. The only comparison his brain could make was a nothingness akin to sleep paralysis.

>[Blood pressure rising rapidly, we need to calm him down... humanely this time.]
>[Is he waking up?]
>[Yes.]
>[Good. Do you believe he's ready to talk?]
>[Please, Sir. Let him regain his identity slowly. This is a delicate process.]
>[Delicate? SHE was delicate. I would rather he feel it all.]
>[Let me handle the recovery. Afterward, he's all yours.]
>[Fine. Three days more, we've splurged enough precious time.]
>[Yes Sir.]

The tops of his eyelids were indescribably heavy as he attempted to open them. Tingling wandered around his face and slowly, he remembered what to do: breathe, move the tongue, swallow, breathe again, exhale, feel the nose. The actions came one after the other until he could see. Above, a harsh light beamed down onto him and he could feel heat. An intricate web of wires spun and twisted their way across his view and to the right, he saw someone. A doctor, he presumed, was covered in a white coat and blue surgical mask. The face was hidden by massive glasses reflecting the room and Kale's pale face. His hair was a dingy mess, his eyes were glossed over, and his skin bore the same hue as the light above. A gray johnny gown was draped across his body.

The doctor began to speak softly, "Welcome back, Kale. This must seem very strange to you, but please take it slowly."

He opened his mouth to reply, but couldn't move his lips enough to form words. Gibberish escaped which prompted the doctor to stand by his side.

"Easy. Let the feeling come back first. Try to wiggle your fingers."

He could feel electricity wind its way down. Ants crawled through his nerves and the ability to turn his head was regained. His hands began to rise; only an inch above his body, but it was progress nonetheless.

"Good," the doctor spoke, "my name is Pierce. Richmond and I have been working to assure your recovery. Do you think you can speak?"

His lips were iron. A numbness infected them and noises as those of a child unknowledgeable of language filtered out.

"That's good. It may take a few hours to regain the feeling. You've been asleep for quite some time."

Kale attempted to rise from the bed, but a roaring fatigue withheld him. His head fell back to his pillow.

"Take your time. I'll return shortly and we'll work again. Feel free to sleep more." It was as if the words carried a potion with them, and he felt his consciousness break apart until once again he slept.

When he next woke, Richmond and Pierce stood over him muttering scientific terminology. He couldn't immediately comprehend their words, but as he regained his bearings, they began to make sense.

"How does it look?" Richmond's voice queried.

"Impressive to say the least. Far better than I imagined," the doctor replied.

"The epidermal layers turned out quite nicely, don't you think?"

"Virtually indistinguishable from the real thing. You're an artist."

"It's a shame my talents were used on such filth. It's time to get him moving."

A hand grabbed him and turned his neck. Richmond's face was inches from his. Bags bulged beneath the angelic man's milky eyes and he was noticeably agitated.

"Start moving. You've slept long enough," he demanded.

Kale pleaded with tumult and pain shot through his body, but his limbs began to wake.

"Sir," Pierce walked to Richmond's side, "Not too soon, this must be done gradually."

"Don't interfere with me," he snapped back, "the blood needs to flow. Once he fully regains feeling, the physical therapy won't take long."

The two men worked to bring Kale upright. As his body postured in a sitting position, he felt waves of blood drop to his legs. Involuntarily, tears fell from his eyes and he fought to move his face. Such insubordination by his own body irked him to his core. He was fully Richmond's slave and no matter how hard he tried, he had no power.

WORK! MOVE! DO WHAT I SAY!

His mind screamed commands to his muscles, but nothing he wished became reality.

"Sir, if you want him to walk again, we need to work his legs." Pierce knelt beside Kale's appendages which hung from the side of the bed and grabbed a calf.

Richmond thought for a moment and did the same. "Kale, focus on the feeling of your muscles."

Together, they began to move his legs slightly up and down. The feeling trickled into existence. One toe, his left ankle, right knee, began to obey one after the other.

"Slowly now. Have patience." Pierce reassured.

Kale groaned slightly, able to conjure the disorganized word, "Ohkwayy."

Richmond observed him with disdain, his face a paroxysm of disgust. "Never in my life, Pierce, have I been afflicted by such emotions." The pale man's eyes locked unwavering on his patient. "Hatred, malfeasance, rage, I feel such things." His low voice echoed in the dark surroundings.

"It is okay to feel as long as you do not *act*, Sir." A challenge decorated the doctor's words.

Kale couldn't understand. A glacial stroke crept down his neck as he stared into the white soulless eyes of the coated host before him.

What's happening? Why is he so angry?

"Try to talk."

He moved his tongue, slapping the roof of his mouth haphazardly. "Whaaat's goiiing onnn?" The memory of speech filled his brain once more and a tired cloud blanketed the neural networks. Kale reached up to his head and whimpered.

Pierce stood and tinkered with an IV line that ran to Kale's right elbow. "Sleep again. I'll run a stable concoction of stimulants through this and tomorrow, you'll be ready. Sir," the doctor stood poised to meet the eyes of his superior, "one more day."

"Very well." Richmond turned and stomped away, his lab cloak flowing as stardust in his wake.

A dizziness filled Kale's brain and he succumbed to the darkness.

[I've never felt this… These wantings, these emotions, they've propagated beyond my control. My hands ache to strangle him… My feet beg to smash his throat… Even when I found Maria out there, I didn't feel this way… I-I've made arrangements.]

[Sir, you must control yourself. No matter how you let these emotions out, just don't show them to him. Go make a simulacrum and kill it if you have to. If you act on these, you're no better than him. It would be a waste.]

46

[I see. You're right.]
[These arrangements... What exactly do you have in mind?]
[It's run our pockets dry. My dear friend happened to be quite the negotiator.]
[So then, you plan to-]
[That's enough. I'll explain once I have the details.]
[Yes sir.]

When Kale awoke next, the blanket of mind haze was gone. He felt new, freshly reacquainted with his muscles, and able to sit upright without assistance. The doctor stood across the room surveying a monitor that depicted his vital readings.

"Ah, that seemed to do the trick." The four-eyed man smiled at his patient behind his mask. "Miraculous what that light does to the cells."

"What happened to me?" Kale's lips moved according to his brain's commands this time, "I don't..."

"Shhhhh, take it slowly," Pierce walked over and took a seat next to the bedside, "you were hurt very badly, but it's okay now. Your body is still on the mend, but you must not be eager to move on your own."

"H-how was I hurt?" his brows wrinkled and he felt his face. Everything was as it should be except his dark hair which stood on end and folded in myriad ways. His hands ran along his body feeling for wounds of which he found none.

"Let's not discuss details right now, but instead try to stand. Here, take my hand." The doctor reached out and Kale accepted the offering. He was pulled gently to his feet and a minuscule dizziness tickled his brain. His legs wobbled slightly, but he stood on his own.

"I can do it." He relinquished the doctor's hand.

"How does that feel? Alright?"

"I'm good... I think." One step, dizziness. Two steps, regulation. Three steps, equilibrium. "I've got it."

Still... What's going on? What in the world happened to me?

"Good! That's great!" the doctor cheered. "Do you feel capable of talking for a moment?"

Kale's mind was swimming with questions, but he considered that now was not the appropriate time to overload his thoughts. "I... I need to rest a bit, then I can."

"Perfect. Let's get you back to bed then."

"Wait. How long was I out for?"

"It's been a month and a half since you were hurt. Forty-two days to be exact."

"A month!" A pain rang through his head and he winced.

Pierce jumped at the signals of pain from his patient. "Okay, lie down for an hour, after that Richmond wishes to speak with you."

Great. That's the last thing I can handle right now.

Steadily, he walked back to the bed and lay flat on his back. He felt the blood in his body churn and as soon as his eyelids met, he was out.

Richmond was silhouetted by the bright lights above as he shook him awake. "It's time to talk."

Kale's eyes glazed over as he opened them to the harsh iridescence. His thoughts were a jumbled mess, but with time and a few deep breaths, he found his composure. "I... Hang on... At least let me think for a second."

"Think all you want. Let it come back to you. The more guilt the better."

"W-What are you talking about?"

"You should've remembered by now. We've given you more than enough medicine."

"Remember? Remember what? What happened to me?"

The scientist's impatient face scowled. "Unwilling to confess your sins, are you? Very well," the white hair was combed across his head in perfect order, yet he had massive dark bags beneath his eyes, "by your hand *Le Lien* was attacked by a Jötunn, or sentinel as we called them."

"A sentinel?" Kale saw flashes of the mechanical face.

"Our home was ravaged. My heirloom... and yet... that's not the worst of it," a deep growl burned in his throat as he spoke, "Phoebe was killed in the attack. You, Kale, killed her."

The words stung his mind. He couldn't comprehend what the chalky scientist said. "Phoebe... What?" He would never do such a thing. He would never hurt Phoebe. "I don't know what you're talking about!"

"Lying, imprudent, filthy amnesiac!" Richmond sent a fist flying into his face. The force knocked Kale off of his bed and his arms, still feeling like gelatin, failed to break his fall. His shoulders hit the floor, sending pain across his back. A trickle of blood fell from his nostril and a sweltering warmth ran through his cheek. "Think! Remember! You don't get to escape the consequences of the sins you've committed! Not against my family and my home!"

"I'm serious!" Kale yelled back, wiping the crimson liquid from his face, "I have no idea what you're talking about! The last thing I remember is going to sleep in the room you gave me and the-'" Something flashed in his mind: a vision of an orange and gold access card.

No. No. No. How could I have been so stupid? The boss even warned me to throw it in the sewer!

"Richmond, look…" he raised his hands out in front to defend from any more strikes, "I didn't know. There was a city guard's access card in my pocket. I had no way to know that thing would attack."

"Oh? A swindling gang member didn't know those cards had trackers?" a maniacal laugh broke from his mouth and he slammed the wall, "Stop the charade!"

Pierce quickly slipped out of the room, quivering.

"I'M NOT LYING! When I told you I quit my plan I was telling the truth!" Deceit filled his eyes.

"Still you lie…" Richmond's vexation snapped to a calm and relaxed composure. The sudden change sent a flood of fear throughout Kale's body. "No matter... Whether you lie or tell the truth makes no difference anymore. Your soul now belongs to me." The host smiled from ear to ear.

"W-What do you mean?"

"Well, in case your memories don't return naturally, allow me to further elaborate on the transpired events. That sentinel not only destroyed this hotel and stole your precious access card, but it killed Phoebe in the process. And as it so immorally walked away, it sent a shot through your stomach, evaporating your internal organs."

A cold paleness consumed his face. "Phoebe was killed? I was..?" his eyes fell and his hands roamed around his midsection.

"But it seems you were the lucky one. The shot missed your heart just enough to keep you alive. Not her… No… It's never that fair…"

Kale couldn't reply, only staring with wide eyes.

The host adjusted his lab coat and straightened his yellow tie. "My precious star, the very thing you wanted to steal for monetary gain, allowed us to restore your body through cybernetics."

"Cybernetics? You put machines in my body!?" Adrenaline began to pump in his veins.

"Indeed. It's quite a marvel what one can accomplish with an infinitely efficient power source, as well as certain other properties of The Well's magic. When you were shot, the lower six ribs, your right lung, sections of your spine, stomach, arteries, liver, and kidney, were instantly destroyed. Your heart and brain majestically managed to continue functioning for a time. We immediately began operation. You did, however, die on us a few times, but our clever machinations revived you. It was quite the process to restore your consciousness."

He couldn't speak. The deluge of reality sent him spiraling. Fragments of memories appeared and then quickly slipped away and he focused his thoughts on remembering.

I died? I don't understand... Phoebe is dead... It's my fault?

A whirl of guilt flamed and churned in lachrymosity. He wouldn't hurt her. She was too pure, too innocent, and undeserving of such a fate. He wouldn't... yet he had...

"Needless to say, I've outfitted your new biotechnology with specific measures of my own to insure nothing like your little stunt ever happens again. As I said, your very soul belongs to me now." Richmond took a seat and eyed him harshly. His hands rested on his knees.

"Please... Tell me what happened. I wouldn't hurt her," he pleaded, struggling for breaths.

"Intentions mean nothing. Our world operates on actions and your actions brought tragedy. We guess it was when the sentinel first broke the wall. She was ripped apart. A steel rod from the hotel's construction tore her like the talons of an eagle. It took an entire day to find the rest of her body. Worst of all, it was Astrid who saw the leg. " His voice became exceedingly low, "this was the devil's work."

Kale's hands rose to his head and he brought his knees in.

Her blood is NOT on my hands. It's not my fault! The city did this! If those cowards behind their walls cared for the people suffering outside this wouldn't have happened! I never would've been forced to take it.

A blurred vision of a sparkling blue shoe appeared in thought but swiftly gave way to a tangled red leg. Her leg. He whispered under his breath, "I'm not the devil."

Richmond paused. "What did you say?"

"It wasn't my fault!"

"Oh?" The pale man grabbed his subject's shirt and pulled him towards himself, snarling, "If not you, then who?"

"The city."

"The city?"

"They made the slums come to this! They keep us out! If it weren't for them, we wouldn't have to be so desperate!"

Something stirred in Richmond when he heard the words. Kale couldn't determine exactly what caused him to peel his eyes and lower his gaze in a form of twisted understanding. But there was a fire in there, one that had just been stoked. "Because they keep The Well from us."

"It's them! It's their fault!"

"The Aureate."

"Yes! They did it," Kale hissed.

He let the thief go and stared into his eyes. "I don't trust you, Kale." The contact between their pupils was not direct, however, Richmond seemed to stare at something beyond physical sight. "The Well was the single greatest blessing this world has ever seen. There are people... devils rather... that now lock those secrets behind walls and sell the key for profit. As an animal, you only saw to do the same with your own interests in mind. I will not."

Kale gritted his teeth.

"But now," Richmond rose and spread his hands apart like a priest, "you and I may see eye to eye if only a bit. It's just a shame what it took to come to this."

He shifted around and pulled himself up to stand equally with the host. "So what then? What now?"

"I have a plan in place, but there is someone else I need to converse with before I grace you with my knowledge. Rest another day and if you feel up to the task, visit the lobby. You're free to roam but be warned, I am watching, and if you cross me in any way, then you will *actually* die." He turned his back to the patient and began toward the door.

The next day, Kale found his way to what remained of *Le Lien*'s lobby. The medical ward he'd been confined to connected to the bottom hallway of residential rooms, which in turn wound like a coiled snake around the lobby.

A smell of sweet incense rose to his nose. The wall opposite the hotel's entrance had been rebuilt to a certain extent; a giant mass of what looked to be metal stood in its place, allowing a cool breeze and streams of outside light to filter in at the sides. The chandelier had been rehung where it once stood, though only a few bulbs remained lit and several arms were missing.

Offset in the corner were red candles surrounding a hallowed portrait of Phoebe. Her bright cheeks wrapped perfectly around a gleeful smile that stretched far across her face. Golden streams of curled hair fell across her crinkled eyes and Kale began to weep.

I didn't do this. This wasn't my fault! I would never hurt her...

Chapter 4
Perdition

He'd woken with tears in his eyes and in a pool of sweat, unsure of how to feel.

Kale recalled the conversation with Richmond. Perhaps, if only a little, the host saw the city as the true perpetrator. But he had a worse thought. He would have to face Astrid; he, her sister's killer. But he questioned, did she feel the same way about the incident as Richmond? Would she resent and despise him or did she see it as an action of the city?

That morning, tension hung in the air like a thick smog. She was pale when he next saw her. Her gaze never left the floor. Still tightly bound in the multi-pieced suit, Astrid tucked her head in her hands above her lap. Even in her grief, her makeup was perfectly applied. There didn't appear to be a proper way to begin conversation and as Kale sat next to her, sweat fell down his back. Richmond had ordered the two to meet him beneath the chandelier in the lobby where Phoebe's memorial stood conveniently in perfect view to their right.

He had cleaned himself up enough before meeting the two. The sentinel's attack had destroyed the further half of residential rooms from the hotel's entrance, but luckily, his was spared. The plumbing systems had been repaired somehow and his mind felt slightly more at ease after a warm shower, though an immeasurable pit clenched his stomach. He'd been given the completed suit that Buchannon had been toiling away at. It was comfortable, lightweight, and tight in the right places. A new tie was presented along with it. This tie, as opposed to the marigold one from before, was azure and as he ran his hand along its suede surface, his eyes admired the color.

"So then," Richmond began after they had gathered, "I do realize the difficulty in this situation. Believe me, we've been struggling." The host's eyes locked directly on Kale while he spoke as if to reinforce the culpability he already felt. The scientist's yellow suit had been traded for a solid black button-up shirt and jeans. The appearance was unnatural to such a man as Richmond, yet oddly suited his direct tone that morning. "This collapse has left us mourning, suffering, and at a loss for words. To say what happened was indescribable is simply not enough. Kale, we know this happened because of you,"

The words made him wince.

"but I find it unnecessary to berate you further. It's been over a month since then and we must move forward. Now, the time for action must begin. As you both are well aware, my goal is to challenge the Guiding City's current practice of hoarding its wealth. The energy, power, and knowledge must be returned to the world, though, even I know this is a grandiose ambition."

"You can't just sneak into the most advanced city ever created." Kale managed to chime in, raising his gaze. Astrid's head turned slightly at the words, but she remained still. "I've tried before and it got two of my friends killed. How are you supposed to do this?"

A grin crawled up Richmond's cheek, "I have a plan. You two, follow me."

A plan to get into the city? How could he...

He took a step towards them and extended a hand out to the disconsolate girl, ignoring the thief who stood on his own.

They walked together towards the metal door of Richmond's lab which had several new dents on its surface and slightly bent outward of the wall. In silence, they descended the dark staircase down and circled the star. Luckily for Richmond, the sentinel had failed to uncover his deepest secret. Kale stood across from Astrid who still cast her eyes downward and he could see sorrow written on her lips.

The host stood at their side.

"My plan is this: you two will infiltrate the Guiding City and learn the secrets of The Well so that we may distribute its generosity to the public and the world."

Kale's head whipped to the host. His eyes widened.
Astrid was unfettered by the lofty plan.
"Us?" Kale processed the words, "You said... IN the city?"
"Yes, that's what I said."
He couldn't believe the words, "You're sending US?"
Richmond couldn't hold back a prideful snicker and leaned forward, resting his hands on his creation. "It seems you have some questions."

Wait, wait, wait... He can get us into the Guiding City? There's no way...

It took a moment for Kale to organize his thoughts. "First of all, how do you plan on getting us inside? My father and I spent years trying to figure that out."

"I've made preparations. I will not expose my insider, however, he has proven vitally useful. We've secured two entrance tickets to the city and a residency in the southern quarter."

This can't be real!

"You're serious?"
"Indeed."
"But, even if we get in, what are we supposed to do once we're there?"
"That will have to wait until you're inside."

Kale's head wrinkled in thought. "What? You're telling me you don't have a plan?"

The host's eyes thinned. "I *have* plans. More plans than you could fathom. I was foolish before. The sentinel attack revealed my weakness. I had brushed away the possibility that they would move again."

He gulped. He and Richmond had made the same dire miscalculation.

Even though the boss warned me...

"-but don't worry," Richmond reassured him, "I will assist you as you go." His hands fell beneath the star to a drawer low to the ground. Rising from the compartment were two metallic squares about an inch in length. "These will be our means of communication during your mission: neural transponders. These devices will self-integrate with your phonic receptors to allow undetectable telecommunication. They're equipped with a subset of cloaking protocols that instantly cease signal projection whenever a wave-"

"Hang on," Kale's mind had begun to break, "I don't understand all that. Like mind reading?"

Visible irritation spread along the scientist. "Almost... Anyway, these will need to be implanted behind the ear. It's quite a painful, but quick procedure. You need only press it behind the bone, and it will implant itself. It's like a phone, Kale, but less cumbersome and untrackable. Pierce will help you put them in in an hour."

Something far more pressing had started to bug him. He eyed the technology nervously, crossing his arms over his chest, "When are you planning on sending us in?"

Richmond took a deep breath.

"Your appointment for admission is in four days."

That soon! I don't understand... How are we supposed to do this?

"Look," Kale spoke with a shaking uncertainty, "I understand how much this means to you, and believe me, I have my reasons for wanting to get in the city, but don't you think we're a little in over our heads? I don't think Astrid is ready for this either." He looked over at the slumped girl who didn't budge at the words.

The scientist's face grew deadly serious and he glared at Kale. "Don't speak for her. You have no right."

He replied with silence.

"We will succeed, I will assure it." Richmond stared unflinchingly into Kale's eyes. "I'm not one to dwell on emotions, but with tragedy comes opportunity." The host led them toward the staircase to the lobby. "As much as I hesitate to admit it, the fact that you are here, Kale, has allowed me to develop much more efficient plans."

Infinite questions flooded Kale's mind as he was sent away to his room. While leaving, he turned a glance back to Richmond and Astrid. An invisible dynamic was constantly communicated between the two. During the meeting, he could tell there was more going on in her mind besides what her droopy body language projected. He was excluded from their knowledge and in a situation as dire as infiltrating the city, a lack of information could get him killed.

Is he trying to trap me?

Kale scoffed as he turned the handle into his room. This game of cat and mouse irritated him to his core. No matter what wits he could use to battle the mind of the scientist, the game was rigged against him. He ran a hand beneath his suit and poked at what were supposed to be his ribs. It didn't feel any different, but the cybernetics beneath his skin contained a security measure against him, at least according to Richmond. It could be a bluff, he thought. After all, he hadn't been conscious during the procedure, but a month and a half had indeed passed simply based on the changes to *Le Lien*'s construction. Even if there was no trap within the cybernetic ribcage, he had been told that the new technology was to be implanted in an hour.

I'm so trapped... For all I know, they could've placed gadgets in my brain. But if I stay here and play along, will I really get into the city?

His inner monologues were interrupted by a knocking. The taps against the door were gentle.

Phoe- oh... right... Who would want to talk to me right now?

Rising from his bed, he shed his suit coat and rolled up the sleeves of his white button-up to answer the door. He took a deep breath and opened it to find Astrid standing in the frame. Her face was downcast, but her suit was well-maintained and straight. There were no stains around her eyes from tears, but visible stress could be seen written on her face.
Kale frowned.
"May I come in?" she queried, strongly, eyeing the floor.
"Umm, yeah, sure..." He gestured to the relatively untouched abode. The room was comparatively similar to its state before his arrival, only a jacket hung on the wall and the bed was slightly ruffled. "Here, sit." He drew out a chair from the desk.
"I'm fine standing." Her voice was harshly monotone and she stood promptly near the door.
"So then," Kale crossed his arms, standing a few feet in front of her, "What're you here for?"
"I... I have something to say."

I'm not prepared for this...

He braced himself. "Okay..."
Astrid's eyebrows rose slightly and she took a deep breath. "That night, when you first arrived, I was afraid to speak to you. Richmond, Phoebe, the others, they were the only ones I'd ever really talked with. I can admit, I've never had to deal with the outside world and its troubles. I've seen how bad it is, but I never felt it, not until Phoebe disappeared that day... Richmond always made it seem like a distant place. It could never touch us."
He hesitated to respond. "She told me after I'd found her crying out there. We took refuge in an old parking garage and I lit a fire to keep us warm. She told me it was the first one she'd seen, only ever read about them in books."

"She loved books." Astrid smiled slightly, continuing to stare at her feet. "Her favorite one was about a witch. It was a really simple and cliche story. The witch put a curse on a princess. She was jealous; wanted the life and the castle that the princess had, though in the end like a lot of children's books, it was kindness that broke the curse."

"I tried to be kind to her."

"Perhaps. She saw it that way. After all, she was the one that told us to let you stay. To her, you were kind."

Kale could sense the tension in their conversation. "What are you trying to say?"

Astrid's soothing recollection began to fade. Her face fell, bending a frown that hid behind messy blond hair. "Your intention may have been kindness, but it wasn't enough to stop the curse. You brought the cruelties of the outside world here through our doors."

So that's it then. She still hates me.

"It wasn't… I didn't mean for that to happen."

"I know. And I know that no amount of hate from me is ever going to bring her back. It's been over a month and I still look for her down the halls…"

A lump stole his throat.

She continued, "I don't know if I'll ever find it in my heart to think of you the way she did." A pause followed and her hands clenched into fists. "Either way, I'm stuck with you now. We have a mission we have to succeed in, for Richmond's sake. We owe it to him, *you* especially owe it to him."

"I… I know."

"That's… all I can manage for now," she began towards the door, refusing to look at him. "Just think about what I said."

Without a look backward, she was gone.

She never looked at me…

A brief period of solace allowed Kale to recollect the strange interaction, but not nearly long enough to understand her true feelings. He could only reason that it was weird.

I can't shake the feeling that this is some sort of trap…

He returned to the bed and continued to ponder Astrid's words until the clock struck the time for the transponder injections.

It's better if I go. I've done enough harm.

He decided to leave.

The other tenants of *Le Lien* were nowhere to be seen, but he could hear scuffling as he slithered by shadow into the lobby. Richmond surely was down in the lab and Pierce would be preparing the imminent procedures. The thought of any more machinations intruding on his autonomy made him shiver. If he allowed them to tinker with his body again, he would be bound even more to the will of the host. It would be better for everyone if he left.

Before any eyes could catch him, Kale stood in front of the hotel's entrance.

I can leave, right? Nothing's going to happen if I step outside…

As nervous sweat built beneath his shirt and jacket, with which he'd replaced the hotel's signature suit, the doors parted. Chill and humid fog collected above the dirty ground outside from heavy rain that had begun to fall, ideal for an unnoticeable escape.

I don't care anymore. I'm done. Even if he were to send me into the Guiding City, I'll just be a slave… I won't fall for it.

Gritting his teeth, his feet flew from the lobby, out into the murky streets of the Old Baltimore slums. Mud splashed beneath him and he squinted his eyes. His thoughts had become a jumbled mess of adrenaline-induced survivability and fleeting madness.

What am I doing? Where can I go? There's no one. Nowhere…

Despite the rain increasing with each passing minute, the sidewalks and ruined streets remained packed with pilgrims. He shoved through the crowds, drawing growls and yells from every shoulder he struck.

The jacket over him had grown drenched and heavy and loudly, he screamed a curse into the air. Nobody cared. In the slums, curses were as common as greetings.

Fifteen minutes had passed since he'd left and he wagered that Richmond would soon hunt him down.

I… I can go back to the cove and beg. The boss won't kill me… I think… I could tell him about Richmond's star… but…

After nearly thirty minutes of running, he took a breath of calm. Beneath the towering dilapidation of an old museum, he noticed the spot where he'd met Phoebe for the first time. His eyes could only stare for a moment.
    The Vulture's cove wasn't far, not when he knew the perfect route to get there; the slums wound like a labyrinth, but he could navigate it blindly.
    Out of the corner of his eye, a glistening shimmer stole his attention. The Den Mother's roost poked above an alley he trod.

She won't accept me back.

The only option, a desperate gamble that he decided through emotion, was to tell the boss of Richmond's plan. Perhaps they could make a deal. If Richmond was serious about the tickets into the city, then he could wager them, but the star… That would be his valuable secret.

That's what I'll do. That's all I can do. If I tell him, I can prove that I'm still useful. Of course, I won't tell him everything, only enough to show that I'm worth keeping around.

His jaw stuck forward as he came upon the final turn to the cove's entrance. The rain was becoming unbearable, like a blizzard of water, and he noticed that the number of pilgrims crowding the area had diminished. Still, his feet stomped through puddles until he stood in front of the flickering neon sign. No light shone in the clear door that led down to his father.

"You won't find them there. They've moved to a new cove."

Kale froze.
It was impossible.
    A voice called from the opposite end of the street, blanketed in the loud pattering rain. It was a voice he knew all too well. The last voice he wanted to hear… Richmond's.
    "Business has been booming as of late. They've afforded a more structured headquarters."
    "H-How did you…" Kale could barely muster the words, spinning on his heels to see the pearly coat of the host through the heavy mist. He couldn't

see his face, but it was impossible not to recognize the prompt shoulders and cold demeanor.

Slowly, the host drew closer, unfazed by the showers. "You know, I meant the words I said. What did I tell you would be the consequence of viewing my work?"

"How did you find me? How the hell did you know where I'd be!?" His skin was pale and shivers of fear tightened around his neck.

"Don't be stupid. You honestly think I wouldn't have my ways of knowing where you are? You, the one who knows my deepest secret, the one I have every right to be suspicious of." Richmond's head stood higher than Kale's and the milky eyes cast a spell on him, one that prevented retaliation. "Perhaps I overestimated your usefulness."

"I…" Kale couldn't form words. He was paralyzed by confusion, fear, and indecisiveness. "How did you find me?"

"A simple tracker was placed inside you when we reconstructed your ribcage. It was an obvious decision to make."

"Tsk." He relinquished himself to the situation. Richmond was in control. "No normal person would think like that."

"I've stolen your freedom. I told you, you are mine. And you have quite the debt to repay me."

"I never asked for this." His eyes didn't leave the ground. "This isn't what I wanted."

"You chose. You chose to see the star. You chose to keep the access card. If careless freedom is what you wanted, then you chose incorrectly."

Kale raised his head, hands clenching at his side. "No, I never chose anything! From the moment I was born, I've had a lethal hand on my shoulders. First, it was my father's, now it's yours. I didn't want any of this!"

The weight of the rain calmed slightly, allowing trickles of light from The Well to penetrate black clouds above. Richmond turned his back to the thug, staring up at the rays. "We all have a hand on our shoulders, Kale, an invisible hand that is the consequence of The Well's arrival. It dug its claws into us that day, but only a few will ever wriggle from its clutches. I intend to be one of them."

"So that's all there is to me then? I'm just going to be your slave forever? Go ahead and kill me. Seems like that's what you're planning anyway."

"Your father told me that his son would be a door in need of kicking down." The host dropped a hand to his pocket, "he was right."

Kale's eyes squinted slowly. "What?"

From the pocket came a small remote, glinting silver light along its edges. Richmond wound it into his hand. "Ten US dollars added to the purchase.

Twelve hundred per ton of steel, five per pound of copper, silver, and gold, well... I drained the supply."

"You... You're lying!"

The lab coat spread apart as he waved his hands about. "I told him I needed a few extra hands. I needed ones that could act, one's that had no options, and he sold them to me for a measly ten dollars." He chuckled, "enough to buy himself some cigarettes for the afternoon."

"Shut up!" Kale leered at the arrogant man before him, beginning to see red between the soaked hair which covered his eyes. His breaths were labored and he could feel the cortisol boiling in his veins. "In all my years as a Vulture, I never met you!"

"That's correct, but I've known you for a long time."

How? How would he know me? Not once did I make a run to that hotel... But... Maybe there was a reason the boss never sent me...

"That doesn't make any sense!"

"It's important that the boss doesn't reveal his most extravagant whales to the lackeys. We can't risk things getting... tricky."

"That's why you were suspicious of me the second I went into the hotel. You lured me into that trap!"

"No, Kale, *you* were the one that asked about the star. I simply welcomed your curiosity."

He grunted at the words. "You're lying!"

Richmond turned back and stared deep into his eyes. "I know your policies. When a member is removed from the ranks, they're removed from this world. Twice, I've saved your life now. You have my watchful eyes to thank for the fact that you even lived to see my good will."

"So, I'm nothing more than a tool. A tool with a ten-dollar price tag? One that you let wander after buying?"

"Correct. And you wandered right where I needed you to."

Kale let loose a laugh, falling to his knees in the water. His hands felt something beside him. A round stone, perfectly fitting between his fingers. "Screw it." Standing back to his feet, he readied his hand beside him. "I guess I have to fight my way out of the clutches too."

Richmond paid the threat no quarter. "Well then, what a perfect opportunity to test this." His thumb pressed the remote.

Kale felt a strange sensation at that moment. His ribs erupted in a plume of pain that spanned the entirety of his body. The joints of his arms became lightning, the ends of his feet turned to stone, and the synapses within his brain screamed in anguish. A splash rang out as his body hit the ground and Richmond stepped above him. He couldn't move an inch.

"It would seem my little machinations did the trick." He stomped on the paralyzed thief's wrist and withdrew the stone. "That reminds me, we need to take one more precaution before I send you into the Guiding City." He withdrew a small blade from his lab coat and began to run the edge along Kale's face. His eyes crossed to watch the shimmering metal. "That sentinel saw your face. Which means we need to make some… adjustments to your appearance."

He couldn't scream as the knife's edge penetrated his skin and the lightning caused his brain to fail.

Chapter 5
Aarnivalkea

[It is said that the Guiding City boasts a painstaking surplus of all things good and holy. The Aureate commands the citizens in silence, weaving an invisible web of fingers that pull and prod to their will. It is an illusory freedom, a hyperreality as Plato described. The shadows appear tangible, frightening in the eyes of the prisoner, keeping them in the cell of their own will, and the puppeteer grins unseen. Yet, there is a way to bring about their downfall. You two will be tasked with unraveling the many mysteries of The Well's light. If we can decipher a means by which to reroute its power to the slums, then the pilgrims will do the rest. My precious little star currently only receives a fraction of what lies beyond those walls, however, I will not sit idly by. While you infiltrate the city, I will be developing stronger conductors and distributing them around the slums. I know this task may appear impossible. As of now, we have no definite way to establish a current from The Well to the outer walls. After all, It took five years just to create this puny machine.]

He could hear the words, and comprehend their meanings, though the darkness of his subconscious withheld his view of their speaker. It was Richmond's voice, he knew, but he wondered where the words came from.

[Now, for The Well, the knowledge we've gained so far is… limited to say the least. The light excreted from the earth is paracausal in nature. It can act in ways no wave in our current understanding of physics should. The first aspect observed was the Midas touch, or the ability to turn objects into a form of gold. It's understandable why the Aureate would withhold such an ability from the general public, after all, for a society to survive it must have a monetary structure. If such power were to leak over into average hands, then the entire economic standing of the world would crumble to bits, but that is not of concern to me. The Well's second observed property mysteriously returns order to the human construction. Diseases are cured in its light and as a result, the life expectancy of the Guiding City's inhabitants has tripled. Finally, as we are all familiar with, the light bears a galvanic power similar to that of electricity, though it suffers no interference, no limitation, and no cause for an initial generation. This third nature of The Well is what we must acquire and take advantage of. The ability to advance humanity should not be limited to one economic class or culture. This withholding by the Aureate is unacceptable and I have sworn my life to see the natural order and equality of the world be returned.]

Am I dreaming?

When the light pierced his eyes again, a new room presented itself. It was darker than Richmond's workshop, illuminated by blue currents running through symmetric wires that lined the walls. A single source of white incandescence radiated cold light onto his head.

The scientist paced before him with his arms folded on his chest that held a bloodstained lab coat against the wind of his stride. His white hair was not combed but wildly fell around his upturned nose. Astrid stood to the right, her chin fixated on the host and her left hand gracefully ran along her opposite arm. She had returned to her upkept appearance of suit and tie that tightly followed the curvature of her body. Her golden hair was braided into a winding strand that fell across her right shoulder.

Kale recognized his situation clearly now. No matter how hard he tried, he was eternally bound to Richmond in servitude. If he chose to resist, he would be electrocuted into paralysis and if he chose to run, he could effortlessly be found. He hatefully glared at the prim-and-proper man in front of him. A blazing fury festered behind his eyes and he shook in anger. Behind the chair he sat in, a chord bound his hands, rubbing a red irritation into the skin. He hadn't yet seen the damage done to his face, but he could feel deep scars running from his right ear across his nose and down the bend of his left cheek. A taste of iron polluted his tongue and his muscles ached in unbearable soreness.

I'm screwed… There's nothing I can do but be a good servant, following his every wish and command. But the last thing I'll do is be weak.

"Once again," Richmond's voice spoke deeply; a muscle twitched in his jaw as he noticed his vassal come to, "I find myself victorious over you. When are you going to learn?"

Kale spat a blob of crimson onto the floor and bent his brows in reply.

"Filthy dog."

Astrid disdainfully tilted her eyes down at the compromised delinquent. "Why can't you just do what he says?"

"That's easy for you to say," Kale snapped back, "seems like you get special treatment while I get the fist."

"Only because it's what you deserve," she retorted.

"What happened wasn't my FAULT!" His words echoed thricefold throughout the metal room and he stomped with the final word. The breaths escaping his nostrils whipped like steam from an engine.

Astrid stepped forward, preparing a litany of words, but Richmond raised a hand and she recoiled back into her resolute posture.

"This morning, Kale," Richmond flowed his speech, "I watched two doves roost atop the patchwork wall of the lobby. I'm sure you noticed how it doesn't seal all the way. It's made an ideal spot for nests. Did you know that when fledglings fall and leave their nests, the parents watch from afar? Even if the drop may kill them… Their souls are bound to the eyes of the parent. It's my watchful eyes that saved you."

"I didn't need you to save me! I can survive on my own like I always have." The black tendrils of his hair only partially hid the burning pupils beneath. "You keep me here against my will and won't even tell me the truth about it all."

"You will receive the truth in due time." Richmond's theatrics followed his words as his hands dipped down like a king offering dirty water to a beggar. "However, I must first remind you of your situation. You've no choice but to do as I tell you from here on out. Remember," a finger pointed into the air, "this was your decision. Twice, I gave you the option to not delve into my secrets, yet you insisted, so any appeals for more of my good will shall fall on deaf ears."

He's right… It was my decision, but how in the world was I supposed to know this would be the result? That's what I get for being so arrogant…

"Then tell me what you saved me for! Why do you care what I do?"

"You want the truth, then? I'll tell you." Richmond bent over and lowered his mouth beside Kale's ear. "To help you," he whispered.

"Help?" Kale laughed in irony. "Sure."

The scientist waved his hands around the air, "It's true. I'm here to give you an opportunity at redemption. I'm giving you the chance to get into the city."

"What a load of crap. You want to get me killed."

"Everything I told you earlier accounts for the extent of our knowledge regarding The Well and the Guiding City. Personally, I've only ever had the luxury of a brief visit with my insider, so I am regrettably unfamiliar with the customs and happenings among the common folk."

"Wait." A trickle of sweat fell from his head. "You mean the words I heard just then? I thought I was dreaming."

"I see my little transponders are serving their purpose." A toothy smile followed. "That's good. I'm confident that between our conjoined minds, a solution can be discovered."

He implanted it while I was out?

A squealing pattern of beeps interrupted the speech. Reaching into the pocket of his lab coat, Richmond withdrew a small pocket watch. "Ah, It's time to meet him."

"Meet who?" Astrid looked up at him.

"The insider. We've arranged a simple hearing. Come, follow me outside."

The two began to turn away, leaving Kale bound to the chair he sat in. "Hey!" he yelled at their backs, "Don't leave me tied down here! Where're you going?"

A white eye turned back to stare at him, "How do I know I can trust you?" Richmond asked.

The younger man let out a chuckle between threatening struggles. "What do you mean? Can't you kill me anytime you want?"

Richmond took several slow steps towards him, "I would prefer not to," the words left his mouth as his hands began to toil the binding on his subject, "You CAN still serve my purpose, but I am more than willing to maim and reconstruct you all I like." Kale shot a shoulder towards the scientist who jumped back reflexively, "Ah ah ah," his hand raised a small remote, "I wouldn't do that if I were you."

"How about this then," the thief suggested, "you let me in on your meeting and I promise not to kill you when I get these bindings off."

"I believe we already saw how that threat played out."

"But you still need me, don't you?" he bargained.

A sneer followed the words, "The single greatest purpose in the world is to protect the greater life of all things. Currently, I am the most qualified for that purpose, therefore I have an ethical obligation to avoid death. If ever my heart were to stop, my toys beneath your skin will decimate your neural networks. In other words, you are the fledgling and I am the parent. If I die, you die. Our twin souls are eternally bound. Isn't that charming?"

A boreal boom shot through Kale's veins and his eyes snapped to meet the host's grinning expression.

You're joking... I knew he'd have put countermeasures in place so I couldn't just kill him, but... That's going too far...

He hung his head slightly, "Is... Is that true?"
"Entirely."
"Then, I really am stuck in this?"
"Indeed."

That's it then... There's no going back. Father sold me to him. The Vultures will kill me if I ever manage to go back and even then, Richmond works with them. Maybe this is the best for me...

The host stepped awfully close, practically touching foreheads with him. "If I were you, Kale, I'd end these foolish threats now. Let me put it bluntly, there isn't a single person alive right now that gives a damn whether you live or die. I'm giving you a chance that your father and your entire organization have been chasing since the gang's inception. You CAN be useful to me, but I can also replace you with another if I so desire. I see the potential you have, so suck that repulsive pride back into your thick skull and accept my gift. I'm through with these games."

He gulped, unable to speak.
"Have I made myself clear?" the pale man growled.
The bound thug let out a sigh of defeat. "Let me join your meeting and I promise I'll cooperate."
"There you go," Richmond patted his head, "good boy."

The insider was not to be seen directly. His identity was wholly confidential to everyone except Richmond, as expected. The three exited the front doors of the hotel and Richmond stood at their head, motioning for them to follow to the left corner of the building. The sky was gray with winding clouds and voices of the slumsfolk littered the air. The host flattened himself against the brick of the hotel and stuck a hand out to halt his two followers.

Peeking around the corner, a hooded face with yellow bandages covering the eyes stared at them. A scruffy chin moved as the first words left the insider.

"*Ça fait longtemps, dis donc.*" His voice was exceedingly deep. Kale couldn't understand the French.

The scientist smiled, "Indeed. What do you have for us?"

"A status report. My duties have found me venturing through many places within the Guiding City. Recently, several of the clerics have been reciting their communions but there is nothing of note hidden in their messages. However, the big news right now is the upcoming election for the governmental exegete."

"Exegete?" Richmond asked, "a special cleric for the Aureate?"

"Yes," the insider replied, turning his covered eyes towards them, "There is debate among the council as to who'll be appointed. It is quite the opportune time for your infiltration. I understand these two have v never been. Have you educated them?"

The scientist raised a hand to scratch the back of his head. "We've had several interruptions in our endeavors recently," he eyed Kale with disdain, "I haven't quite had the chance."

Astrid tapped Richmond's shoulder and offered him a questioning look. Kale watched the two closely.

"I see," the mysterious man continued, "then, you two, listen well. This disagreement has left the Aureate fractured for a short time. They currently campaign against one another for their respective candidates. Due to this, commotion has erupted and security is spread thin. It's reached a boiling point. Certain factions aligned with the politicians have occupied liberated zones throughout the city. Without a conjoined government, they no longer have individual authority to deploy military interference, however, security drones patrol the streets at various times. You will need to be careful to avoid their suspicion."

"So," Kale interrupted, "what're we supposed to do once we get in?"

"We've arranged a dwelling for you two to live in in the heart of the city, though, I regret to inform you that it is quite small."

Astrid pushed past to get a word in, "How small?"

The insider's face stoically stared back, "The original preparations were made for you and your younger sister. All we could afford was one room in the commerce district."

Her eyes widened like she was suffering from a heart attack and a paleness leaked through her generous makeup.

"Huh? You mean I'm going to have to share a room with her?" Kale stuck a finger at her.

"No way. I can't do that!" She protested.

"Keep your quarrels out of this!" Richmond separated the two. "You're going to have to deal with it. Astrid can contact me any time she needs to, so don't try anything."

Kale remembered the security measures constructed within his body and cursed. "As if I'd do anything. Just tell her to stop treating me like I'm a thug and we won't have an issue."

"I've only said things you need to hear," she mumbled.

Richmond turned to Kale and held up the frightful remote.

He gulped.

"So then," the insider continued, "listen carefully to the information I've gathered. The Aureate is currently comprised of six members, each ruling equally in power:

The first is a man named Alastor Jalaal, a pompous diplomat so enthralled with his wealth that he'd do anything to show it off. He even has a golden castle right on the border of The Well.

The second member is Rachael Hemming. She was CEO of the leading auto manufacturer before The Waking but has since dabbled in politics among other sciences, quite like our host here.

Third is Moriarty Jacobs, a financier long ago, he doesn't seem to care for politics. I don't even know how he came to rule, but if I learn more I'll be in conta-" A horrendous string of coughs exited the insider and he bent over in pain.

"Woah," Kale reached towards him to help, "you okay?"

A dark and scarred hand blocked him and the strange man found his composure. "Y-Yes I'm fine. Allow me to continue."

Richmond didn't flinch at the man's condition.

"Fourthly...*cough* is Damian Shikov. He spends his days outside the Guiding City. My guess is that he likes the power, but not the chains of an office. You shouldn't hear much about him.

Our fifth member is Dr. Brianna Sky, a lawyer in the past, now one of the most compelling and corrupt leaders the world has ever seen. They call her the 'Machine Goddess' in the streets and it's been told that she gave half herself to bind with technology. I've only heard rumors, but they're enough to scare me. You two, do not get involved with her in any capacity."

"What in the world?" Astrid cringed at his words. "The people of the city sure sound strange."

"Finally, we have the one I know least about, Gilgamesh. It is a name scrawled among the others. No one knows if they're human, machine, or another name for The Well, however, they're included among the rulers. *cough* That's all I know."

Kale's jaw hung wide while listening. It was intriguing. Their anomalous nature caused him to imagine the world beyond the walls. "So," he began, "you said they're all competing to have their cleric elected? What exactly does that mean for us?"

"As I said before, this is good. The security measures in and around the city have been allocated thinly. You should have little trouble moving through and *cough* gathering information."

"But where do we even begin?"

Richmond raised a pale hand to silence him and spoke, "Let's let our insider get back to work. We can discuss this later." He turned to the cloaked man, "You may leave now, thank you."

"Yes Sir." The Insider offered a low bow and was gone. A handful of coughs trailed his departure.

Kale turned to Astrid as they began back into *Le Lien,* keeping a good distance behind their host. "What's up with that guy? Is he sick?"

"I don't know," she responded in an equally befuddled tone, "all I know is that he was someone Richmond rescued after The Waking and since then he's been working for him."

"Why'd he have his eyes covered like that?"

"I guess it's so we don't figure out his identity, but yellow is Richmond's signature color. Maybe it shows his loyalty. You know how he likes that kind of stuff."

"That's true."

I didn't expect her to actually talk to me…

The two of them were ordered to gather in a special dining room accessed through a door underneath the winding staircase of the lobby. It was new to Kale, a red-carpeted expanse lit by similar fountain lights as the rest of the building, though the walls were covered in dark hardwood architecture. A long table stretched for a great distance in the center of the room. Decorative streaks of yellow wound between the grains of its granite surface that stood on many petrified tree trunks.

He whistled in admiration.

As they walked in, a perfume of garlic and red wine climbed his nostrils and he felt a sweet nostalgia deep within. Three plates of steaming steak and potatoes were prepared at the closest end by hands unknown to him, accompanied by a glass of dark and bubbling wine. Richmond folded his coat over a large captain's chair and took the end seat. Kale felt his mouth water and swiftly dove to dig in, which was met by a hiss from Astrid.

"What?" he argued.

Questionably, he glared at her, but quickly realized the lack of etiquette and reluctantly withdrew his suit coat, draped it over the back of an ornate chair to the host's right, and rolled up his sleeves before returning to the plate. Astrid did the same on the opposite side. He eyed her as she moved. Her shoulders were tightly bound in the undershirt, so much so that her arms, stiff as sticks, struggled to find her utensils.

Get a new suit already…

"Eat for a moment," Richmond began in his elegant voice as he sliced a piece of medium rare steak, "then we'll talk."

Such a delicacy had never before graced Kale's tongue. The steak, perfectly seared and salty on its edges, oozed a warm and buttery liquid as his teeth pressed it together. The peeled potatoes to its side fell apart when his fork prodded their centers. After stuffing his mouth, he took a sip of the drink that flowed with a hiss down his throat. It was sweet, followed by a tinge of alcohol only recognizable enough to please but not annoy his taste buds.

"Now this," he spoke with bulging cheeks, "is how you bribe me, Richmond."

The scientist brushed his hair back and produced a sinister grin, "Good."

After a few minutes of heavenly teeth gnashing, a silence ensued as a result of their filled stomachs.

Richmond broke that silence. "So then, I'm sure your brains are eagerly awaiting clarification about the next few days. What questions do you have?"

Kale shot a hand in the air, "The Aureate, the members are weird. What's up with them? They're some sort of government?"

"They're the presiding governors of the Guiding City, an oligarchy that decides laws, monitors economic distribution, and oversees mass events. You'll have to find a way to slip under their noses."

"How're we going to do that?" Astrid asked.

"That's the great uncertainty isn't it…" Richmond rested his chin on a palm. "Frankly, we don't know. The situation in the city, as our insider said, is volatile at the moment. You should use this to your advantage. Security is scattered and now that I've changed the topography of your face, Kale, you two shouldn't be a cause for suspicion."

Kale remembered the events of the day prior. His hand traveled to his face and traced the cut that ran across. He looked around and picked up a silver saucer beside him, inspecting his reflection. Among the many scars on his face, this one stood out. It ran deep across his nose and down his cheek. He felt a sense of sadness about it, then brief anger, but managed to gulp down the thoughts. "Right," he replied softly.

"Your priority should simply be gathering information. As you know, I'll be accompanying you through the transponders while I see to matters here at *Le Lien*. There is still much work to be done in designing means of distribution of The Well's power. In two days, I'll bring you to the gates and you'll find your way to the dwelling. Unfortunately, I cannot travel into the city with you."

"I still don't like the idea," Astrid complained quietly.

"It doesn't matter. You'll make it work."

Kale gulped, "We just know so little."

Richmond stood to his feet and pushed in his chair, leaning on the tall backrest of it. "I understand your hesitations in this endeavor, but you have no choice. I'm fully confident in you two to deliver."

Astrid raised her eyes to meet the scarred delinquent that sat opposite her. Both of them frowned and slowly looked away.

"What do you think about it?" he asked.

"I'm a little scared," she said plainly, "this is so overwhelming to me."

"It's the same for me too. At least we're not on any kind of time frame for this."

"Ah, but that's where you're wrong." The host's words cut the air. "It is imperative that we capitalize during the confusion. We *must* have a concrete plan in place before the Aureate is restored and the city's usual security measures resume. I estimate a month at most."

Equally, Kale and Astrid's faces turned ghastly.

"A month…" he whispered.

"When we enter the city, you'll have to find your way to the dwelling. The insider has fashioned a makeshift map." Richmond fumbled around his lab coat and withdrew a rectangular piece of steel. A button rose in its center that he pressed, causing the metal to split. The two sides were pulled apart by his fingers and a blue glow emanated between them. Small dots like stars appeared on the blue light and lines began to dash from point to point creating a detailed cartograph of the area. "Among the 'exceedingly complex maze of metals,' as he describes it, are many districts of the city. The commerce district will be your new home." He pointed to a dot in the center of a circular intersection of several paths. "The southern commerce district sits closer to The Well than any other residential area. Your home will be on the eastern side, where the district connects to the city's academic university. We worked hard to create the ideal reconnaissance location for you and from what I've been told, the university allows guests on a regular basis. Perhaps starting there would suit your early days well. Learn as much as you can about The Well and its properties without raising suspicion. Remember, you are citizens now. You need not be nervous."

"You say that, but still... There's plenty of danger." Kale leaned into his elbows, the golden face of a sentinel flashing in his mind.

"All you need to do for the time being is focus on information gathering and relaying such information back to me." Richmond's voice was surprisingly calm and he stroked his chin in thought. "Don't be fearful, but don't *ever* forget the mission."

Astrid sat up resolutely, making strong eye contact with her superior. "I promise I'll do everything I can to make sure we do what we need to."

"WE," Kale sarcastically butted in, majestically waving a hand downward, "will do everything we can."

The host smiled to himself, "Take tonight and tomorrow to collect yourselves. I have my own work to attend to." He threw his coat over his shoulder and walked over to Astrid, placing a hand on her head, "I'm going out for the night, but I'll return first thing in the morning. Kale," he eyed him with a deathly stare, "I'll be watching."

Kale brushed his hair back, "Always so suspicious of me? Don't worry I won't do anything."

Of course, I'm going to take a look around...

That night, he lay atop his bed, staring at the ceiling with intense contemplation.

He turned to a digital clock resting on his nightstand. Bright red numbers flashed 12:14 on the face. The lights of his hall remained dimly lit after the sun went down and he poked his head out of the door to check for wandering faces. Even after all his time spent in *Le Lien*, he still had yet to meet several of the guests and with that uncertainty, he had to be extra careful.

Wearing the darkness of his suit as a cloak, he matted his hair down to block his face and crouched over, weaving through the densest subsections of shadows unblemished by the fountain lights. As he found the top of the spiral staircase leading down to the lobby, his squinted eyes scanned the floor. As far as he could tell, it was uninhabited. Slowly and quietly, the tips of his toes lead him to the ground level. The light from the chandelier was turned off and the few incandescent devices did little to illuminate the room. He could pass unseen.

I just want to look at it.

His hands found the smooth keypad. Sweat dripped over his brow as nervousness began to set in.

He tapped: 5507 to which the sliding of the lock responded in kind. The metallic staircase down presented itself and trickles of golden light from the star pulsed at a relative speed to his racing heart. With each step down, he thought of turning back, but his body refused. The star shone brightly against his eyes which were adjusted to the previous darkness. His hands inspected the interlacing metals that formed the miraculous machine's construction. It was warm to the touch, not hot, but pleasant like it wanted to be beheld. He traced the wires that exited both sides of the cylindrical device, watching the winding ropes transport infinite power graciously out of the room. It truly was a marvel that Richmond created such technology without the tools of the city. He drifted into deep thought.

[It seems I was right to have my suspicions.]

Kale jumped so high in the air that he felt the tips of his hair bend against the ceiling.
The web of nerves in his body froze in fear and his eyes darted around feverishly. The sound of Richmond's voice resonated in his mind like a thought, not of his own, but automatically broadcast through his sensorium. "H-H-How… What's going on?" he shakingly spoke to himself.

[Did you forget about our transponders? They work fantastically don't they?]

He let out a nervous chuckle, slowly bringing his hands to his pockets. "I g-guess they do."

[What were you doing sneaking around my workshop at this hour?]

"Nothing! I swear!" Kale prepared himself for a sudden blast of electricity to erupt from his ribs. "All I wanted to do was look at it. I couldn't sleep."

[Then, did you get a good look?]

The nervousness began to dwindle and he brought himself to a fixed posture. "I was just admiring it. You want us to gather data on The Well so I thought I could start by observing this."

[Thinking of the mission rather than stealing?]

"Yeah…" A small chuckle followed, "Also, I wanted to know what you went out to the slums at night for."

[And why would that be your business to know?]

"Trust," he quickly replied, unsure if it was the right word. "If I'm part of this then I want the truth."

Richmond's voice over the transponder paused for a moment and a light sigh followed.
[I suppose you're correct in feeling that way. Trust would be a good thing to have, wouldn't it?]

"Then you'll tell me?" He couldn't help feeling slightly surprised at the exchange.

[Very well. I'm meeting an old friend. You see, I couldn't build the star with the available tools, so I had to resort to hidden markets for the parts required. Electrical conductors are very in demand as you might imagine and we're going to need every piece of scrap we can get our hands on for this mission.]

Conductors… Like copper and steel?

"I see." Disappointment began to crawl through Kale's body as he heard the words and slowly he inched his way back to the staircase. "So, who's the old friend?"

[Your father, Kale.]

Chapter 6
Cleric

Kale frowned and sank to sit on the cold bottom step. "Right…" The idea of Richmond's acquaintanceship with his father made him want to vomit.

[Your father and I have a very useful relationship.]

"Does he know?"

[Know?]

"Does he know where I am?"

[Considering my purchase, It's likely.]

"Does he ask about me?"

[Is that knowledge important to you?]

"I don't know."

[No.]

"I see."

[I shouldn't need to tell you the psychology of your father.]

"He's never cared about me."

[He cares about his organization.]

"Yeah. He does. And I guess that means he doesn't care about me."

[He cares about getting into the city.]

"But not for his family."

[That depends on what one considers family. To your father, The Vultures are family.]

"You know what I mean."

[I do.]

"Does he know about your plan?"

[I'm not sure that's something you should be concerned with.]

"You don't trust me?"

[I trust myself to make the right decisions.]

"Then, how about a truth for a truth?"

[You want me to ask you something?]

"I'll promise to tell you the truth, whatever you want to know, but you have to answer my question."

[What makes you think I want to know something about you?]

"Just go with it. For my sake."

[Very well.]

"Then, ask what you want."

[I want to hear this from you then. Why did you decide to help Phoebe?]

Kale grew cold.
The question made him sick. "I... I thought that if I helped her, whoever she belonged to would give me a place to stay." The answer made him equally sick.

A long pause followed the words.

[Your answer, Kale, is no. Your father's best quality is that he doesn't ask questions about his clients.]

He snickered mockingly. "So, he's inadvertently helping you destroy the utopia he wants so badly… and he doesn't even know it?"

[Utopia? No, not at all. The Guiding City is no utopia. They are without meaning. Those people have no experience, no subjectivity. They're inhuman hedonists with no image beyond their own. They are animals, and you know I hate animals. We are doing the world a service by exterminating such meaningless pleasure-seeking. Had I the means, I would do it myself.]

The ire in Richmond's words drove Kale to thought, but he couldn't bring himself to feel the same emotion. "Right now, I don't care too much about servicing the world. It's been too cruel to me."

[And that, Kale, is animalistic thought.]

"Whatever." He rose from his slouch and began to leave. A faint light trickled from the hotel lobby, through the crack of the steel door atop the staircase.

[I expect you to come to an understanding, and I expect it soon.]

"Give me some time. Right now I don't know what to feel."

Kale completed the trek up the staircase and opened the door to find himself standing face-to-face with Astrid, who looked particularly surprised. Her chin curled up and a stiff hand attached to her hip. She wore a long coat of black fluff that zipped up from her knees and a golden light shone off of her left shoulder, likely an old gadget of Richmond's.

"Great." He mocked her before she had the chance to speak. "I'm in trouble now, aren't I?" He spoke to the transponder without breaking the girl's eye contact.

[Good luck.]

Richmond exited the transponder's call with a small beep.

I hate him...

"What're *you* doing down here this late?" she interrogated him with forceful verbiage.

"Don't worry," he said, irritated, "I already talked to the boss." He tried to walk past her but was stifled by a hand to the chest.

"Empty your pockets."

"What? I didn't take anything."

She held up a small gray remote. It was the same one that activated the shock in his ribs. He shuddered slightly and his eyes locked on the device.

Kale's limbs froze. "You have one of those?" he whispered.

"Yep," the corners of her lips twitched slightly like she was withholding a prideful snicker, "better do what I say."

Kale frowned and his shoulders slumped when his hands found his pockets. He folded them outward, revealing only lint and void. "See?"

Her hands crossed over her chest and she put distance between them. "Then what were you doing down there?"

"None of your business! I was talking to Richmond the whole time."

She sighed, looking at the floor and bringing the remote back to her pocket, "Anyways, I guess it's good that you're here. Call it strange, but I wanted to talk to you. Things are eating at me that I need to get off my chest."

He stood straightly, eyeing her suspiciously but genuinely intrigued by her words. "What do you mean?"

"Can we go sit?" she pointed to the leather seats that surrounded the dimly lit coffee table of the lobby's center. Phoebe's memorial glowed behind her with flickering candle flames.

"...Sure..." he equivocated slowly.

Astrid sauntered in front of him, tugging at her coat even though it hung loosely around her. He watched her body language, analyzing what it meant. She constantly expressed discomfort, insecurity, and fear, but all other signs about her told otherwise. She spoke with confidence, stood upright, and never backed away from him. It could've been a quirk of hers, but given the situation of Richmond's mind games, she was greatly predisposed to his suspicion.

He sat down slowly, eyes not leaving the girl across from him, and sank into the chair. He rested his hands widely apart. She took her seat, crossing her bare legs and folding her hands evenly in her lap. She noticed his eyes and dodged the gaze swiftly. Tinges of pink flushed in her cheeks and for a second, he felt his heart rate increase.

Don't fall for it... It's probably just an act.

"So then," he broke their silence, "what is it?"

"Um..." she cleared her throat and brought a hand to her mouth, "I can't tell this to Richmond and I figured you'd understand a bit since we're kind of in the same position, but- I need to be honest."

"Wait," Kale held up a palm to silence her. He closed his eyes and lowered his head slightly. "You just said 'honest.' I need proof that you can be honest with me. I... I can't handle any more lies."

Her brows bent in frustration and he noticed her arms flinch slightly, but her composure was maintained. "Shouldn't I be the one saying that? Let's not forget how everything you told me that first night was a lie. Richmond told me who you really are."

"It wasn't all lies... well, some of it..." He mimicked her motion, confronting her upturned face with his own. "But I'm willing to turn over a new leaf."

She squinted. "What if you're lying right now?"

The tension irritated him. "I'm not."

She stayed silent for a minute, their eyes locked. An invisible contest waged between the two until finally, Astrid withdrew. "Then how about this?" She stuck her hand out, curling all of her fingers in except for her pinky which reached out to him.

"What?" Kale asked, inspecting the offer.

"A promise," she said shyly, "Phoebe and I used to make them."

He looked at her hand with hesitation. "What kind of promise?"

"In the books we read, a promise means you have to do something. I promise that going forward we can be honest with each other." Her lip quivered slightly. "For the mission, we have to have trust."

"So you trust me enough to make a promise?"

"It only works if we trust each other."

"And you're willing to do that?"

Some undecipherable emotion overcame Astrid which caused her to drop her head. Kale didn't immediately understand it. "Something made Phoebe trust you. Even if you may have had selfish reasons for helping her," she spoke softly, "the fact is that you brought her back. You saved her that day and for that, I'm grateful. There's good in you, somewhere. Richmond wouldn't be so sure of you if there wasn't."

There was a spell in those words. Something clicked inside him. Kale guiltily hesitated for a moment. He pictured the little girl's smiling face, her happiness when she returned to her home. The image came with pain. Slowly, he met Astrid's soft hand, wrapping his pinky around hers. "I promise."

So that's it. I can't play these games anymore... Surely, she wouldn't make a promise like this as a way to trick me. Hopefully, this means the beginning of trust.

"Then," Kale pocketed his hand, "a truth for a truth."
"What do you mean?"
"We each ask a question and no matter what, we must tell the truth."
"Okay, let's do that."
"You start."
A small grin grew on the girl's cheeks, alluding to a deeper understanding, the ability to be truthful he supposed. "Ask me a question then."
He thought for a moment. "That first night, Phoebe told me she wasn't related to Richmond, and you told me he wasn't your father. That was a lie wasn't it?"
She sighed, "since you brought it up, yes, that was a lie. You could tell?"
"Tsk." He looked away. "It just *felt* like a lie, like everything else."
Astrid reclined slightly, "I guess."
"Why?" Kale raised an eyebrow, "that seems like such a weird thing to hide."
She scratched her head. "This is going to sound crazy, but my sister was raised without the concept of parents. He wanted to shelter her from reality and give her a life free of the world's problems. There's too much sorrow out there. She didn't need to know."
"So that was one of Richmond's twisted experiments?" He looked back to the memorial, still flickering the jubilant face of the little girl. A deep pain twisted his stomach into knots, but he took a breath and it faded slightly.
"I guess you could call it that. He didn't want her to have the pain of losing our mother."
"What happened to your mother?"
"She died shortly after Phoebe was born. She was out to get food at the markets, like any other day, but she never made it back. Richmond, or... father, found her body in an alley not too far from here. She had been strangled and who knows what else..." The green eyes fell to the floor. "On the outside, it

doesn't seem to bother him, but that man has seen more tragedy in this world than anyone else."

"I guess your mother was a good person. You two seem nothing like Richmond." He sat forward slightly, resting his weight on his knees.

"She was an angel, always worried about others rather than herself. It's who Phoebe got that side of herself from. As for me, I wish I could be more like her. I don't see myself in my father, and with my mother, I always felt out of place. The love the two shared for one another was so strong and unbreakable that it made me feel intrusive."

"What was her name?" Kale inquired.

"Maria," Astrid replied with a quivering voice. She paused for a moment, then looked up to meet his eyes. "That's a truth from me. Now it's your turn."

"What do you want to know?" A single strand of black hair fell across his eyes. His jaw held stern.

She thought for a few seconds, resting her chin on her hand, and then spoke, "Why did you sneak into Richmond's lab?"

He sighed, "I wanted to look at the star… And I guess I wanted to know what he went to the slums for, but I got my answer." The thought of his father's hatred stung as he recollected Richmond's words. "He caught me though."

"He watches us," she said, looking around the lobby. "He told me what happened after you left yesterday. He tracks us, but I don't mind it. After Mother died, he's been so cautious. It wasn't only to spy on you, Kale, he cared for you."

"What?" Kale sat up and crinkled his brows, "How could he care about me after what I did?"

There's no way that monster of a human could care for someone. Obviously, it's only to protect his assets and give himself the upper hand if he ever needs it. That's the kind of person Richmond is. As if he'd ever feel compassion.

"It's pity. He's always looking to the greater good. He's an amazing person."

"I don't want his pity," he hissed and reclined back into the chair, crossing his legs. "Anyway, what was the thing you wanted to talk about?"

She frowned and copied his action of sitting back. "I wanted to tell you that I'm scared. I can't bring myself to tell Richmond, but I'm terrified of what we have to do."

He took a second to observe her and thought to himself. "I am too. Twice I've seen those sentinels do what they do. It's horrible. To me, there's nothing scarier." The visions of his comrades being crushed beneath unfeeling metal stained his mind. The black lenses of eyes and sharp machinery caused him to sweat.

"I know he said we have nothing to worry about and we're just going in as common citizens, but still..." Her head fell into her hands and strands of golden hair extended between the fingers. "It's like the vision of that thing is scarred in my brain! I can't sleep anymore because of it, I can't close my eyes or I see its face, and I can't even think back about the good memories of my sister or I see her body!"

Kale clenched his hands together, trying to hold back his own emotions. He opened his mouth to speak but hesitated as he saw Astrid whimper. Time slowed. He'd never experienced someone so vulnerable... so *honest* before.

I have to be the bigger person. I have to leave it all behind. The boss, The Vultures, everything... This is my chance to start over for something better... I guess...

He lowered his voice in a seemingly unwelcome attempt at comfort, "I know your pain."

Is that the right thing to say?

The eyes that stared back held a color so deep he felt an infinite truths lay beneath the pupil.

"Kale?" Astrid began to speak, turning her head slightly, but retaining eye contact. Her hands found the edges of her coat and wrapped it tightly around herself.

He crossed his arms and raised an eyebrow, "yeah?"

"Can I trust you?"

He brandished a half smile, untellably genuine and equally forced, "I promised, didn't I?"

"Then," she held down the bottom of her coat as she rose to her feet, loose golden hair stuck to the tear-dampened cheeks, "thank you." Her face turned down to look upon his. Her eyes squinted with soft tinges of red around their edges. Her lips curled upwards in a satisfactory show of appreciation.

He couldn't understand it. Through all of his manipulations and false words, she chose forgiveness, or so it seemed. Yet, as always with Astrid, it didn't settle well with him. There was something more, he was sure of it. Whether something dark, something beyond comfortable companionship, or something extraordinarily benevolent, he couldn't tell. Her appearance of a normal girl with a deep devotion to her father couldn't be all that the frame of a well-to-do woman held beneath.

Can we actually trust one another? I wouldn't trust me…

"Forgiveness," she turned to walk away, "will take some time." The suspended ball of light followed her shoulder.

Well, that's a start I guess…

"Wait." Kale said, rising from his seat. "Why did you come down here?"

Without turning around, she replied, "I just needed a moment to myself, happened to hear you down there." She climbed the stairs feeling the cold railing.

A moment longer he stood in the lobby. After she'd reached the second floor and he heard the ding of the elevator, he traveled the path back to his room.

Richmond returned early the next morning, bringing with him several tattooed men that carried heavy loads of scrap metals on their shoulders through a side entrance of the hotel. Kale had risen early, dressed in loosely fitting jeans and a black shirt. The hotel's laundry was filled with leftover clothes from various pre-Waking guests and the crew had taken care to assure they were well maintained for future necessities. When he found the lobby, Richmond yelled to him from outside.

"Ah, Kale, come help us with this load."

Kale, uncertainly looking at the dusty morning roads of the slums, curled a brow at the man as he walked outside. A chill air greeted him. A large cart, fortified by steel wheels and a hydraulic piston motor, stood in the street with a hearty supply of various rusted and reflective metals in its bed. Several unkempt pilgrims stood eyeing the supplies from the sidewalks nearby and the two hired-hands cursed at them in German. They'd have to fight to get a piece of the wealth, and although violence in the slums was as common as dirt, the muscular thugs deterred them by appearance alone.

"You sure it's a good idea to bring other people here?"

"Yes, yes, they're fine. They know their bounds." The host smiled at the men who grunted in passing. Their eyes locked on Kale as they passed and one nodded to the other.

A chill went down Kale's spine. "Vultures?"

"Yep." Richmond's white hair gleamed in the morning light, and he held a hand up to block it. "They're new to the crew, easily under your father's thumb, and eager to prove themselves. It's best to take the ones with the most consequences here so they can't think about trying anything… dubious."

"Do they know who I am?"

"It's doubtful. That is a measure I took to ensure this works out well." He slapped an arm over Kale's shoulder, pushing him forward slightly. "Go grab some metal and help out, I'll see to breakfast being prepared."

As he walked to the assortment of scrap, he eyed the members carefully. He could sense a skeptical gaze glossing him over.

I need to check…

With his thumbs, he signaled a small V, and extended the rest of his fingers out past the wrists as wings; the recognizable hand sign of The Vultures. When the gang was first formed, they commonly used it as a means of hidden communication, a symbol that a brother was nearby, though as the gang grew, they needed a permanent brand. Tattoos became the normal practice of initiation. Once a Vulture, forever a Vulture with the only unmaking being death itself, except of course in Kale's case.

If they recognize it, they'll definitely know who I am… but if not, I'm in the clear.

The thugs wrinkled their heads in confusion and one spoke up, "You gonna help us out or not?" His accent was thick.

Kale let out a thankful exhale.

I'm relieved that they don't know me… But… What if they did? How would I feel then?

Burying the thoughts, he hopped up into the cart and grabbed a long bar. It was heavy and he felt the muscles in his back stretch as he raised it above his left shoulder. The sun beat down, casting a warmth onto him among the chill air from the salty sea to the east. He felt a calling deep within, of the worlds beyond, but was quickly ripped from his thoughts by a smack of iron to the back of his head.

Kale bit his tongue, stifling the insult that he almost yelled at the brutish thug. Working with dirty scrap was uncomfortable enough first thing in the morning, and he figured picking a fight would only make it worse. He couldn't deny the faint greeting of nostalgia though.

After about thirty minutes of painstaking work, the sun had begun to rise a quarter of the way through the blue sky. Wispy clouds lined the air and the smell of freshly cooked bacon exited *Le Lien* by way of a smoke cloud that traveled from the front door.

Richmond's head poked gleefully from the corner of the entrance doors and he called to Kale loudly, "The food is ready. You can stop the work now."

Thank god...

A pile of metals had been created in the lobby next to the door of Richmond's lab. Steel beams and wires stood taller than his head like silver bramble and he wiped a bead of sweat from his brow. The regulated temperature of the hotel lobby embraced him like a comforting hug. Kale walked to meet Richmond at the dining hall entrance where plates had been prepared. Buchannon, the old tailor, was hunched over a hearty serving of eggs, covered to the edge in crystalline salt. He cringed at the overly seasoned dish.

"Who're the cooks?" Kale questioned the host as he entered the room.

Richmond had returned to his white lab coat and marigold suit and stood lazily against the doorframe. "No chance to meet them, eh? The two chefs, Reba and Maryland. They're very nice women, I'm sure you'd get along."

"Maybe I should pay them a visit sometime…" He found his way to a seat at the opposite end of the long table, sitting in front of a plate of scrambled eggs and crimson bacon. "Where's Astrid?"

"I haven't seen her this morning." Richmond bent his eyebrows. "Actually, why don't *you* go get her? She scarcely stays in her room for long."

"Huh? I don't even know where her room is." He stuffed a forkful of egg in his mouth.

The host crossed his arms, placing a leg against the wall. "415. Take the elevator to the fourth floor, it's the sixth door on the left. You two need to become better acquainted anyway."

"Can I finish my food first?"

A sigh hissed through the air. "You can do it now, or I can make you… Your choice."

the thug spoke with bits of egg on his tongue. "Do you really have to threaten me every day? Chill out a bit."

Richmond spoke between his teeth, "it's because you make me threaten you every day."

Kale groaned and dropped his fork, propping himself up with his arms. "Fine."

"415, Don't forget."

"Yeah, yeah, I won't forget."

Forcing me to work all morning and now I can't even enjoy my food? I can't stand the way he's always against a little relaxing.

The elevator let out a resounding **DING** as it reached the fourth floor. The ceiling bore small holes throughout as a result of the sentinel attack allowing thin beams of light to trickle in. The hall stretched for a long distance of red carpet, where several overhead lights failed to shine. Kale stuffed his hands in his pockets and stepped lightly down the path. One, two, three, four, five, six... Astrid's room stood before him. He sighed. He didn't feel like talking to her. The next day held enough stress and he was tired from lifting metal all morning, but slowly, he approached the door.

He raised his knuckle to knock but paused at the sound of sniffles.

Great... She's crying... I can't handle any guilt today.

He tapped the door three times. "Astrid? It's me. Richmond told me to come get you."

The sniffles grew louder, and he heard her choke for air. "D-D-Don't come i-!" She struggled between coughs.

"What's wrong? You okay?"

Staggered gasps ripped from behind the door and he heard a clattering sound of something falling. "S-S-Stop! Get out of my head!"

What in the world? Something's wrong...

Kale shivered and felt the handle. He tried to turn it without pushing the door open. It was unlocked. "Hey!" he said with a slight panic, "I'm coming in."

She whimpered and groaned but choked for air simultaneously. "Ah! N- I can't..."

He turned the handle and leaned against the door, prompting her to cry as it opened inward. The room was dark, and a smell of harsh perfume filled his nose, sucking the air from him. He brought his hand up to his face as he looked for her. Knelt down the floor, Astrid was slouched against the bottom of her bed. She was covered in a bedsheet that had been ripped from the mattress and still tugged against a corner hidden from view. His eyes traveled upward, following her body, which he could tell was naked beneath the thin sheet. It was terror he felt, though, as he saw her face. The girl's hands were clawing at her hair and her mouth was open, bearing teeth clenched together. The whites of her eyes glowed with a bloodshot red, staring back at him with a deep cry for help. But between the eyes, centered on her forehead, a golden mark sprouted tiny emanations of light, faint enough to see in the dark.

"What in the-"

"H-Help me, please…" she cried softly.

Frozen, he stood for a moment, unable to act. His eyes locked on the golden symbol, shining as a third eye. She wasn't wearing any makeup.

Tears fell from her eyes. "It's talking to me…"

"You…" he whispered, "you're a cleric."

Chapter 7
Purgatory

With cold hands, he grasped her forearms as she shivered with uncontrollable spasms. He could feel her pulse throb outside the skin.

"I need you to get a hold of yourself. Try to calm down," he halfway spoke the words to himself.

"I-I can't!" She yelled, "It won't stop!" She rocked back and forth, hissing between her teeth. Pools of water began to form in the corners of her emerald eyes.

"What's it saying?" he reluctantly inquired.

"I don't k-know… I can't think!"

He thought for a moment, unsure what to do. A panic began to build and he feverishly looked around the room. Her fur coat from the night before hung from a steel hook in the wall and he rose to retrieve it. The sleeves of his shirt had grown wet from her tears. Carefully he nestled the coat over her shoulders and wound its sleeves under her hands. "Should I call Richmond? Can he help?"

She jumped at him, gripping his arms tightly and she yelled, "No! I don't want… I don't want him to see me like this!"

"Then what! What should I do?" Kale frantically asked.

"Just," she took a deep breath that escaped in fragments, "just stay here… p-please. I'm scared that I'll lose myself."

He couldn't control his lower lip which held his mouth slightly open. He couldn't blink. The golden light from her forehead commanded his attention and he felt fear.

"But why not? He'd be able to help," he bargained.

A frustrated yelp left her throat, "I can't. He'll think I'm weak… Please… It'll go away soon… When this happens, Phoebe used to… She kept me from slipping away…"

Sliding down to the floor, Kale wrapped his arms around his knees. His shoulder pressed against hers and he cast quick looks to check on her condition. The pain seemed immeasurable. Pale lines had formed along the trails of her tears and her hands, though slowly fallen to a self-embrace around the coat, quivered as a metronome. He dared not speak.

90

Time crawled without haste. It felt like hours between her breaths, yet only minutes passed. Slowly, the crying came to an end, but the condition of her body lingered. As her breathing regulated, Kale could stand it no longer.

I... I have to do SOMETHING to help...

With an anxious tinge, he placed an arm around her shoulder. Her hair tickled as it wirily poked at his skin. She flinched and was cold. Lightly, he pulled her in. "It's okay. It's almost over." He didn't know if they were true, but the words felt appropriate.

Astrid didn't challenge his action but instead allowed her body to fall against his. "T-Thank you," she whispered, closing her eyes.

A clock ticked on her wall and through all the confusion and horrific images he'd seen, he hadn't noticed the noise. His chest hurt from the consistent panic and the weight of her head on his lap only amplified such feelings.

Twenty minutes of silence passed. His eyes never left the clock's hands. The inner monologue of his brain counted each and every second and after the first ten minutes, she'd fallen asleep. Every ounce of his manhood prevented him from waking her.

Ugh... How'd it end up like this? Richmond is probably getting all kinds of ideas right now...

After what felt like days, her eyes began to open. A fickle drool had collected into his jeans, but his mind ignored it. Her pupils turned upward and met his. He could see the recollection happening in her brain. A crimson hue climbed from her cheeks with each realization until it became entirely red.

She nervously sat upward and drew the coat tightly around her body. "I'm... Oh gosh... I'm sorry!" The opposite wall received her attention.

Kale hesitated to reply, "it's okay."

A period of silence followed.

"So you really are a-"

"Yes," she cut him off, clearing her throat. "I'm a cleric."

A bashful tension prevented eye contact between the two and Kale twirled a strand of black hair between his fingers, covering his face.

"Does he know?" he prodded.

"He knows, but... I've hidden these from him... as much as I can... The episodes."

"So, just then, that was The Well speaking to you?"

She replied shakily, "It's extremely rare, only happens a few times a year, but always without warning."

"What'd it say?"

She paused for a moment, bringing the bed sheet around her over the coat. "*The light is not alone... The light is here... The light blesses all... If the gift is not for all... You need only wish it.* That's roughly what I could gather. It doesn't use words, but I know what it's saying."

Kale looked over to her questioningly, "What does that mean?"

Her head fell to her knees. "I wish I knew. It's terrifying."

"Looked that way."

Another pause followed.

"When it spoke, I felt strange... like it was angry."

"Angry at who?"

"Everyone."

A knock came from the door.

The two jumped slightly at the sound and distanced themselves from one another quickly.

"Astrid? Is everything alright?" It was Richmond.

Kale spoke up, rising to his feet with legs like jelly. "Yes! All good!"

Astrid froze.

Crap...

"Oh, I see... my apologies." The host's voice trailed away.

He brought a hand to his face and cursed beneath his breath.

A soft giggle escaped the girl next to him and he turned to look at her. She smiled. "I guess you need to clear that up."

Shyly, he looked to the floor, "What should I tell him though?"

"Just say I was having another fit. He'll understand." She stood and found her composure. Her face was heavily stricken by the stress, but leagues better than when he'd found her.

He inspected the clock which read 12:07. "Breakfast *was* ready when I came to get you, but now it's probably cold." Without turning another look at her, he found the handle to the door.

Astrid's face rose, "That was the first time it's happened since she... I was scared that I wouldn't have someone to keep me sane, so- Thanks."

"No problem."

He left the room.

Richmond stood in the center of the lobby, resting his angular chin on an enclosed hand and inspecting the massive pile of various metals that had been roughly placed outside his lab. His snowy hair was combed backward along the top of his head and the lab coat was donned to match.

Kale's shirt was heavily wrinkled and he straightened his appearance out slightly before approaching nervously.

"I swear that wasn't what you thought it was."

"Oh, I understand. I'm quite glad you two are getting along now," the scientist replied.

"I wouldn't go that far, she was having a fit."

"Ah, so you became the consoling hero?"

Kale sighed, "You could say that."

Richmond turned around to meet his eyes and crossed his arms. "We have less than twenty-four hours now. How are you feeling?"

He paused for a second, looking at the floor. "Nervous. My only memory of that place is a bad one."

"I know Astrid is too. She puts on such a facade of confidence around me, but even I can tell that it's only a facade." He placed a hand on his steward's shoulder. "Be kind to her, Kale. We all know how much pain has befallen us these past months."

A small amount of guilt welled within him, but with the feeling came an equal amount of reassurance that trust, though of uncertain measurement, could be attained.

Kale raised an eyebrow accompanied by a snicker. "Is that sympathy I'm hearing from you?"

Richmond stared at the ceiling. "I wonder…"

Kale didn't see Astrid again that day. For a reason he couldn't immediately discern, his only desire was to retreat to his room until the next morning.

That night the air was cold. Traces of glistening moonlight flowed through the window that he'd tried to cover, but due to the sentinel's damage, the glass did not fully seal the frame from the outside breeze. Without changing clothes, he wound himself beneath the bed covers.

These are good people. They took me in when I had no place and all I did was destroy their livelihood. Phoebe is dead… Phoebe is dead and it's my fault… It's my fault…

It was a strange feeling.

After sleeping for several hours, Kale woke uncertain of his location. Out of all the dreams he typically had, none came to him during the slumber. He questioned it, knowing he'd experienced a tale within the mind, yet being unable to recall any details whatsoever. He turned to his digital clock on the nightstand, which flashed the time 3:18am. In just under five hours, he'd be taking his first real steps into the Guiding City. He still couldn't fathom it all.

His thoughts lingered on the wondrous technology he'd discover in the coming days, but something bit at his heart, an overwhelming desire to apologize. To apologize to everyone, Astrid and Richmond, even those he'd never met here in the hotel. He couldn't focus on the mission until the guilt was gone. Standing from the bed, he walked and placed a hand on his doorknob to exit, but hesitated. Now was not the time. Surely, everyone in the hotel was asleep at that hour. It would be better for everyone's sake if he sucked it up and waited.

Am I that afraid of my own emotions?

He returned to the bed and stuffed his face into the pillow.

Early in the morning, the alarm buzzed a hateful tune, ripping Kale from his sleep at 6:00am on the dot. He groaned and slapped the top of it, knocking it from the nightstand, but failing to stop the sound.
Richmond's voice ripped through his brain at the same time.

[Good morning, you two. It's time. Please wear your suits and be in the lobby by seven. I expect no tardies, Kale.]

He yelled back at the air, "You know, you never told us how to shut these things off."

[Maybe if you're good, I'll fill you in on that feature.]

Rolling over into his pillow, a sigh of disgust was absorbed by the fluff, and with little motivation, his legs reached the floor. Bits of dark still shone from the poor window of his room and he walked to gaze outside. The slums were in a deep state of sleep. From his view, he could see people shivering on sidewalks, using bits of trash and scrap as headrests. Some paced along the way, but with no destination and no purpose. The slums truly were a terrible place to live.

We're going to change this… That's what it's all about. We're going to fix this world.

After a rejuvenating shower, a long session of slicking back his hair, and toiling through the motions of putting on a full suit, Kale proceeded down the staircase to the lobby where he found Astrid talking with Richmond by the front door, Buchannon asleep in a leather chair, and two women he hadn't yet met by the kitchen-Reba and Maryland, he assumed. He slithered his way over to Richmond and Astrid who were deep in conversation and interjected himself between them. Pierce, the doctor, was nowhere to be seen.

"So it's time then?" he said.

"Indeed," Richmond replied, crossing his arms and working his face into a stern expression, "today's the day. Today, you will take your first steps into the Guiding City."

Astrid folded her hands at her waist. She was fixed up significantly more than the last time he'd seen her. Her suit was still noticeably undersized, but her hair was brushed back straight and makeup covered her face. "I can't tell if I'm nervous or excited." Her voice was hesitant.

Richmond leaned forward and placed a hand on each of their shoulders. He smelled of freshly applied cologne and was dressed in his yellow ensemble, surprisingly, without the lab coat. Cologne, among other things, was an extremely rare delicacy in the slums. It was likely he'd been saving it for special occasions such as this. "You two have nothing to worry about. The fact of the matter is that you are nothing more than average citizens now. You have absolutely nothing to be afraid of." He wrapped his hands around their necks and pulled them both in for a hearty hug. Kale cringed at the motion, but Richmond was stronger than he'd imagined. "I'm fully confident in the both of you to succeed. Have some confidence."

Astrid fully embraced her father, tightly clinging to his neck. Kale managed to free himself and stuffed his hands in his pockets.

"Now then," Richmond continued, letting the girl go, "it's time to leave. Everyone say goodbye."

With those words, Astrid ran over to the two women in the lobby and jumped in their arms. Various *I'll miss you*'s and *Take care*s came from them, but Kale stood alone by the door, uncertain of who to talk to. He hadn't grown particularly close with any of the residents and he doubted if any of them would care about his leaving. In his mind, the devil that destroyed their home would be parting in good riddance.

To his shock, Buchannon stood from his chair and hobbled over to the young man. He stood slouched and offered a few words, "Be careful with that suit. I worked too hard on it for you to mess it up."

Kale smiled in partial relief, "I'll try to. No promises."

Astrid and the two other women strode to the spot where he stood. One stepped up to him first. She was a skinny woman, looking to be in the later years of her life. Her hair was silver and curled and she wore a long and loose nightgown where two slippers poked out from beneath. "I don't believe we've met yet."

"No, we haven't," he replied, "I'm sorry I didn't come by."

"Oh that's fine," she snapped dismissively, "we're always busy anyways. But I'm glad I got to meet you before you leave, you be nice to Astrid, ya' hear?"

He smiled at her. "I'll be as nice as she is to me."

"I have something for you," the other woman chimed in. She was sizably larger than the other, but something about her drew him in, like an unspoken acceptance. "I figured it's best if you take it."

"What?" He asked, surprised.

"This was the last one she made." The woman reached into a pocket of a long cotton coat she wore and withdrew a small piece of paper. "She drew everything."

Kale unfolded the gift by the edges and saw a rough depiction of a man and a girl walking along a street. He recognized his brown jacket from the first day, colored in crayon, and blue shoes on the feet of the girl. He couldn't look for long, or some unwelcome emotions might have appeared, so he folded it back and stuffed it in his pocket. He couldn't reply.

The woman smiled and gave him a parting hug. "She'd forgive you. Remember her."

She would forgive me?

Richmond broke up the ceremony and pulled the two away from the others, "We have to be at the gate in thirty minutes and we have a few blocks to walk. Let's get going, shall we?"

As the three of them moved to exit, the tenants of *Le Lien* called their farewells and waved at them. The double doors on the entrance hissed apart and the crisp morning air greeted them. Kale looked at his feet and the crimson carpet of the hotel's lobby. It would be the last time he'd see it for a while and he imagined that the slight pain he felt at the thought of leaving probably affected Astrid tenfold. Her entire life, or so he had been told, was centered around *Le Lien* and the people within. The shock of stepping into a future of unknown strangers, unfamiliar circumstances, and starting anew would be significantly more difficult for her than for him who lived nomadically.

The doors slid shut behind them.

The gate to the Guiding City was approximately three blocks away from the hotel. They would have to walk for a mile through slum dwellers seeking money and the fact that all three of them wore expensive suits would only make things more tricky. Richmond led them and strode with full confidence in his demeanor. His hands were in his pockets and his legs shifted weight around with a slight swagger. Kale and Astrid followed close behind, darting their eyes at each penny-hungry pilgrim. Confused chittering broke out each time they passed and heads turned, following their every step. Astrid cringed as a used needle crunched beneath her shoe.

"I don't like this," Kale spoke to the girl beside him. "Watch your pockets."

She replied with a frown, "I don't either."

The host turned back to them with a solemn stare "Remember, these are the people we're trying to help. In all their squalor, in all their poverty, and all their misfortune, they deserve the world just as much as anyone beyond the gilded walls. They are the reason I work. Don't ever forget that."

The looks from Kale and Astrid turned from disgust to pity at the sight of the hands reaching toward them. The faceless and nameless beggars became people with problems and they realized that the only difference between them was a lucky birth.

A stench of mechanics filled their noses as the Guiding City drew closer. The gate was clear in their view now. Golden towers and buttresses stuck out from the giant wall, perfectly aligning with The Wells light that climbed into the heavens. It was like magic how the street transformed from dusty and dirty, littered with bricks and grime, into a perfect path glistening with polished quartz.

Peering down from the towers were guards of the city, uniformed in golden armor that matched the tinge of the walls. On their heads were yellow helmets holding blue visors in place that contained technical infinities he couldn't even begin to comprehend. For armaments, each guard carried a long silver rifle. Richmond whispered to them that the rifles fired fragments of The Well's light. Typically, the light of The Well reformed human construction, but the minds of the Guiding City developed a way for it to do the opposite. The ontological rounds fired from the guns swiftly dismantled their targets, reducing them down into atoms. Accuracy mattered little.

A voice bellowed down to them as the party reached the gate's base. "Admissions?"

Richmond waved for the two others to stand back and reached into his pockets. The guards' rifles turned the barrels towards them. Kale felt a chill crawl down his spine.

"Here," the scientist yelled back, holding up two gold and orange identification slips.

"Into the scanner," the voice commanded back at them.

To their left, a small terminal emerged from the ground. It was shaped like an old restaurant intercom but was perfectly rectangular. A slit opened at the top where Richmond deposited the access cards.

The machine spoke to them, [*Southern commerce district, eastern residence wing, studio 385, Astrid Vanhannen, admitted, Kale Matthews, admitted.*]

"Huh," Kale turned to the others questionably, "Matthews? That's not my-"

Astrid stomped on his foot discreetly, hissing, "shhh!"

He straightened his posture and looked ahead.

A fake name? I guess that makes sense...

"Proceed." The guard's voice bellowed.

With a loud whirring, the massive golden gates began to part. As the doors drew separate, he felt sweat roll down his back. He expected long crystal roads, flying cars, and strange people walking between the prismatic skyscrapers, but something different greeted them. It did not lead into the streets of the city, but instead to an interior. Decorative marble floors formed a circular pattern on the floor. Overhead a giant chandelier made of diamonds shone fractalized light throughout the room. An overwhelming excitement filled the two new residents and they began to walk forward, but Richmond, however, did not follow their steps.

"It seems this is where I have to leave you." He retrieved the two identification cards from the machine and stuck each one out to them accordingly. "I can't accompany you into the city."

They both knew it, but neither had fully processed the reality that the genius behind the whole operation could not join them. Astrid stood speechless, looking back at him with deep disappointment.

Kale spoke up, "What are we supposed to do now?"

He replied, tilting his head, "you knew I couldn't join you. Go ahead, enjoy the luxuries of the city."

"But without you," Astrid's voice trembled, "I don't think I can do it."

"Have you two already forgotten?" Richmond tapped his temple. His eyes showed visible sadness.

[I will be with you all the way.]

Astrid ran to him for a final hug. Kale stood behind her, frustrated, but feeling the drawing in his pocket. He opened his mouth to say something but closed it back. He turned to look at the new future that lay before them. At the back of the room was a desk, yet no people stood behind it. Blue holographic words were projected on the rear wall that read: *Guiding City Linear Railway*.

Something new emerged within. No longer was he nervous. The fear and hesitations of the night before were nowhere to be found. Before him, a new life awaited, the potential to start over. He could now atone for his sins, make a new impact on the world, and create the future that his father never could.

"Richmond!" he called back, "you can count on us."

The host removed his daughter's arms from around him and turned her towards the city. "Go then."

Astrid continued to protest but gradually found herself following Kale forward and the two of them took their first steps into the Guiding City.

[Good luck.]

Kale turned a parting glance back to see the host's face one more time. Something was different. Astrid hadn't noticed, but below his nose, his lips twisted into disgust and the gate of the Guiding City closed between them.

Chapter 8
Eternity

A harmonic voice over an unseen intercom alerted the two new arrivals after the gates closed: [*Welcome to the Guiding City. Linear railway boarding will now commence. Please scan ID vouchers and board your respective cab.*]

Kale and Astrid looked around the room in confusion. There were no other people to be found. The shining marble interior reached high above them and the only sign of habitation was a hallway leading out the back.

"I don't understand," Astrid said, "what are we supposed to do?"

Kale studied his surroundings. "There's a door there. I don't see anything else to do." He pointed to what appeared to be the exit.

As they passed below the new doorway, they stared down a golden corridor. They began to walk down the hall, tension building with each step. Golden light blinded them from ahead and both mentally prepared to see the outside. The relatively low light had caused their eyes to adjust accordingly and they couldn't make out what lay beyond, but slowly, they approached the exit with lifted hands.

Stepping through the harsh luminescence, the terrible winds of the outdoors whipped against their bodies. Kale looked up. Stretched before him was a world incomprehensible from anything his imagination could've conjured. The Guiding City presented a setting greater in scale than anything he'd been told. The city, as he could see, was built on a decline, gradually falling towards The Well. Of course, he couldn't see to the bottom, but skyscrapers taller than the clouds reached high up into the heavens. Their golden architecture twisted and bent in ways that buildings shouldn't. Many of them reflected The Well's light, bouncing translucent rays around as spectral craft resembling diving birds of prey danced through the air without sound or direction.

To their right, one of the railway cars hovered between four rails that stretched for miles like a tangled web. A speaker shouted: [*Linear railway car seven, departing now, destination: northern urban core.*] With a bass-filled resonance the air rippled. Purple waves bounced around between the rails and the car, charging. Then, the train shot forward at a speed undeterminable. As he watched, he couldn't see it move, but fragments of its image appeared in broken strands along its path.

Their mouths stood agape at the sights. A clear view charted a course through the city until it met a wall several miles down. Sidewalks lined the bases of the buildings allowing uniquely dressed citizens to walk, hover, and collect throughout. Small drones littered the streets like bugs around a vibrant light, hissing and beeping as they flew.

One zipped right over Astrid's head, blowing her straightened golden hair out of place, and she ducked to dodge it. With a small buzz of infinite movement, the drone found a point between them and stopped. [*Identification vouchers, please.*] an automated voice spoke. A lens produced itself from the main body of the drone.

"Oh, right," she said, retrieving the two cards.

A small ray of blue light scanned the cards and the machine replied, [*Southern commerce district, eastern residence wing, studio 385, Astrid Vanhannen, admitted, Kale Matthews, admitted. Please board car 26 in the left terminal.*]

With a faint hiss, a train car appeared at supersonic speeds to their left. It was gold and sleek like everything else in the city but had no visible doors or means of entry.

[*Please board car 26 in the left terminal.*] the drone said after the two stood aimlessly inspecting the cab.

Kale looked at the drone with a baffled expression, "how?"

[*Please board car 26 at the left terminal by the starboard accession hydrotank.*]

"Huh?" he replied, drooping a side of his face.

"Kale, look over here." Astrid found a sealed door on the nearest side of the car. It broke apart in fourths, each shard sliding into itself until a full entrance was presented before them. The entire interior of the vehicle was filled to the roof in a deeply blue liquid. There were no seats, no obvious places to stand.

[*Please enter the gelatinous hydrotank for pressure regulation. Please note, your breathing will not be inhibited. You will not be submerged.*]

"It wants us to go in the water?" She looked at the substance, disgust written on her face.

"I guess we don't have a choice do we?" he answered, sticking his hand into the matter. He felt nothing. It wasn't wet. "Woah…"

[*Please enter the gelatinous hydrotank for pressure regulation. Please note, your breathing will not be inhibited. You will not be submerged.*]

"Well, here goes." He stepped inside. It was as if he'd entered a dark room. He felt no resistance from the 'gelatinous' liquid as it was called. "It's... weird. I'm not wet."

Hesitantly, Astrid followed him, releasing an obligatory "Ugh" as she winced upon entry. When her entire body was inside, the door slid shut and reformed itself perfectly sealed, causing the interior to grow pitch black.

A tiny feeling of fear grew between the two. The darkness lasted for a few seconds while a speaker in a similarly automated voice spoke, [*Linear railway car 26, departing now, destination: southern commerce district.*]

Sounds of systems whirring to life sprang forth, but their attention became completely captivated by the walls of the car growing with light. The exact image of the outside was projected internally. The two looked around in amazement. They watched as the image stretched and contorted. The car moved, but faster than the light could reach them and they felt nothing; no pressure, no movement, no inertia, but after about three seconds, the car stopped. They had arrived at the new destination. [*Linear railway car 26, arrived, southern commerce district stop E.*]

It was beyond all comprehension, an expanse of architecture no physics could accept. The commerce district was below them, according to the internal image of the car, situated between many colossal buildings. Halfway up from the ground level was what looked to be a town square, although it was more of an octagon. Many people in various outlandish attire wandered and collected about. Several children ran and played in the streets where colorful mercantile stands lit with iridescent glows sold things he couldn't quite make out from the distance. An aroma like the clean air after a rain traveled fluidly into their noses.

It was gold. Everything was gold, almost to a nauseating level, but he couldn't shake the feeling of overwhelming awe. Luckily, the blue sky still shone through to accommodate the bland choice of color. He and Astrid both were unable to speak at such a sight.

The side of the car buzzed open and the image was gone from the walls. Without haste and with a pinch of caution, they stepped out onto a platform where a humanoid robot tinkered at a terminal of buttons and levers. It was about five feet tall and a spindly assortment of mechanics. The face was blank steel, but it turned to look at them as their feet met the pavement and the liquid within the railway car sloshed back into place. [*Astrid Vanhannen, Kale Matthews, please step onto the transport bay, it will guide you to the ground level.*]

"Is this… real?" Kale said to the girl who stood beside him, equally bewildered. A strong wind blew his suit coat apart and he stood against it, admiring the cityscape.

"I think," Astrid replied, their eyes both traveling among the infinite moving lights below. Before them was a square of floor with intertwining rails around its perimeter, embossed by steps to climb aboard. The robot stuck a hand out and pointed at it, gesturing stiffly. The transport bay, as the machine called it, was an advanced form of an escalator. Kale recognized the idea behind it; they'd made good sources of small metals in The Vulture's old scavenges of abandoned malls.

"So we're just supposed to hop on?" He raised his eyebrows at the machine.

[*Please step onto the transport bay, it will guide you to ground level.*]

"I guess these things are only programmed for necessary responses." Astrid pulled on her suit coat.

Kale sighed, fixing his jacket back into shape, "Alright then." his polished loafer met the platform which whirred to life. A faint purple glow formed around its edges. Slowly shifting to the middle, his fingers met the railing and he clung tightly to it. Astrid followed behind him.

Once they were both aboard, a fourth wall of railing rose from where they'd entered and they became locked in. "I don't like it," he said.

"Neither do I. I almost can't comprehend it…" her voice trailed off as their transportation device left its dock and began down the air.

Their path was a descent toward the town square. As they traveled, it wasn't fear they felt, but rather a minuscule excitement. A new future would begin once their feet met the ground, a future in a new world, a chance to start a new life, and a billion uncertainties along with it. Through the slow dive below, the buildings around them appeared to twist, but they couldn't tell if it was kinetic motion or a trick of the light.

Another drone followed their path. It was marked with a green polygon on its main body, an icon he couldn't distinguish.

The transport bay clicked into place at the foot of the commerce district, a few blocks away from the town square and the rails fell. The drone turned to them. [*Please provide your identification vouchers. I will mark a path to your destination: Southern commerce district, residence eastern wing, studio 385.*]

Astrid held them up and an orange light from the drone scanned each card. [*Map encoding completed. Please press the navigation icon on your vouchers to access the map. Pleasant travels.*]

"God, I'm tired of hearing those things talk," Kale muttered under his breath as he was passed his voucher, "and how many times are we gonna have to scan these things?"

"I don't even know where to begin…" Astrid looked around their new environment, ignoring his pessimism. Her clothes had become tightly clung to her figure from the strong wind and she tugged it away as her face panned through the numerous people scurrying about. Their style was strange, like formal wear, but with various flamboyant adornments. One woman she eyed wore a purple dress that matched her skinny body, although along the shoulders were sharp yellow spikes resembling a large V. She talked with a man who was covered in a jacket that fell to his knees, but his chest was grossly exposed. It was thin, not like British trench coats of old, but rather like a silk garb. Lining the bottom was a thick circle that ran fully around him and connected the bottom of the jacket. Kale cringed at the sight. Everything was so out of the ordinary and he felt a sickness begin in his stomach.

"You're not about to see me in one of those." His eyes fell to his voucher. "Let's figure out where we're staying. I'm not sure I can handle much more of this right now."

"Even so," Astrid said quietly, her eyes drifting along the spires that stretched into the heavens, "after being in the slums so long… Isn't it amazing?"

He followed her gaze and became entranced by the sight. "Yeah…" Mystically shaped cars silently traveled through the roads in perfect unison. Their wheels, at least among the few that had them, appeared to be stationarily, yet in motion.

The Guiding City… I'm really here… Mom wouldn't believe it.

"A couple of newcomers, I imagine?" a man's voice came from their left, a New Zealander's accent. It was a guard, like the one he'd seen atop the walls earlier. Kale became immediately tense and averted eye contact.

"Y-Yes we are," Astrid replied to the man, "we've just arrived and are quite lost."

"I see, looking for your place?" The guard removed his helmet to reveal a dark face. His hair was buzzed to the skin.

"Right. We're supposed to be in the eastern residence wing, but all of this is too confusing." She motioned at the buildings which appeared to intertwine with themselves creating a sense of misdirection.

"Don't worry. I've seen a million others in your position, ya' get used to it. Now, can I see your vouchers?"

"Oh, yes." She held her's forward and the guard retrieved it from her hand.

"Okay then," he inspected it and pressed a finger to the surface, summoning a small holographic map of the area, "take the first street on your right down three blocks and the entrance is on the left. It's a big building with a sign on the front that says: EASTERN WING SUITES AND STUDIOS. Once you're inside there'll be an elevator. Just scan your voucher and it'll do the rest."

"First street on the right, three blocks, then it's on the left," she repeated it to herself and looked down in focus, "got it."

"You know, it's a lucky thing that you're in the southern commerce district. It's one of the only ones not claimed."

The two looked up at him, "Claimed? What do you mean?"

The guard raised an eyebrow and folded his arms over a large golden vest he wore. "Well, ever since the election campaigns started, there's been disarray in the streets. Factions are squabbling over territory to promote their candidate. Us officers are spread too thin… The whole thing's a mess…"

Kale perked up, "Wow, I had no idea!" He lied.

"However," the authority continued, "you'll have no problem with them here. As of now, the Globalist Sympaths occupy the manufacturing district's factories at the southern border a few blocks back. To the west are the Axis Extremists. If I were you, I wouldn't go west at all. They're a very dangerous bunch. The sympaths are closest, but they don't do much to cause trouble outside of their area. Aside from those two, you won't have any issues going North or East, at least as far as the academy. It's a few miles east and open to the public. Keeping it neutral was one of the only things the Aureate could agree on… but don't go any further into the waterways. The Skyridge Aeonic Order controls it. They tend to keep quiet, but I don't trust 'em. Not with her history…" He sighed. "Anyways, just follow those directions and you'll find your residence in no time."

A pause followed his words until Astrid interjected, "Thank you, we'll be on our way then."

"Oh," Kale lifted a hand before the guard turned away, quietly leaning in, "do you know where I can find any bars around here?"

His companion scoffed at him, "Kale! That's the last thing we should be worried about right now."

"What?" he replied, shrugging, "I need something to make me feel at home."

The officer laughed, "Yes. You see the town square over there?" He pointed at the alleys that ran in all directions between the ever-tall skyscrapers. Golden cars without windows slowly wove and parked along the sides. "The third way marked by that large orange sign is where restaurants are designated. We have a few bars and clubs there. Either way, all the information you could need can be found with the touch of your vouchers. Just touch the icon that looks like a globe and ask a question. The Aureate's AI network is incredibly advanced."

"Thank you, sir!" Astrid quickly took Kale's hand and walked to their right. Once they were out of earshot of him she spoke quietly, "You heard what he said, let's not go anywhere near those places."

"Tsk." he turned away, "*You* don't have to, but I can't take this country club atmosphere. It's a little *too* rich."

"Whatever. If you want to get yourself killed go right ahead. I'm going to find where we're staying." She bent her lips smugly and let go of his hand, marching off to the street the guard directed them to follow.

The uncomfortable thug snarled, "Wait, I'm coming!"

The streets were much busier than he'd originally imagined. Though it wasn't comparable to the slums where hundreds of smelly and derelict vagabonds huddled like rats. The people of the Guiding City marched along the sidewalks in perfect order. Their eye-catching clothes drove a tinge of madness through his brain and he felt he'd never belong in such a place. Various drones hovered around the crowds broadcasting commercials of different items: a new set of glasses that connected you to a social network, a nanotechnology pill that could cure cancer, the newest car that ran on magnetic inertia, and a suggestive advertisement about a lifelike robot that could take the form of any man or woman. The latter of which prompted a sickened gag from Astrid.

The thing that Kale found the strangest, however, was that everyone appeared happy. It was as if all the actions they took at the present moment were of their own choosing. He inspected the faces of those they passed. Every single mouth showed a content smile.

Are they really happy here? It's almost creepy how perfect it seems…

When the two reached the end of the first block, their black suits and ties blew wildly from the wind of a passing rail car that flew by overhead. He followed its distorted image as the gravitational technologies refracted the light around. The rail ran further into the city towards the light of The Well and he wondered where its destination lay.

"Come on," Astrid said, pulling her suit in tight, "We're almost there."

As they continued, the citizens moved out of their way, as if an unspoken acknowledgment of their ignorance was passed between everyone as a collective and respectfully addressed. Both of them walked slightly tilting their gaze to the black loafers on their feet to avoid the wandering eyes until they found themselves outside of the structure the guard had described.

It was a fantastically tall building, reaching beyond puffy clouds that shrouded the heights of its construction. Their mouths fell in wonder. At the entrance were glass doors built for giants. Atop the doors, flowing along the ever-rising glass was a large neon sign broadcasting EASTERN WING SUITES AND STUDIOS in alternating colors. Kale attempted to count the floors:

20, 40, 60, 80, 100, 120, 140, 160, it just goes on forever…

They stepped forward, prompting a reaction from the entrance which parted at their arrival. Kale led as they stepped inside the building and an immediate smell of expensive coffee filled their noses. The lobby was enormous. Massive crystalline chandeliers hung from the tall ceiling, and various mahogany tables and leather chairs were scattered about around large screens showing sports, sitcoms, and other unrecognizable forms of media. Kale found himself drooling in thought, tallying the cost of every item; his calculations came out to millions.

Tall vases housed multicolored flora along the walls, but In the center of the dark green carpeted floor was a cylindrical golden elevator.

"That must be what he was talking about." Astrid pointed out.

Kale studied the room. "Do we need to check in or anything? I mean, there is a reception desk over there." He pointed to their left where a marble counter was set up. A young woman stood promptly behind the desk wearing a red uniform. She looked to be a late teenager and had amber hair tied in braids that wound around her shoulder. When the two newcomers looked over, she greeted them with a sweet smile.

Woah, she's cute.

He eyed the girl, inspecting her face. She wasn't particularly attractive by old-world standards, hardly his type, but a sudden realization made him uneasy.

Everyone's faces… There's no mud on them… Everyone is clean…

"I guess it wouldn't hurt." Astrid followed him over to the desk.

"Hi!" The girl gleefully began a rehearsed phrase. "Welcome to Eastern Wing Residential Suites and Studios. Have you already reserved a residence?"

"It's studio 385, it should've been booked a few days ago." Astrid said, scanning around the room.

"Okay, great! Let me see here…" The girl began feverishly tinkering with a screen in front of her. "Astrid Vanhannen and Kale Matthews? May I scan your vouchers?"

Kale's voucher was snatched from his hand and offered to the receptionist.

"Alright, you're all set. It appears your luggage is already waiting for you! The elevator is already pre-programmed, just step inside and it'll take you there. Your room will be the 14th on the right!"

With a smile and without words, the gawking young man was pulled away from the desk. The receptionist waved at them in parting.

The hallway of the third floor was a ridiculous assembly of further nauseating gold: golden carpet, golden walls, golden doors, yellowed fluorescent lights, and thankfully, silver number plates. Their room, as told by the receptionist, was the fourteenth on the right, number 385. Waiting outside the door were two large suitcases that neither of them recalled packing and attached to handles at the top were each of their respective names. Astrid scanned her voucher on the door and with a click, it opened.

It was a fairly simple room, though not large enough to house the tension between them. There was a tall, mahogany dresser against the right wall, a desk with some kind of orb hovering above a thin base atop it, an ornate rug that covered roughly enough space for them to avoid one another physically, a gray lounge chair in the corner, and a final thing that nearly drove Astrid to a full panic; one twin sized bed against a completely transparent back wall. Outside the window, the Guiding City stretched out in fractals and the light of The Well reached high into the sky, filling the room with gold. To the left of the entrance was the bathroom which was surprisingly large compared to the rest of the room, though its technology seemed to have not advanced since The Waking.

"Oh…" she hissed as she entered the room.

Kale's eyes narrowed as he inspected their new home and sighed when he set down his luggage.

The door shut behind them.

A chill crawled down Astrid's spine as she turned to look at him. His face was stoic and he found a seat in the closest chair.

"I can tell you've got something to say." He waved a hand at her. "We're probably thinking the same thing."

A bead of sweat fell from her brow. "Well... This wasn't what I had in mind."

"Yep," he turned the chair toward the desk along the wall and plopped his feet upwards, "me neither."

"So," she continued, folding her hands on her waist, "I think we need to lay down some ground rules."

"You pick what you want. I'm used to sleeping on the ground anyway."

"Firstly, obviously, I get the bed."

"I figured."

"Second," her attitude became sterner, "don't touch me, don't touch my clothes, don't talk to me at night, and I will always be first to the restroom."

"You think I'm a monster?" He attempted a laugh but could tell something about her was discomforting.

She sat on the edge of the bed. "Look, this is going to be hard for both of us, but at the end of the day," the words were difficult to conjure and she turned to look out the window, "I'm still just a girl. This is all so new to me."

He looked up between fallen black bangs that covered his scars. He watched his hands for a moment and picked at calluses on his palm. She was right. "I get it."

They sat in silence for a moment, unsure of what to do or say until a certain familiar voice sounded within their minds.

[Hello, you two. How are you finding the city?]

Richmond's fatherly tone brought Astrid's hands to her face. "We've just arrived at the studio. The city, its... greater than we could've ever imagined."

[That's good. I know this situation might be overwhelming at first, but I believe things should get easier in time.]

Kale snickered, "I don't think I'll ever get used to this. I thought the hotel was bad, but this is on a whole 'nother level."

Richmond chuckled at the thought.
[It is quite a shift from the slums, isn't it? Things are beginning to move very quickly. Think of it as a nice... vacation.]

Kale's head flew back with a sigh, "Unlike you rich folk, I've never had one."

Astrid interjected, "We'll make it work, but I don't exactly understand what to do."

[I expected that. Your residence has been strategically placed close to the Guiding City's main academy. According to our insider, this is one of the only unoccupied zones free of factional conflict. The academy is open to the public and houses an infinite number of books. All of the declassified research into The Well can be found there. All I ask of you is to collect knowledge and report to me any interesting discoveries.]

"Yes Sir," she replied, tugging at the bottom of her suit. It was a gesture of nervousness, the thug noticed, but of course, she couldn't let Richmond see that.

[Don't worry, you two have nothing to be afraid of.]
The transponder beeped signaling the end of his call.

Kale stood and stretched his arms, "sounds easy enough."
"Yeah…" Astrid sat in deep contemplation of something. Visible frustration wrinkled her forehead.

He raised an eyebrow at her for a moment before saying, "What're you thinking about?"

She quickly met his eyes but turned them away with equal speed. "I miss him."

For a moment, he considered shooting a smart-aleck remark, but the sight of her downcast posture caused him to decide against it. He could tell she was in pain. Hearing his voice only cemented the fact that it would be weeks, months, or perhaps even years before they saw him again. Once inside the Guiding City, it was a nightmare for the average citizen to leave. The simple truth was until the mission was accomplished, they would never be able to go back.

Kale undid his suit coat and threw it over his shoulder, "I'm going out."
Astrid looked up in desperation, "What? We just got here. Where're you going?"

"To explore. Gonna wander for a bit… give you some space." In a roundabout way, he figured she would appreciate the gesture.

She rose to her feet and stood squarely in the middle of the room, "Please. Let's take time and figure this out."

"That's what I'm letting you do. I'll go away for a bit and check out the scenery. In the meantime, you set your boundaries, get unpacked the way you want, and I'll come back after you're finished. I know how you women are."

The words seemed to completely catch her by surprise. Her eyes, in contrast to the past expression, beamed with direct precision at him and he wondered whether it was fury or something else that drove it. A muscle twitched in her stern jaw.

"I- I don't want to be left alone."

While looking at her frustration, Kale realized a stark truth that had avoided him for a while now. The two were opposites. Astrid, with her pompous upbringing, represented order and strategy. She sought to plan every modicum of her endeavors so that nothing went wrong or surprised her. Perhaps that was the reason behind her ticks and constant adjustment of her clothes. Was her need to constantly look professional the outward sign of the internal struggle? He could only imagine that his presence, of wild and uncontrollable impetuosity, caused every action he took to be a challenge of her worldview.

I should really be more gentle…

"Don't worry," he offered her a smile, "take your time. I won't go far. I promise." He stuck out his hand, extending the pinky.

His words dropped her guard and she stared at his hand for a minute. Then, the corners of her mouth curled upward and she met his pinky with her own. "Then," she reluctantly admitted after looking away, "I'll handle it." Her arms crossed over her chest. "But don't do anything stupid… Please."

"I won't." He turned and exited the room.

As Kale reached the fancy ground level of the residence wing, the transponder in his brain beeped to life once again, causing a panicked jump.

[I noticed you two are a distance away from each other. Are you alone?]

"You know," he said between gnashing teeth, "I'll NEVER get used to that."

[This is an important message, Kale. Are you alone?]

He walked around the elevator and took a seat in one of the many arrangements of fine leather chairs, conscious to avoid any possible prying ears among residents. Warm light shone down from the chandeliers, but he found a spot of shadow. "Yes, I'm alone. I left her in the room to get things sorted her way. Give us both some space to take it all in."

[I understand. That's likely for the best. Anyways, there's something I need you to do. Something only you can do.]

"Already?" Kale propped his feet on a table in the center of the chairs and placed a hand over his eyes. "I don't like the sound of that."

[Your mission will be different from Astrid's. It's true that she'll be doing simple research, but you will be a bit more... hands-on.]

"Richmond, what are you talking about?"

[Take some time. Get used to the city. I've arranged a meeting with the insider for tomorrow, but I'll explain the details of the situation later.]

He scoffed. "Get to the point."

[Very well. Your mission, Kale, will be to infiltrate the southern Globalist Sympath faction and gain their trust. They can prove to be useful allies.]

A sheer cold crept through his body. He stood to his feet and darted his eyes around the room. Sweat began to fill his sleeves. "Wait... Hold on... You can't be serious... I JUST got here!"

[I am.]

"But the insider said the factions were dangerous and violent gangs."

[Then you should feel right at home.]

He laughed and dropped his head to his lap, falling back into the cozy leather. "So this is your way of getting me killed... I see."

The scientist's voice donned a tone of compassion.

112

[I do not wish for you to die, but the opportunity is far too great to pass. You see, this particular faction shares the same mindset that we do. They believe the greater world is deserving of The Well's blessings. It's natural our paths would cross.]

Kale assumed a serious demeanor and rested his chin on a palm. "If they're a political faction, it won't be easy to gain their trust. What're you thinking?"

[You're correct, which is why this operation will be... shaky. I've delved into your history among The Vultures. This was the opportunity I was talking about. I can use you.]

"You want me to deal?"

[The negotiations of these modern and sophisticated factions are not the same as dealing with poor and uneducated rabble. You'll have to work your way in.]

"And? What about them? I know it's a gang, but do they have a leader?" His brain toiled in thought.

[Yes. The insider will know more than I, but for now, I'm told it's a woman and she doesn't deal well with men.]

"Great. When it comes to women, I'm still trying to figure out Astrid."

[Astrid will come around in time. She's not as complex as you might imagine... At least from what I can see.]

"I think we're natural opposites."

[Kindness, Kale. Simple kindness. That is how you'll gain her trust.]

He sighed. "You know I'm not very good at that."

[Figure it out. Now, that is the extent of my knowledge. Ponder it through the night and the insider will contact you tomorrow.]
The transponder beeped and he was gone.

Kale muttered to himself, "You're going to get me killed..."

Chapter 9
The Devil's Lair

    The outskirts of the Guiding city were easier to walk among than the busy streets. He'd covered a few miles in one direction, traipsing along sidewalks and alleyways, eager to avoid the common citizens. None of the creatures, he could hardly consider them human, were forthcoming and it made him feel as though conversation would be impossible. The blanketed happiness on their faces disturbed him. When he'd exited the hotel, he considered flirting with the receptionist, an opportunity he'd never attempted in the slums, but figured it would only bring further conflict between Astrid and himself, so he did not.

    The sun had begun to crawl down the western half of the sky and hidden itself behind The Well, although one could say the two were virtually indistinguishable in terms of radiance. There were little shadows for him to slither through and everywhere he went, he could not escape the gold. It had been about thirty minutes since his departure and Kale reasoned that Astrid would be done organizing the room, but he couldn't bring himself to return… not yet. The officer from earlier told him about select bars and clubs nearby, perhaps he could find a semblance of 'home' there.

    Psychedelic lights among the mercantile stalls of the town square made his head spin and he watched his reflective shoes as he walked. The air was cold and through all the gigantism of the city, it couldn't block the salty gale of the Atlantic. He searched for the large orange sign of the correct alleyway to trod down and found it after turning a full one-eighty. Words flashed, GUIDING CITY DISTILLERIES AND PUBS.

    He'd figured that the people occupying an area of alcohol and roughness would be a bit more down to earth, but he couldn't have been more wrong. They were the same, strange, and remarkably content. His lips frowned and he jammed his hands in his pockets as he slipped inside the nearest pub.

    Gold, gold, and more gold greeted him inside. The workings of his stomach churned. After sliding through a rotating glass door, the tables were organized perfectly resembling diamonds around the central part of the room. A tap bar occupied the back, clean as the rest. The walls were adorned with pictures of the Guiding City's skyline and various shipments of cargo. Kale found a seat at the bar, away from the alien citizens where he stared blankly at many tall cylinders with nozzles for pouring drinks. The human element of mixing had been entirely automated. Indistinguishable chatter filled his ears and the music playing throughout was surprisingly bland, just like everything else.

"Hello?" He yelled down the bar towards a door leading into the back, "Where's the bartender?" Heads turned from the customers, collectively interrogating the ill-mannered newcomer.

A hand tapped him on the back and he angrily spun around to see the perpetrator. It was an officer, but surprisingly, it was the same officer from earlier that day. His shaved head reflected the golden lights above. Bright, olive eyes and a slouched left arm caused Kale to let his guard down if only a little.

"Found your way here?" The man released Kale's shoulder and took the seat next to him.

"I did." He replied, "not quite what I was hoping for."

"You want something like the outside?" the officer queried.

"Yeah," Kale rested his elbows on the bar, "all this gold... It's too much."

The other man laughed, "ya' get used to it. It was the same for me at first." He began tapping on the bar and a screen appeared beneath his fingers. A wide assortment of concoctions shone and he swiped between them. "What will you be drinking today, Kale?"

"How do they taste here?" His eyes traveled amongst the selection.

"However you'd like."

"Bitter. I need to be reminded of the *real* world."

"I understand. Whiskey?"

"Bourbon."

The guard nodded. "I saw you walk in. I can't drink in uniform, but I'd be happy to pay your tab." He withdrew a voucher from a pocket on his vest and scanned it on the screen. From the door in the back, a humanoid robot like the one he'd seen at the transport bay walked forward with a small glass. It stood stiffly in front of the farthest cylinder to the left and filled the glass halfway with an amber liquid. "A nice introduction to the city, if I may."

"So," Kale began as he received the drink, "you said it was similar for you at first, how long have you been here?"

The officer grunted and reclined against the bar. "Fifteen when The Waking happened... I lived in Fredericksburg growing up after my family emigrated from Wellington. My father was a sheriff and when it happened, we were forced to move. His job was to investigate the damage, search and rescue type stuff."

"So you've been here since the beginning then?" Kale took a sip and cherished the burning to an extent.

"Yes, but it wasn't always this way."

"Golden?"

"No." The officer hung his head, "closed."

Kale's eyebrows rose as he took a sip of the burning liquid. The taste was exquisite, easily the best he'd had, but due to the perfection, it lacked a certain human element. It tore down his throat, but he didn't flinch. "Oh?"

"When we first started," the Kiwi man reminisced aloud, "It was meant to be a symbol for the world; a 'haven of modernity' as they called it. The vision… A great city for all and anyone… But as you can see now, it didn't work… Sorry to bore ya' with the philosophy."

The finely dressed thug swirled his glass, dragging his drink along its edges. "Nah. It's interesting. So why not? Why hasn't it just… opened?"

"Lots of reasons." His voice grew low, "mainly economics. I see it, the reasons why, but I wish it wasn't the way it had to be. Can you imagine if the walls suddenly came down? It'd be a war! Tons of people would die and any remaining armies wouldn't hesitate to flock and claim what scraps they could sink their teeth into. Sometimes I wonder if this really is the most humane way of keeping society intact. Although, it makes me happy when I get to welcome new people. You newbies, you're more human."

Kale remained silent.

"But… How'd you end up getting here?" The officer's eyes, which had been absent from Kale throughout the entire conversation, turned to his scarred face.

Slurping the final remnants of stinging drink, he slammed the glass down with a curiously loud force. It wasn't intentional, but it succeeded in switching his brain into a defensive mode. "A gift… from a friend."

"I see."

The story Kale told the officer was one he'd practiced in his mind many times after the failure of lying to Richmond. In this fable, he was one of many children, the product of an English professor and a corporate bookkeeper. He'd gone to university, away from the family home, but was left to the slums after everyone was lost in The Waking.

It stole sympathy from the guard and he offered to buy Kale another drink, but a beep of the transponder in his head caused him to search for a means of ending their conversation.

"Thank you," Kale began to sweat as the beeping continued, "I didn't catch your name."

"Peter King. If you ever need me for anything, mention my name in your voucher. The icon with the helmet will connect you immediately to the garrison."

Peter waved goodbye as Kale slipped out of the bar and into the colorful street.

After the beeps continued and drove him to insanity, he talked in return while weaving through the strange city-goers. "What? Who's calling?"

Astrid's voice filled his mind in reply. A nervous tone formulated her words.

[Kale? I wanted to check on you. You've been gone for a while.]

Around that time, a pink hue grew in the eastern sky. He still wasn't sure if he wanted to return to the residence. He wanted to explore a bit longer, yet her voice somehow provided a tinge of comfort. The collar of his shirt had begun to wrinkle from the sea's humid corruption in the air and the coat had become heavy. The road smelled of sweet food being cooked in the restaurants a block over. "I'm good. You done?"

[Yes, I think we can make it work once you get back. Where'd you go?]

Kale looked towards the south once he returned to the town square. The stalls had begun to close for the day and the area became noticeably less populated, but past the linear rail station at which they'd arrived, was a gilded gate with a sign that read in gigantic lettering: SOUTHERN FACTORIES ROUTE C. Suspiciously, he watched as a hooded figure tinkered with something on the gate's outside, prompting it to crack slightly and allowing him to slip through. The image he spotted was only faint and the distance was far too great for him to make out the details.

That's the area the sympaths occupy...

[Kale?]

He'd gotten so engrossed in thought, he'd forgotten to reply. "Yeah... I'll be there in a bit."

[O-Okay.]

A quiet beep followed, signaling the end of the call.

His thoughts lingered on the figure entering the factory district's gate. Were they a member of the sympaths? Was that the entrance to their occupied zone? Would they be willing to negotiate? Was he supposed to simply walk in? An infinitude of questions flooded his mind.

I can't relax right now… Should I have asked the officer about the sympaths? I could've gotten more information…

The synapses of his brain fired in rapid precession questioning the very nature of his identity. As a gang member himself, he shouldn't have been so nervous and he reckoned it would take something grand to clear his head.

He didn't know where it came from, what sent it, or what it wanted. Its blue lens flashed a beam of light that scanned him head to toe, fixating on a spot in his side where Richmond's machines had been integrated. It was a sleek drone, silver unlike the golden ones throughout the Guiding City he'd seen so far. The rotors behaved differently, rotating at supersonic speeds in 360 degrees of motion like translucent spheres. It didn't talk. It simply looked at him and no one around paid it any mind.

The machine maneuvered like a hummingbird and Kale tried to swat it away, but it dodged his hand and shifted to another side, beeping.

"What d'you want?" He stared into the lens, irritated and with a raised eyebrow.

Three small lights flashed on its side and it continued to beep, but turned and began to fly away. Kale didn't move, which it noticed, and flew back to him, beeping once again.

"You want me to follow?" There was an undertone of concern in his voice, and he looked around. The complacent faces of the citizens chattered and observed the immense advertisements. Neon signs buzzed and flashed to distract all attention. They shifted around him like ants without acknowledgment, inhuman and empty.

But Kale folded his hands in his pockets and began to walk behind the drone.

What is it? It doesn't talk like the others. I don't think it's the police… I didn't do anything wrong…

They passed between massive golden spires with infinite movement beneath their surface. Loud music from within shook the surroundings, golden polygonal cars drove in the streets all at the same speed, and a giant hologram of an Aureate member, Alastar Jalaal according to a nameplate beneath that shot fireworks out of the sides, waved and laughed with a hand on his fat belly.

Kale scoffed.

The sheer vastness of the Guiding City was enough to bring anyone unfamiliar to a feeling of utter insignificance, but as long as he watched the drone and followed its shimmering body, he could tune out the sights.

Was it an invitation, a trap, or a taunt? He didn't know, but he needed to learn more about their new home. Curiosity could not be limited, and after all, they had arrived as citizens, nothing more and nothing less.

The drone led past the edge of the commerce district to massive golden signs that read: SOUTHEAST WATERWAYS. Kale remembered the words of the officer who'd met them after arriving. This was the occupied zone of Skyridge's Aeonic Order.

He cursed under his breath.

This is a mistake… But… I can just take a look around…

It was a dark expanse, lit by bright blue lights traveling along unkempt wires that bordered a concrete walkway. Huge, black ocean waves sloshed over the sides spewing seafoam into the air. He could taste the salt. Although it was still daytime, The Well was so bright, that the shadows of the great buildings between this district and its light left perpetual shadows. There were no guards, no gates to ward anyone from meandering in, but as he had traveled with the drone, the Guiding City citizens had grown fewer and fewer. It was ominous, and his instinct told him to turn around, but every time he hesitated, the drone would beep and fly circles around his head. There was a reason it wanted him, and he had to know why.

The walkway was cold, and Kale's predisposition to darkness gave him courage as he slipped between the thick shadows. The drone buzzed with excitement as they traveled closer to its destination. He had yet to know where they were headed, but massive warehouses began to come into view. They were tall, so tall that fog created by the splashing sea withheld view of their tops. Orange sparks blew from mechanical arms that were constructing something within. Small robotic frames walked around carrying loads of metals and wires. Kale recognized them. They were the same humanoid machines as the one that operated the linear railway terminal. There were hundreds, all performing various tasks. He couldn't tell what they were building.

But the drone still wanted him to follow, so he did. The frames paid him no mind, turning their heads in confusion, but resuming their work. It sent shivers down Kale's spine, and he pulled his clothes in tight in an attempt to make himself small.

It was like being in a storm. Not beneath, but inside the cloud, as the blue lights of infinite wires shimmered and mist blew all around. He was teetering on the edge of his bandwidth, but the drone finally stopped when they reached a rectangular building. There were no windows, no adornments, and no color except for giant letters that read SKYRIDGE TECHNOLOGIES on the side. A singular door presented itself and the drone scanned a keypad on the outside. Kale hid behind his bangs of black hair which had grown wet and hung over his eyes.

Every nerve in his body screamed for him to turn around, but he couldn't. The door opened with a hiss and a low mist flooded from its edges. It was cold inside. Despite Kale wearing his layered suit, he shivered. Maybe it was the temperature, maybe it was fear, but goosebumps crept along his arms and his hair stood on end.

Inside the room, the drone hovered to a spot on a silver wall where it tilted vertically and attached itself like a magnet, prompting the lights on its central module to be turned off. The room was dim, lit like the outside in a haze of azure. It was a swamp formed entirely of wires and biomechanical fluid that bubbled in electrically charged tanks all around. He could tell by purple spouts of lightning that crackled with each fizz. He could see morphology beneath the liquid. Something was being created, and he didn't want to know what.

Kale took to the shadows. There was a reason the drone wanted him. There had to be.

That reason made itself abundantly clear as he reached the opposite wall of the room and a gigantic blast of white light locked on him. Kale's stomach fell.

Positioned at the end of a floor like water that lied about its physics and caused him to stumble was the outline of a head. It was a machine, a skull of chrome, held together by light and power. The eyes made him uneasy. They stared directly at him, devoid of life, but moving with intention in three layers. It spoke with a woman's voice subsumed in harmonic hisses.

"You are like me."

Kale didn't move. He knelt, attempting to escape the harsh light, but peered upward at the face. "W-What?"

"Machine. Something more than human. There aren't many of our kind in this city. With The Well's ability to reconstruct flesh, it's rare to see devotion like yours." The face spoke.

"I-," he found it difficult to form words. "I'm a human."

"Yes," it replied, "but we found something on the inside. Tell me, what is its purpose?"

"I don't know what you're talking about." Kale rose to his feet, his loafers slipping on the perfectly smooth metal that covered the room's floor.

"Really? My envoys don't make mistakes. They're designed to seek out biological machines. They bring me additions to my collections. Would you like to see it?"

He looked around. Sweat grew on his forehead and he quickly wiped it away. "Collection?"

"That's right. Take a look." The walls, hidden from sight by the bright lights, began to slide apart.

Kale squinted to see. Lining the walls in uniform spaces were numerous mechanical limbs, weapons, and webs of tubes. They were difficult to define: a metal forearm with a seven-fingered hand on its end, a set of four lungs with fractaline wires protruding on all sides, and triple-jointed legs with a ball and socket attachment. All of them were made of metal.

The face spoke, its eyes traveling along Kale. "So tell me, what is YOUR integration?"

"I-I don't know…" He couldn't run. He couldn't slip away. There weren't any signs that he was captured, but a stark fear of the unknown held him in place.

"Then why don't we find out?"

From behind the face, humanoid frames like the robots he'd seen outside began to march toward him. Their appendages were outfitted with various surgical tools and they all locked their faces forward.

He yelled, turning away, but an immensely strong grasp snagged his arm. He grunted and kicked at the spindly robot, sending it on its back.

At that moment, the massive face began to laugh without motion.

"Don't worry, I'm only kidding." It spoke with a playful mockery. "The look on your face is priceless!"

Kale's teeth were gritted in deep fear, his cheeks the color of quartz. "What do you want with me?!"

"I told you already. I want to know about your integration." The frames stood on standby aside, clear fluid dripping from their arms. "This is Skyridge Technologies. Here, I manufacture these frames. They do require a measure of bioavailable proteins to reach their full potential, but I'm always discovering new methods of perfecting them... Which is why I would like to learn how yours works. My drone identified joint cooperation between the machines under your skin and your neural networks. It would benefit me a great deal to research you."

"Look. I don't know who you are or how you found me, but I'm nobody's experiment." The statement felt like a lie.

"Well, that's a shame... My name is Brianna Sky. I own this facility and I can make it worth your time if you were to work with me."

Brianna Sky? This machine is a member of the Aureate! But... The insider specifically warned us about her... I wonder what he knows.

The words caught Kale's attention. He coughed. "What're we talkin'?"

The voice jested. "Let me run a few easy scans and then you're free to go. I'll have these frames give you a microdose of fluids that will navigate your networks and relay the information to me. I can't say it's comfortable, but it'll be over before you know it. Afterward, you can choose an augmentation from my collection and I'll have it attached for free. Sound like a deal?"

His eyes traced along the wall of machines. "Sounds intrusive."

The thought of more cybernetics in his body disgusted him, but he imagined himself with a metal arm or supercharged brainpower and began to consider the offer.

"Not at all. We are the innovative leaders in human and machine integration. The best in the world. We'll take good care of you."

He brought a hand to his chin, eyeing a silver arm that had wires like hard muscles. "What would that thing do for me?"

The face noticed his curiosity. "Strength. Mobility. Diversification. That arm can turn you into a superathlete as soon as it's placed. Never rusting, never rejected, and you won't even be able to tell."

What would Richmond think if I got a cyborg arm?"

"But you'd have to cut off my current one?"

"For now. It would be a seamless removal. However, those that work with me get their perks. I'll let you touch the light. With The Well's paracausal abilities, it can be reformed when exposed. It's a win-win. So what do you say?"

More machines under my skin... As if! I don't even know what's in there right now! No way another machine-crazed scientist uses me. I doubt I'll have a choice, but If I stay on her good side, maybe I can slip out before she attaches it...

Kale laughed at the thought, raising his hands in the air. "Whatever, I'll take it. Somehow I doubt you'd let me leave if I said no."

The face snickered. "Good choice."

It was difficult to discern what caused it, but everything went dark. He could tell he'd lost consciousness, and there was a ringing in his ears, but something was different. He coughed. A glob of orange liquid flew from his mouth and splashed on the floor. It tasted like lemons. "What the-"

"Welcome back! The scan went great." It was Brianna's voice.

"What'd you do to me?" His eyes darted around, he hadn't moved from before. The silver skull stole his view.

"An artificial ribcage, biochemical dispensaries, mechanical artery connections, but the neural pathways... I would've never thought to... Even beyond that, there's more... It's a marvel. Who created this?"

Kale wiped his face, staring harshly at the machine goddess. He felt violated. "I... What are you talking about?"

"Your machine, I want to know who made it."

For some reason, I feel like I can't mention him... They told me not to trust her.

"I don't know." He found his footing and postured to meet the gaze.

The voices chuckled. "That's a lie."

"I'm serious."

"I'll give you one chance to reconsider your answer." The frames around the room switched to life and turned their sparking blue heads to watch him.

Kale gulped. He was in too deep. Staying here would only mean more traps and snares. "Look," Kale raised his hands, eyes switching from frame to frame, "I was kidnapped by a scientist and-"

Before he finished his sentence, he spun on his heels and sprinted towards the door he'd entered. The frames began to march, reaching out with their wiry arms. He slipped beneath their reach, kicking the nearest robot square in its chest. Their spindly construction made them easy to fight off.

"Don't go," the face spoke after him, "we were getting along so well!"

Kale spied a glistening shelf at the laboratory's entrance. Lined along the walls were metallic files, sticking out of the wall. He didn't know what they were, but they appeared to have value. "Since I didn't get my payment, I'm taking what I want!"

"You can run, but I know what you are!"

Ripping them from the wall, he dodged the grasping hands of metal and disappeared into the night.

The entrance of the eastern residence wing grew brighter as the sky darkened. For a moment, Kale hesitated to enter. The metal files from the lab fit loosely beneath his jacket. He wouldn't tell Astrid about what happened. Not Richmond either. He needed to reflect and assess what he'd stolen.
Scanning his voucher on the door to studio 385, he watched his feet as the door dragged open. Astrid sat atop the bed with her knees crossed, staring out the window at the light of The Well as it climbed the quickly darkening sky.
 She turned her emerald eyes over her shoulder to look at him upon his return. She'd changed out of her suit into a fashionable flamingo robe and her hands were busy braiding her hair which was halfway completed. The makeup was gone from her face and the mark of the clerics shone dimly on her forehead. "I can feel it," she spoke quietly without context.
Kale forgot about his mission.
He stood paused in the doorway, eyes locked on her unnatural appearance. The yellow glow of her clerical brand mesmerized him. It was the first time he'd seen what she looked like without the professional applications and the strain of incredible distress. Her eyes, lacking the dark outlines, appeared noticeably younger and vulnerable. Her skin was light and he could feel the softness through sight alone. After about a minute, he responded to the strange statement.
"What?"
"The Well. I can feel it." Her hand gently traced her cheeks and touched the glowing spot on her head. "It's like a pressure, something I need to do. It doesn't hurt, but it's there."
Kale looked to the right and saw that the chair he'd reclined in earlier was no longer there. In its place lay a small mattress, covered in a finely sewn blanket and one pillow. The chair had been moved to the opposite wall, pushed under a desk next to the closet. "Is it telling you something?"
"No." Astrid turned back to the window and continued toiling with her golden strands. "It's comforting."

"Interesting." Kale took off his coat and hung it on a hook from the wall.

"I unpacked your suitcase. I think Richmond prepared them for us. There's a lot of his old clothes in yours. They should fit."

The clothes inside fascinated Kale. There were sweatpants, graphic tees of bands long lost, a blue tracksuit, and three pairs of well-worn jeans. No matter how hard he tried, he couldn't imagine the scientist wearing anything from the selection.

"I heard he used to be different back then." Astrid finished fixing her hair and took a seat on the edge of the bed. "Buchannon told me stories about how he was an athlete before The Waking. He held the school record in the long jump."

Without reply, Kale chose dark track pants from the suitcase and made his way to the restroom to change. After shutting the door and removing the suit, he eyed the spot in his abdomen which had been replaced by mechanics. His ringers ran through the valleys of his ribs. The color and texture of his skin appeared the same, but he could tell from the feeling there was something noticeably harder and colder than bone lying beneath. He touched the soft skin behind his ear, feeling a metal square, the transponder. It made him sick. His arms and muscles had grown skinnier during his time in *Le Lien* and due to the injuries. Without the long walks in the sunny streets of the slums, his skin had lost some color. It left a sour taste in his mouth, the slow deprivation of his original identity.

No more machines... No more cybernetics. I am NOT an experiment.

Kale analyzed the objects he'd stolen from Skyridge Technologies. They were silver on their edges, identical to the Insider's 'map' he'd seen Richmond open before they'd entered the city. He peeled it apart. Blue and orange light flashed to life in the center revealing sprawling topography. It was a shipyard, he could tell by the flowing ocean waves and a maze of large containers.

Is this part of their zone?

There were words at the bottom.
- MAIN PROGRAMMING (ENVOY DRONE)
- MANUAL SENTINEL BASE (PILOT)
- REPLICANT SPIDER ASSEMBLY (COMBAT DRONE)

- DISCARD WASTE PROCESSING (FRAME)
- COLLECTIVE PROGRAMMING (GILGAMESH PROTOCOL)

What is all this? Sentinel?

His finger hovered on the word SENTINEL and the map rescinded. The light zoomed into a warehouse on the northern sea border, bypassing the roof. On the inside was the outline of a massive humanoid. It was a sentinel, he could tell, but slightly different than the ones he'd seen before. Something about it was less advanced, fashioned with axles and pistons in places where the others wore wires. He scrunched his eyebrows.

Are they building a sentinel? But Brianna Sky is a member of the Aureate… She wouldn't need to…

At that moment, Kale quickly shut the map, folding it into his shed jacket.

This is gonna get me in trouble…

As he returned to the room. Astrid spun around towards the window, dodging the sight of his exposed torso. "So then," she said with false confidence in an attempt to hide her embarrassment, "where did you go when you went out?"

"I checked out the bars."

"Oh," her eyes fell, "I see."

"I ran into our friend," Kale continued, "that officer."

The words drew the girl's attention and she furrowed her brows, "You did?"

He sunk into the chair on the western wall. "He seems normal enough."

"Tell me about it."

Kale took a deep breath. "He said he's been here since the beginning, that it wasn't always meant to be this closed-off city of elites. Originally, it was supposed to be a haven where people could work with The Well's energy. He doesn't like what it's become."

"So it sounds like he could help us, right?" She leaned in.

"I don't like working with the police. It's too risky."

She sighed, "That figures."

"What's that supposed to mean?" Kale crossed his arms, covering his tattoo.

Astrid looked to the ceiling, reclining back on her hands. "Why don't you leave that stuff behind? You don't have to be a gangster or thug anymore. Richmond's given you a chance."

The statement punctured something deep within him.

As if she knows. She couldn't understand what it's like to struggle… It's in my bones.

"Look," he withheld the impulse to argue, "I'm trying, but there's a part of me I can't deny."

She thought for a second, almost visibly excited by the statement. "I understand it's all you've known, but we're trying to help. You and I are doing something good. We're gonna help a lot of people."

He considered the words. "Maybe."

A silence followed.

"So," he broke the silence, "tomorrow… What'll you do?"

She scurried around the bed and found her voucher. "Here, look." her hands tapped surreptitiously until an orange hologram appeared. It was a spinning map of a crazily structured cathedral surrounded by multi-walled polygonal buildings. "The academy tours start at nine in the morning, I figured it would be a good place for us to start our research. This is a map of it. They meet outside the library, which is that church-looking building, but that's all I know so far."

Richmond told me I have to meet the insider tomorrow… But he never said when… or where.

Kale attempted to cover up his rising anxiety. "Sounds like a good plan."

His face did not reflect the calm and relaxed nature of their conversation. Instead, he failed to control the stark frown on his lips and stared blankly at the floor.

An awkwardness began to coat the air before Astrid spoke again.

"You scared me," she whispered.

"I scared you?"

"You were gone for so long. I was alone. I don't like being alone."

"Sorry."

He couldn't meet her eyes, but a faint red welled in his cheeks.

Softly she asked, "Are you still grieving?"

The words cut deep.

"It's not that," he said lowly, turning away, "I'm just stressed."

She whispered, "Right…"

A pause followed.

"Do you still think about it?" He asked her the question, yet considered *his* answer.

"It's *all* I can think about."

He didn't reply.

"But I understand the situation and I'm working on moving on." Her eyes traveled toward The Well. "It doesn't hurt as bad anymore."

His arms fell beside him, "I've tried to convince myself that she would've… forgiven me. But it always feels like I've just earned a spot in hell."

Lightly, Astrid walked over to him and grasped his hands between hers. "Don't think like that! Never in her life, did Phoebe ever think badly of someone. That night, when you helped her and first stayed at *Le Lien*. She was so excited and thrilled that she got to share her happiness with someone new."

"Then…" He looked up to see her, but his black hair blocked the sight. "What about you? Have *you* forgiven me?"

She let go of his hands and took a few steps back. "I… I'm working on it."

"If only I could go back… I wouldn't have-"

"Kale," a nerve ticked in Astrid as she heard his words, "I know I was hard on you at first. It was wrong of me. What happened was a terrible accident. You couldn't help your nature, not when the world is so cruel. But since then I've learned that there is good in you. I think maybe I'm starting to see you the way she did… If only a little."

Kale sunk his head into his hands. "I see it every night. The same dream over and over. I walk her to the hotel, but my mind… it screams for me to not enter those doors." He didn't include the reality of Richmond's predestination. "I just want to bring her back to you and leave… I-"

A cold hand on his shoulder caused him to stop.

She was close. Her fingers felt like ice. "That's enough." She was so close to him, he could feel the heat of her breath as she spoke at a whisper. "We're here to change everything. You can redeem yourself."

He raised his face. "Why are you doing this?"

Her cheeks grew red and she turned away slightly, "I don't know. I could tell you were hurting somehow." When she looked back at him, presenting an unsure smile. "I thought it was the right thing to do. Like you did for me that day."

He remembered holding her during the unexpected communion with The Well. Perhaps she didn't entirely see him as a dreg of the slums. Perhaps she saw something deeper, something he couldn't. The massive number of stimuli on his mind caused his head to ache. "Thanks."

She looked down at her voucher and noticed the late hour time had crawled to. "I asked the receptionist on the bottom floor for another mattress for you." She pointed to the makeshift bed on the floor set aside for him. "It's small, but it's all that would fit."

"It'll work." Kale rose from his chair and his muscles rippled with the motion.

As the two of them slid into their respective beds, a tension tugged when the light of the room fell to darkness and Astrid tapped a button on the window, causing it to grow completely black. The Well was blocked out. He thought about her, about what she could be feeling, about the contrast of her recent actions compared to their first meeting. He couldn't understand it.

What does she see?

The thoughts carried him to a dark slumber and visions of Phoebe, shadows looming in his wake, and a single white strand of light climbing The Well.

After a few hours of much-needed sleep, a beeping startled Kale from his dreams, causing him to gasp awake with a sharp vision of Brianna Sky's mechanical face. He yelled.

[Kale. Wake up. Now.]

It was Richmond.

"Huh? What's going on?" He whispered under his breath, careful not to wake Astrid who was in a deep dream. He could tell she was sleeping heavily by one of her legs hanging over the side of the bed and the dim light of her cleric insignia shining against the wall.

[It's time. He's waiting for you. I need you to get out to the street as soon as possible.]

"Are you serious? Right now?"

[Yes. He's waiting. Get dressed and hurry. Well... I hope you're already dressed, but put on a fine appearance for him.]

"Yeah, yeah, I got it. Gimme a sec." He quietly rose and fastened the expensive attire in a meticulous effort of silence. Before exiting, he felt the metallic Skyridge apparatus that hid within his suit pocket. With a pinch of hesitation, he reasoned it would be wiser to have it handy. Slipping out the door and down the elevator, he shivered when the cold air of night whipped against his body and blew his hair in every direction.

He looked around. The nighttime streets of the Guiding City were surprisingly empty. Various lights still shone from the many skyscrapers and The Well lit up his surroundings, but the shadows were deep. Richmond's call had not yet beeped, so Kale knew he could still be heard.

"Where is he?"

[Look around, find him. I was told he's ready now and had made his way to you.]

Kale's eyes darted between the colossal walls and shadows of architecture. On his left, the corner of the residence wing led to a pitch-black alleyway. "He doesn't like to be seen, right? I'll go somewhere dark and he can come to me."

[Yes, that is likely where he'll be.]

As he walked towards the darkness, he heard a faint sound, a string of coughs and the clearing of a throat. "Found him."

He squinted down the alleyway to see the outline of a man blindfolded and cloaked. A deep French accent greeted his arrival. "Welcome, Kale, I am deeply sorry for the inconvenient time of our meeting."

"Don't worry about it." He warmed his hands on his hot breath. "Whatcha got for me?"

cough "As you have already been told, you are expected to infiltrate the southern Globalist Sympath faction and convince them to join our cause. This will not be easy."

"Yep. That's all I know. How am I gonna do that?"

The insider cleared his throat. "A few blocks south is an entrance to the southern factory district. The reason I've called you here at this hour is due to the weekly cleaning of the gates. Even though the area is illegally occupied, the city still requires the outer entrances to be maintained. The gate will be opened.

You'll have to find a way to slip inside. I'v- *cough* I have traveled down into the area myself. It is a road of abandoned buildings, still forged with metal and brick. They have scouts in the windows that watch for trespassers. I was fortunately undetected, but I know that if you are seen they won't shoot… Well, at least not at first."

Kale's head hung and he hid behind his dark bangs. "Somehow, I don't believe you."

"The sympaths are organized beneath a captain, a fierce woman, and a lower-ranked scout who acts as her hands. Despite their politics, they are not kind. I wish you the best in your endeavors with these two."

"Wait, that's all you've got?" Sweat began to crawl down his neck.

"For now. The gates will be opened at… *cough* seven. Make sure you're there on time."

He threw a hand up, "Hang on. Astrid and I are supposed to tour the academy at nine. What am I gonna do about that?"

The insider turned to leave. "I don't know. Perhaps you'll have to skip. Now, I can't stay long."

"Hey, before you go, an officer told me to avoid Skyridge Technologies. What do you know about that?"

I already know why… Should I tell him what happened? No… Richmond would scold me… But does he know more?

The insider hummed lowly. "Not as much as I'd like. Brianna Sky is a bit of a mystery, but I've never heard anything good. If I were you, I'd listen to that officer."

"Right…" Kale replied, "thanks."

He appeared to be swallowed by the darkness and was gone. Kale did not attempt to follow.

Richmond chimed in through the transponder.
[You won't be attending that tour.]

A long exhale broadcast his discontentment. "That's going to make her angry… and I finally got on her good side."

[She can't know what you're doing. Aligning with the sympaths can be our key to taking this city and granting the blessings of The Well to the greater world. Kale, you can be the savior. But her clerical status is an enormous risk. She cannot be involved.]

"So how am I going to explain this to her? She'll think I've ditched." He slumped down against the smooth wall of the residence wing, remembering Astrid's complaint about being left 'alone.'

[I'll speak to her about it, but I'll be forced to provide a less-than-adequate excuse for your absence.]

"Make it a good one… please."

[I'll try. Now, I wouldn't recommend returning to the room, otherwise, you might wake her. The gate opens at seven.]
With a beep, he was gone.

Kale yelled a nasty curse to the dark, echoing loudly through the alley. An aching pain flared in his jaw as he clenched his teeth together.

I'm going to die… He's going to get me killed…

A vein popped out from his forehead among the scars. He felt deep anger at Richmond for forcing him into the role. The thought of walking down an abandoned trail into potential enemy territory was terrifying. All he wanted was to return to bed and tour the academy with Astrid in the morning.

He did not return to the room, as instructed. Instead, the foggy allies along the town square provided ample cover to get away from the occasional citizen that gleefully rose for a morning walk. Orange rays had begun to blaspheme his friendly darkness.

After meandering for hours, it was time to infiltrate. Sweat accumulated under his jacket from nervous pacing and Kale found himself standing beneath the words on the golden gate, SOUTHERN FACTORIES ROUTE C. It was a colossal wall of pure gold, separated down the middle by magnetic plating and a keypad for voucher interfacing. He reasoned that no ordinary vouchers would allow access into a closed zone and looked around discretely for whoever would come to open it. There were no blemishes, not even so much as a scratch on the surface.

6:54am… Should be any minute now. What's there to clean anyway?

Then, from behind him, a large vehicle in the shape of an old freight truck hovered slightly above the ground, emanating a similar purple light as the railway. With a low hum, it advanced towards the gate and he swiftly escaped its path. Atop the golden machine were two guards without helmets, yawning at the early hour. Kale watched from a bench surrounded by greenery nearby.

The two men slipped off the top and walked over to the gate's interface tapping it with their vouchers and with a low rumble, the doors slid apart, granting access to the southern factory route. He'd have to find a moment when they were distracted to slip inside. Many citizens had begun to flock around the town square and linear railway station and with each new arrival a pressure built inside Kale's stomach.

Is this even a crime? Should I be nervous in the first place?

The guards spoke flippantly among themselves, gathering strange tools from the vehicle and activating analogous drones. It wouldn't be too difficult to slip inside, as long as they remained distracted. He rose from his seat and slowly strode over.

As he reached a close distance, he tiptoed around the truck to their opposite, out of view. They had begun to move toward the gate, readying their tools in hand and continuing to chatter, until they'd disappeared behind the colossal left door. He could do it.

Now's my chance! If I can just not get caught by anyone else...

He sprinted.

Quickly, his feet flew into the unknown dilapidation behind the gate. A fire burned in his head, screaming for him not to, but he continued unfazed.

"Hey! What're you doing?!" A voice called from behind. "Don't go in there!"

Crap! Crap! Crap! I got spotted!

Faster and faster he kept running, deeper into broken-down buildings resembling the slums. Steel arms reached high above, looming like winding trees in a dark forest. The road ahead was long and the morning sun hadn't yet reached it. Deep shadows from the linear railways blocked out much of the sight and he wielded them as cover. His feet ached in his loafers little padding. The air smelled of oil and dirt and a ringing of his head distorted all hearing, yet his path continued. According to the insider's testimony, enemies lurked in windows unseen, watching him, suspecting him, and waiting for an opportune time to capture him.

A picturesque monolith of a brick wall stood between fresh sunbeams, subsumed by massive ancient factory walls a few yards ahead. Kale relished the sight of rest and slid beneath its shadow.

Sweat dripped from his hair like acid rain, creating moist heat pockets within his suit. Despite the chill sea breeze on the air, his skin burned from the running and his breaths escaped in triplets.

What have I done? How did I get myself into this…

Kale's head spun as a tornado of thoughts ruptured his brain. Surely, with all of the commotion he'd created, a Sympath scout had noticed him. If they truly were as advanced and fearsome as he'd been led to believe, then he was compromised the moment he stepped past the gate.

The attempts to control his breathing calmed him down from a state of panic to serious contemplation. The ragged puffs became regulated and his body focused on long exhales through the nose.

Okay… Confidence… I need confidence… I'm here to deal…

But his thoughts became disturbed and the panic painfully returned as a gentle sound invaded his ears and the feeling of cold steel on his neck caused his hair to stand.

"Who are you?" A quiet voice of a young man spoke softly.

Ice slithered through his veins. Kale couldn't bring himself to turn and face the voice's owner. He opened his mouth to respond, but fear silenced his chords.

"If you're not going to tell me, then do you know where you are?"

"I…" Without turning around, he offered a tone that was flat and forced, "I'm here to make a deal… I need to see… need to see your leader."

"Ohhhh, the captain? You don't know how this works, do you?"

He paused. "I need to talk to them. I'm here to make a deal."

"A deal? You sure? It's gonna hurt..." The voice rose to a giddy high note.

"What?"

Everything went dark.

It was strange. He felt nothing. His vision went pitch black and when he tried to remember how it happened, the workings in his brain failed. There was a dream, the remnants at least, of a hand pulling his collar. It wasn't a bad dream. Actually, the feeling was quite nice. But the chanting was loud… very loud.

When his eyes opened, before the light could reach his retinas, a loud cheering erupted. Hundreds of voices screamed down from above, calling for something.

He felt dirt in his hands, and when he attempted to breathe, dust filled his throat. It was the coughing that fully woke him.

He was now in a large expanse of brown. The light of The Well shone brightly in the sky, but all around were dirty people raising weapons in the air and tearing their voices at him. Ruined walls rose high on all sides and he attempted to climb to his feet. When his vision completely returned, he noticed that the expanse was like the interior of a colosseum.

A voice on a loudspeaker echoed boldly through the makeshift arena. It was a woman's, graced with a Russian tinge.

"LET'S SHOW THEM WHAT HAPPENS WHEN PEOPLE THINK THEY CAN *DEAL* WITH US!"

The many surrounding militia ripped their yells in adoration. Once Kale found equilibrium, he studied himself. His clothes were tattered and covered in dirt. He was left to his white button-down and stained slacks, but the jacket and tie had been lost somewhere.

Standing across the area was a young man, shirtless and adorned in ripped cloth. His hair was bleached and separated down the middle. He was athletic but lean. Striations of muscle ran like wires along his arms, contrasting a boyish face that found too much glee in the situation. He stuck a fist stuck in the air and the crowd erupted.

Anger flared like a bonfire in Kale's chest. "HEY! WHAT'D YOU DO TO ME!" The words were instantly drowned out.

The voice over the speaker called, "Go! Show him how WE deal!"
The man rushed forward.

Am I going to fight him? What's going on!?

Quickly, his fingers toiled with his sleeves, rolling them up the forearm. The other man was quick. In a few seconds, they'd meet.

Uggghhh, screw it!

Kale raised his fists in a fighting stance. He was no stranger to combat. In the slums, a child learned to fight as soon as they could walk. Many times in his life as a Vulture, they squared off against rival gangs that would form to challenge their monopoly. The battles would often be finished thanks to their sheer numbers, but one on one fights were occasional for him so he bore confidence.

A grunt left his opponent as a fist struck forward. Swiftly, he slipped beneath, returning a low shot in answer. Neither connected and the enemy laughed in acknowledgment.

"It seems you know a little something." The voice was familiar.

Kale snickered, "Not too bad yoursel-."

Before he could finish his sentence, a kick flew to his left side. Pain erupted in the area of real bone and he buckled over slightly. "That was cheap!" Kale lunged forward, sending a left jab toward his cowled opponent and then a right straight. The skin met slightly and the enemy ate the pain.

As he looked for what was coming next, the attacker signaled a low shot. Kale dropped his hands, expecting to block, but a heel came flying from the right. The bone smacked against his temple and his lips met the dirt. The pain made him dizzy. Black dots littered his eyesight and the crowd screamed.

That hurt… It hurts… Really hurts…

With a groan, he rose to his feet, shifting slightly left and right without the cooperation of physics.

"There you go," the boyish Sympath taunted, waving his hands around towards the crowd, "you can stand."

Pain scorched the gums of his teeth as he ground them together. He hated the man in front of him.

I'm gonna kill him.

He sprinted forward with raised hands. His opponent laughed, carelessly bracing a high guard, but Kale switched at the last moment to a double-legged takedown. His arms wrapped around the enemy's knees, muscles rippling as he hoisted the other man into the air and slammed him down on his back. A pained grunt echoed around the arena. An arm coiled upward, wrapping around Kale's neck. He tucked his chin down, preventing a choke while he struggled to get ahold of the attacker's own.

Alongside the grappling work, he jabbed punches into ribs and his hands burned and popped with each strike. Sweat accumulated beneath his chin and he slipped from the grasp, bringing a strong elbow down onto the attacker's face. Blood spurted forward as a cut opened above their eye. Again and again, he slammed appendages into the other man's face, screaming curses and threats with a blinding rage, but out of nowhere, the opponent found a second wind.

Kale ended up on his back defending strikes as they volleyed down. Fists, elbows, and knees fell onto every inch of his body and pain tore at his skin. He could feel his face swelling and ribs cracking. Blood flowed from his lips, busted in several places and his teeth loosened. Consciousness inched away with each strike.

No, not like this… I can keep going…

With a massive push, Kale flung the other man from atop him. Skidding to the side, both jumped to their feet and simultaneously threw kicks. His foot connected with a chin, but the other's drove heavily into his thigh. His balance left and the back of his head slammed into the hard ground once more.

The transponder began to beep. Someone was calling him and he groaned in frustration.

Ugh, not now!

[Kale?]
Astrid's voice was shaky and confused.
[Where are you?]

He attempted to reply, "I-I'm sorry I ca-"
Before he could recover and mouth the final word, a fist rocked his jaw. White dots littered the world around him and darkness overtook his sight.

Damn. I'm finished…

The next time he opened his eyes, he was on his knees in front of a burly woman, packed to the teeth in hard muscle. She sat strong atop a golden seat, resting her hands wide apart. A dark blue robe parted where cuts allowed her massive arms to escape. Tan combat boots stomped the ground beneath her and tattoos of predatory animals crawled up her neck twisting in a way half alive. Her eyes, like a hawk's, stared down at him between black locks. "You said he came to deal."

Kale struggled around, unable to move his arms. With each attempt, a rustling of chains shook and he realized they were contained apart in handcuffs.

"Yes, captain," A voice, the same as before; the man who found him and the man he fought, replied.

Dark crimson dripped from Kale's mouth onto his white shirt which had been halfway undone exposing the vulture on his chest. His hair fell over his eyes and a scar above his brow leaked inky liquid into his vision. He could feel the puffiness of bruises swelling all over.

"You, trespasser." The woman spoke beneath a large window aligned with The Well. Everything around him was dark except for her image and the man to her right. "Do you remember forests? Where I was from, before The Waking, we had lots of forests, the kind of trees where the roots run above the ground. We'd use them as steps to climb mountains."

He looked up without replying. Between the blood and scars, his face was beyond recognition.

"I always found it fascinating. It was like a web connecting the entire forest. It made me wonder if all trees are connected beneath our feet. We're sort of like that, you think? Here, we Sympaths fight for all the other people outside the walls. We fight for the people all over the world."

Kale glared at her, once again refusing to speak.

"Not amused? You know, we can't make a deal if you don't talk." She leaned forward, resting her head on her palm without breaking eye contact.

"Why…" He couldn't form words beyond a whisper. "Why did you do this to me?"

A pause followed.

"I never deal with a man I can't first control. It was necessary."

He could tell her type by sight alone: strong, powerful, and never hearing a 'no.' "You didn't even give me a chance to explain myself…" He spat red onto the ground in her direction. The insufferable action prompted a clicking sound to the right and her servant drew a pistol aimed at his head. The action didn't bother him, he'd seen it too many times than he cared to recount.

"No, no, Joyner, he understands." She waved down the threat, "Before I allow you to speak, I'll clear the air. Explain this to me; why were you in possession of Skyridge layouts? Heavily detailed ones at that…"

The map! I should've gotten rid of it.

Kale scoffed. "Part of the deal." He glared at them, staring dead into the woman's strong pupils.

The captain crunched her fingers, squeezing a fist. "Are you from the Order?"

Not even giving me time to think... That's cheap.

Kale ignored her accusation. "I have an offer." His throat was indescribably dry. "I've been told that you people are on the side of the slums, want to bring The Well to the rest of the world. I can offer you a partnershi-"

"We don't need a partnership." Her voice boomed through the expanse. "There are no allies in this city other than those already in our ranks." Her statement was absolute, commanding the room. She was, by all standards, a natural leader.

"*We*," he retorted, "aren't from the city. I can give you people on the outside."

She stroked her jagged chin with a hand in deep contemplation. "Go on."

"I represent an organization known as The Vultures-"

What am I saying? I can't speak for them! I'm not even a part of the ranks anymore!

"-We have three hundred men outside the walls. They're metal workers, strong and able to fight. They've been trying to breach the city for a decade and I believe we can work together."

The woman hummed a low consideration. "These... Vultures... Why do they want to breach the city."

The question caught him off guard.

Why? Isn't that obvious?

"Well... they want to be rich. With The Well's energy, they can beco-"

"Then you don't understand our mission." She rose to her feet, casting a deep shadow over him. "You're from the slums? Of course you are. You wouldn't care for our cause otherwise."

"Yes, I lived in that dump my whole life."

"What about now, can you still taste the dust?"

"I don't understand what that has to do wit-"

"If your 'organization' isn't fighting for the suffering people first and foremost, I won't work with them. Don't come to me and talk about profit!"

He couldn't reply. His mouth hung open in disbelief. There was nothing else to bargain. The Vultures were the only thing he could offer to the Sympaths and if they were to refuse, what would happen to him? The cards were gone from his hand.

"You came to deal, yet you're ignorant of what we stand for. If you have nothing else to say, we'll dismiss you." She signaled a hand and the man began to walk over, gun at the ready.

"WAIT!"

The looming elite stood still. Kale hissed, spitting the blood from his mouth, and spoke, "There's one more thing I can offer… a mind."

The massive woman looked down at him over her nose, "A mind?"

Yes… This is perfect…

"Yes. A man. A scientist. A genius! He's created a machine to draw The Well's power outside of the walls."

Her arms folded, flexing veins and muscles like iron cords. "He's sending The Well's power to the slums?"

"I won't reveal his identity, but for you to believe me, I can have you meet him."

"And why would I trust what you're saying right now? Why should we want anything more than we already have?"

"You're at a stalemate, aren't you?" He recalled the words of the insider. "You can't get what you want because the other factions are rallying across the city. He can help."

"So, you *have* done a bit of research." She hummed in low contemplation. "If that's true, we could bypass- But… Why would he risk a crime like that? The Well's energy is the sole property of the Aureate."

Kale smiled, "because he's fighting for the same thing… To bring down the city and offer The Well back to the people who deserve it most."

The captain laughed, "I could use a man like that. Tell me about his technology."

Should I really tell her this? What would Richmond think… But I have no choice… That's all I have left…

The words hurt to speak as his tongue slapped against the cuts in his mouth. "It's a star, a receptacle for The Well's energy, and able to transfer infinite power. His goal is to bring the light to everyone and restore Old Baltimore to the glory it had before The Waking. I don't really know how it works, but I've seen it."

The captain paused, standing still and locking her eyes dead into Kale's view. Time slowed down as the thoughts in her head became impossible to read.

After what seemed like an eternity, she spoke. "Is it true?" Her boots stomped over and she knelt to face the captive.

"Yes."

"Then," the sharp woman began rummaging with her pockets, "the Sympaths occupy a certain number of gates around the southern border of the Guiding City."

"Captain," the scout chimed in, studying her actions, "are you sure we can trust him? He could be an Aeon spy."

"Spy or not," she withdrew the Skyridge map from beside her throne and opened it, leaking blue light into the room, "we've gotten something far more valuable now."

The lackey persisted. "It could be a trap-"

"If that were true, he would've bargained more than a meeting with one man. Besides, we'll be able to track him." From a pocket in the blue robe, she retrieved a small golden object. The form resembled a diamond but possessed several off-shooting spikes bending in all directions. "It's a personal keepsake of mine. Any member of our ranks will recognize it immediately and not harm you. Get him into the city and find us once again." She turned and resumed her place on the throne, signaling her servant once more. "We'll be watching."

"Thank you," He rubbed his swollen wrists as the chains shook in release, "I won't let you down."

"Oh, I know you won't. It's your only choice."

Kale was released shortly after and sent on his way out of the Sympath's occupied zone. He was given a black cloak to cover himself with and a spare voucher that could access the southern factory district's gate. By the time he made it back to the commerce district, night had begun to cast its comforting darkness. His skin was completely stiff from dried blood and the swelling of his face had only slightly settled. If he were to face Astrid, he'd certainly have hell to pay, but he had no choice. The only thing he could think was how terrifying Richmond's fury would be after he would tell him of the deal's terms.

His head hung low as he drug himself bruised and beaten back to the residence wing, deeply uncertain of how the next interaction would unfold.

Chapter 10
Ecdysis

As the sun set in the Guiding City, a cozy bench shrouded by heavy tree branches provided a quaint spot for meditation. The thoughts of his mind conjured a will to contact Richmond and the neural transponder reacted in kind.

[Kale, did it go well? Tell me the details.]

The disconsolate and bruised thug pulled the cloak over his head and spoke almost at a whisper. His face ached with the motion of speech. "It did. I struck a deal."

[Tell me.]

"I'm not sure you're going to like it…" The consequences of Richmond's fury didn't concern him anymore. It couldn't have been worse than the pain he felt at that moment, as adrenaline began to fade and the aches of his injuries returned both internal and external.

[Speak.]

"I've arranged a meeting between you and the captain of the Sympaths. I tried to wager The Vultures as a bargain for their help, but she refused. They were going to kill me… I had no choice but to tell them about the star," he responded in monotone, hiding his eyes behind his sable hair which was thick with sweat.

Richmond paused before allotting a relieved sigh.
[That's good.]

Kale's head perked up at the words. "You're not angry?"

The host assumed a flat tone with his words, devoid of assurance or disappointment.

[No, this works. This is opportune. Now, about gaining access to the city…]

I thought for sure he'd want to kill me for it…

"They gave me a voucher to access the southern gates and some kind of item that Sympath lackeys will recognize. It'll be sketchy, but if we can sneak around guards and officers, I can get you in."

[I see. We'll think on this in the coming days. I want you to rest. Rest your mind. Did you specify when this meeting will be?]

"No. They have scouts patrolling the perimeter of the occupied zone. If I show them that object, we should be allowed in without an issue."

[Good.]

"So," Kale slumped within the cover of the cloak as a chill sea breeze blew in, "what'd you tell her."

[To trust you. She was quite distressed at your disappearance.]

"She probably hates me now…"

[Perhaps. Even I don't fully understand how she feels at all times. She's always been a strange one… unpredictable… emotional…]

"Total opposite of you." He felt along his scarred face. Lumps had formed around his eyes and his lips swelled through dried blood. "I don't think I can face her like this."

[What do you mean?]

"I was beaten… badly. When I got into the district, they knocked me out and threw me into an arena. I had to fight the second in command. We beat each other up, but I got the worst of it."

[That is extreme, but she can't know. You cannot tell her about this mission. Surely you can think of some excuse. She will understand… I think.]

"Tsk. You don't sound so sure."

[I'm not.]
With a beep, his voice faded.

After a long and procrastinated walk back to the residence wing, Kale stood outside the door to their studio nervously. His face was hidden, concealed behind the black cloth and though he held his voucher in hand, his body refused to raise it to the door.

I can't do it... What'll she think? She'll think I've gone off and gotten drunk somewhere or beaten up by the police. What am I supposed to tell her? I can't tell the truth or she'll want to get involved... Why did Richmond make me do this? She probably hates me for leaving her today...

Consumed by thought, self-doubt, and worry, Kale never noticed the door lightly swing open and Astrid's aghast face scan his injuries.
"What happened to you?" Her voice was quiet.
He couldn't reply. Opening his mouth, the sentences stammered into gibberish. Sweat filled his clothes as his eyes raised to meet hers. She wore a new gown, lighter and slightly more revealing than the last he'd seen her in. He rushed past, sliding into the bathroom and slamming the door shut behind him without a recognizable word. He could feel emotion gaining the better of his senses. The caps of his knees hit the floor. The built-up sufferings and panicked feelings throughout the day had yet to manifest themselves and though he'd taken the time outside to attempt to clear his head, the attempt had failed.
"Will you talk to me?"
He could hear her outside the door, pressing against the surface opposite him, as if she was touching the back of the cloak he used to hide his shameful state.

Get a hold of yourself! You're a man!

A silent war waged through synapses of his subconscious. A bitter poison trickled along his tongue as his lips parted to respond. "I... I need a minute alone."
"Are you hurt? Where were you today? I have a lot to tell you about." There was no frustration written in her voice, rather something along the lines of deep concern could be felt when he heard the words.

He wanted, deep down, to tell her everything, to regain the trust and compassion of the night before. If only Richmond hadn't forced him to stay silent about their darker matters, then that trust could remain. Despite the many troubles they had experienced and the ties of tragedy that constantly showed its pure childlike face when they saw one another, an understanding had begun to develop, he thought.

Two differing options presented themselves to him: approach Astrid with confidence and create a fabricated story or withdraw from the situation and avoid her. Neither seemed appealing.

The girl's voice broke his thoughts, "I don't know what you did or where you were today. Father... Well, Richmond told me to believe what you say. I don't mean to pry too much. I know there're things you can't tell me... That's just the way he works... But I'm a little scared. I saw blood..."

"I'm alright." The words were all he could manage. Any more, and he'd tell her everything. After a string of silence, he rose to his feet and began to start the water for a shower. He didn't hear Astrid move.

The warm water stung through his cuts, running between the gaps in his skin. It felt nice, consoling the bruised whelps on his face and ribs. The injuries would heal with time, but he couldn't stay in there long enough to avoid her. Eventually, they would have to talk.

Suddenly a click came from the door. Kale froze. A curtain blocked his view outwards, but it was strange. Somehow, the door was opened.

Her voice shook with timorous hesitation. "I'm coming in."

"What're you doing?"

"I can't see you, but we need to talk." He heard her, around the curtain, sit on the floor. "Let me see your face."

Is she crazy? I can't deal with this...

"I-I can't."

"Why not..."

There were no words to reply. None could properly provide a suitable excuse. He was simply ashamed, genuinely bashful. He didn't want her to see the bruises and cuts, the signs of his defeat. "I'm trapped."

"You're trapped?"

He slid to the bottom of the shower, letting the water run through his hair and drain red into the floor. "I'm trapped between the things I thought I wanted for myself and the things that I believe could somehow be right for me to do... but no matter how much I want to do it, I'm not the one that gets to decide."

A silence followed, but between the sound of trickling water, he could hear the shaking of his breaths. Astrid whispered in reply. "What do you mean?"

"You know? I want to change. I want to do better for myself. I want to leave it all behind. I want to atone for the things I did, but I doubt I'll ever get the chance… I've never had a choice."

The girl sat silent and pondered the words he spoke. She could hear the soft sniffles of his anguish that he tried desperately to hide behind a cough. "Don't say that."

"But it's true. Maybe I'm supposed to suffer for what I did. Maybe I'm gonna have to die just to feel like I made up for it."

Without reply, Kale heard the scuffles of the girl rise from the floor and then the clicking of the bathroom door latch. "You left me alone again."

He sat with his thoughts for a few minutes until the water no longer pleased his body, but felt instead like a burning whip slapping his flesh. Hesitantly, he turned the faucet off and stood in front of the mirror, attempting to dry himself without worsening any injuries. The rough towel stung as it dragged over purple bruises. Fresh blood dripped from his eyebrow.

To his left, a set of clothes had been neatly placed on the countertop, a small gesture of kindness from the girl, he reasoned.

So it's just pity…

After dressing himself and stretching black bangs of hair over his eyes, he exited. Astrid had found a spot on the floor, at the edge of the bed, beneath the light of The Well where she sat on her knees and looked up at him with a stern brow.

"Come here."

A moment passed when his eyes inspected her skin and a reply became impossible.

"Come here. Lie down, like I did to you that day." A slender hand patted the exposed flesh of her thighs.

The ailing muscles of his body relinquished to the call without a word of answer. Kale found himself lying on his back and resting his head on the tender lap. The softness of her body was unlike anything he'd ever felt. The cold metal of his past became a distant and forgotten memory.

"I saw some cool things at the academy today." Her fingers fell to his hair and traced lines between clumps of matted strands and a scent of damp lilacs graced his nostrils. "The library, in the building that looked like a church, has more books about The Well than we could ever read. Tomorrow, I'll go back and find as many as I can take back here. I want you to see it."

An attempt was made to divide his lips for speaking, but he was unable.

"The people, the students and the workers there, they were all very nice and welcoming. It's not like the outside. They can live. They can walk the streets without worry or concern. Imagine if everyone could feel that." She leaned over him, pressing her chest into the top of his head, leading to a flush of crimson that filled his cheeks. "I did a lot of thinking today while you were gone and I realized something. *I* should be the one to fix you."

"I..." the words felt like a ton of bricks, anchoring his tongue, "I'm trying..."

"I realized it's not something you can do on your own and that It's what she would've wanted." Astrid's voice escaped as honey, flowing inside him and warming the cold truths beneath. "There's no point in me being angry at you or hating you for what happened. Had you been able to choose, I know you wouldn't have done it. I have faith that one day I'll get to see my sister again and I know that If I were to face her having hated you, she would be sad."

There was hypnotism swirling as he looked up into the emeralds of the girl who held him. Her golden mark of the clerics eased the troubles in his mind. She was warm, so warm, and softer than anything he'd felt. Her fingers commanded his emotions and with each touch, the pain of his injuries disappeared.

"Kale," she whispered sweetly, as her face touched his, "I don't want this to continue. I want our bonds, mine, Richmond's, yours, and everyone else's at *Le Lien*, to be stronger because of what happened, not hurt. I'm not someone who can live with hate in my heart, which is why I've made such an effort to be kind to you. Richmond accepts you for who you are, but I'm trying to find a way to reach that same understanding. You shouldn't hate yourself." Her forehead rested on his. "Now, will you tell me who did this to you?"

"You know I can't tell you..."

"You can tell me."

"I can't..."

"You can."

He raised a hand to cover his eyes. A silent scoff left his throat and he began to speak. "I wish... I wish so badly I could tell you everything... All I can say is that I'm trying to do the right thing... Astrid, you have to trust me. Things are about to get tough... tougher than anything I've done before, but I just need you to keep being who you are, just like this, and if you can do that, you'll fix me."

The girl took a moment to ponder the words he said, continuing to run her fingers through his hair. "Then, I trust you."

With the words, relief flooded his chest cleansing the insecurities, worries, and doubts of the day. He took a deep breath.

Was that all I was worried about?

"Ya' know," Kale jested as he closed his eyes, "you're breaking your own rule."

She returned a sweet smile. "Which one?"

"You told me not to talk to you at night."

She considered the words, bringing a hand to her chin and turning her gaze to the penumbral glow of The Well. "I still see some light out."

Time seemed to stop when she lowered her head. He didn't see it, but he could feel the radiant heat of her skin slowly growing closer. His heartbeat began to accelerate as the infinite softness of her lips touched him. It wasn't a kiss of love, he knew, but rather a reassurance of a sort that his mind did not fully understand. It couldn't be love. The relationship between the two wasn't deep enough. He didn't love her. She didn't love him. After all, how could she?

Don't fall... Don't let it distract you... Just accept it for what it is and nothing more...

With a resistant mind, his lips savored the taste until she released herself.

Less than an inch apart, she spoke once more, "You're mine to fix, no one else's. I promise to Phoebe that I'll make you into what she saw you to be." Without saying another word, she lifted his head from her lap and climbed into the bed above. He found his composure to sit on the floor and fought the urge to look back at her. The room grew dark as she tapped on the window and silence consumed his surroundings.

This is an act of pity... Nothing more...

No further words were exchanged between the two as the night dragged on and Kale sat awake for hours wondering exactly how the emotions swirling in his mind would find a conclusion.

A haze of awkwardness followed them during the morning's interactions. He couldn't avoid thinking about the night before, the kiss, and the fleeting memory of taste, but she acted as if the night as a whole only occurred in his dreams.

"The library opens at 9, if we can leave here at 8, that'll give us enough time to walk and do as much research as possible." She spoke in a hurry as her hands flew, spreading harsh makeup over her face to cover up her clerical iridescence. "You're gonna think it's so cool. The books just don't stop!" The words bore a childish excitement.

I guess she's like her sister when she's excited...

The girl's flurry of speech continued, "There's a cool model of the Guiding City in the middle of the library. I had no idea it was so huge! We're pretty close to The Well compared to everything else, but the city is just as big all the way around. I wonder if the slums are as bad everywhere else..."

Kale stretched after donning his suit which now had small holes beneath the armpits and dirty stains on the inside from his squabble in the Sympath territory, but after a hearty scrub, its color had been returned to a gleaming sable. "Probably..." He couldn't look at her directly. If he did, he smelled her perfume. When she talked, a heat leapt through his body.

God... What am I, a kid?

The chill morning air whispered between the buildings and web-like rails winding and slithering through the sky. A flock of drones buzzed overhead as the party joined the busy streets.

To reach the academy, they would need to walk two miles east and pass the channel that connected to the Atlantic. The academy was uniquely positioned to observe both the happenings of the Guiding City and receive connection with the greater world, though no one could expect to simply arrive by boat; security measures for such an event involved underwater barriers and if a ship happened to cross without a trading voucher, its crew would never be heard from again.

"It's quite a nice walk," Astrid said as she ducked beneath a small roadside tree. "Yesterday, in the channel, I saw a dolphin swimming."

Kale sniffed the air. The salt had grown to a strong and realized flavor as mist blasted his face from a breeze. "I've never seen the ocean before."

The girl's face lit up at the words. "Really? I'll show you when we get there! There's a big balcony at the back of the library where you can stand out and see for miles. The docks are pretty far away, but you can still make out all the ships and barges passing by."

He didn't care much for the ocean. He'd never seen it and it would never influence his life, so it mattered little, however, he'd happily take a day of books and sightseeing over torture at the hands of the Sympaths.

The sky was especially azure that morning. Sunbeams cut between fluffy clouds and The Well shone into the heavens. Even birds found the weather desirable enough to play and dance among the rays. Perhaps a day such as this could be what Richmond meant by 'vacation.'

After a mile of walking, they came upon a bridge, a golden and ornate construction that both served as a road for the unimaginative and polygonal cars, but also provided gilded sidewalks for foot traffic. The citizens walking along the roads grew noticeably younger as they drew closer. Teenagers congregated in groups sharing their vouchers with one another. They were students, he could tell by their matching uniforms of flamboyant design and flared yellow adornments along the sleeves and pants. On the backs was a crest, a replicant outline of The Well's rays breaking through the clouds. Kale balked at such attire.

Astrid stopped her stride to peer over the bridge's railing. Gentle waves of saltwater tossed and churned beneath them, sending foam along the banks. "Technically, it's just the channel, but there you go, Kale, your first look at the ocean." The water glistened with yellow dots like stars in the crests and fathomless shades of midnight in the troughs.

"It doesn't look any different than normal water…" He inspected the less-than-impressive sight.

The besuited girl stole his arm and pointed to the shallow ripples along the bank. "Look. The water itself isn't any different, but it's what's beneath that matters. The ocean, saltwater, is so full of life. I love it." Past the pointed finger that she extended for him, several crabs chittered and crawled beneath the surface. Colors danced along their shells switching from crystalline blue to a fiery crimson as they moved. The iridescent pallet almost caused them to disappear with the shifting waves, but still, his eyes admired them.

The path leading to the academy was paved in marble, silver, and flawless platinum to reflect the pompous perfection of its architecture. While the space outside was significantly less claustrophobic than the towering skyscrapers of the dense city, the academy allowed many students to roam beneath gentle oaks. Lively foliage was exceedingly rare in the slums as the primary source of green only came from toxic and invasive vines. Billions of fingers of grass tickled the feet of children that played in the courtyard behind a tendrilous golden wall that stretched for miles in each direction. There were still skyscrapers, but the construction of the academy resembled pre-Waking cityscapes, friendlier and more tolerable to the eyes. The library, as Astrid pointed out, was a grotesque assortment of stained glass, fractal spikes, and flying buttresses. Kale had long ago been told stories of Heaven by his mother who followed the Christian faith. He didn't necessarily believe them, but when viewing such an ornate building, he strongly considered their validity.

The two stopped walking once they reached the gated entrance to the courtyard to admire their surroundings. "It's beautiful, isn't it?" Astrid giddily spun her head to sightsee. "I've heard buildings like this still exist overseas. Apparently, Richmond's university had one too that's hundreds of years old."

"It's incredible." His eyes followed the gothic weave.

They began to walk towards the entrance where students flooded into and out of gigantic wooden doors that were outfitted with steel bracings. Kale rubbed shoulders in an irritated manner, clearing a path between the oblivious crowd of adolescents who didn't flinch at the gesture. "Hey, care to move?" He spoke in a careful tone to hide his desire to shove them out of the way. The eyes of a young couple that stared back seemed unfazed until they saw his face. Perhaps it was the scars or the uncomfortable expression it wore that caused them to rush aside, but he didn't care. Astrid clung to the back of his suit coat until they were inside.

She had not exaggerated one bit about the vast selection. To properly number the count of books within the library would take months, perhaps even a full year, Kale reasoned. His jaw fell as the rapid movement of winding staircases and silent hands browsed the thousands of rows that climbed seven stories to the roof which projected a hand-painted mural of cloaked figures bowing to the radiant Well. He felt like an ant would if it crawled into a football stadium. From the outside, the library, though impressive, had not appeared large enough to house the contents within and he wondered if they had instead been transported to another world.

Once he had fully absorbed the enormous interior, Astrid led their path. "I know it's a bit overwhelming, but don't let it intimidate you. I know where we need to go."

He gestured a hand forward and smiled at her, hiding his sense of discomfort among the crowd. "Lead on."

Towards the back of the library and between faces that rudely inspected the 'old fashioned' suits the two wore, the genre of nonfiction research into The Well prominently broadcast itself with a hologram that spun its image and radiated different colored lights. Books of all shapes and sizes were neatly arranged on dark wooden shelves that climbed in rows along a steep staircase.

Astrid marched forward with confidence and climbed a few steps before sitting to inspect a low row of green-spined hardbacks. She brushed a strand of straightened gold out of her eyes and crossed her legs. "I looked into these for a bit yesterday. They're collections of research into the way its light behaves."

Kale became interested and leaned against the shelf at an equal height with her. "This is all public knowledge? That's kinda surprising." He traced the titles at eye level,

- EXPERIMENTAL CONTACTS WITH LIGHT by Dr. JR Redding
- REACHING INTO THE WELL by Cordan P. Watson
- HUMAN AUGMENTATION OF WELL-INDUCED ENERGY by Dr. Brianna Sky
- JOURNEY OF THE RAYS by The Associated Partners of Human Advancement

The third caught his eye and he shivered at the name. "Hey," he tapped the girl's shoulder, "I think we need this one." His finger pointed to the name Brianna Sky.

"Brianna Sky?" Astrid scrunched her brows. "That 'machine goddess' or whatever, right?"

"We need to learn what we can about the Areate."

If I told her about Skyridge, she'd probably freak out…

"Sure, get it."

He withdrew the book, surprisingly heavier than its appearance, and placed it under his arm. "How many can we get? How does this all work?"

"As many as we want…" She became intently focused on the works before her. "As many as we can carry."

For close to an hour, the two skimmed numerous books searching for the ones that could provide the most practical and useful information that they could relay back to Richmond. Only one problem presented itself, all of the books were intently specific to studies. There was no: FUNDAMENTALS AND BASICS OF THE WELL.

Painstaking silence made Kale uneasy as he scoured the shelves for something he could understand, but his toil was interrupted when Astrid gasped. "Hey, come look at this." From the tallest shelf she could reach, her fingers struggled and withdrew a dark red book with a gilded title, THE CLERIC WISHGRANTERS: A BRIEF HISTORY OF GIFTED CHILDREN.

"Wishgranters?" Kale inquired, leaning his head in to see. "What's that supposed to mean?"

"I don't know…" She opened the front page and began to read, "From the time of the first communion and the extensive research into the nature of The Well's light, the cause and reason for the clerics' existence remains a brutal mystery." Her eyes glossed with wonder as she continued down the page. "I need to read this."

He studied the back of the book as the girl fumbled through the pages before him. "Hang on." His hands stopped her from turning further. "There's no author."

Confused, Astrid turned it over and checked every corner. "You're right." Opening the front page where the usual publishing information would have been, she found a small footer written solemnly in tiny lettering at the bottom: *A special thanks to the one who knows, Gilgamesh.*

"What do you think that means?" Kale turned his nose upward and sighed.

"I don't know. Either way, we should start small. Let's take a few and work on reading."

With 5 large and dusty books in hand, Astrid led him to a circular desk in the center of the library where two cheery and strangely content receptionists tinkered on holographic screens. Their faces made Kale uneasy and he browsed a nearby aisle. One spoke up after receiving the books and placed them in an orange carrying crate that somehow felt lighter than the combined weight of the books. "These items must be returned one week from today. If we don't receive them back after the allotted time, a late fee will be charged to your vouchers. If we have not received the late fee or books after two weeks, then the full monetary charge of the books' current market value as well as tax will be taken from your voucher's respective accounts. Please make sure to take care of them!"

With a respectful thanks, Astrid found the secluded thug and tugged on his arm, "Come here, I didn't get to show you yet."

"Show me what?" he inquired.

"The *real* ocean. Remember?"

They stepped to the back of the cathedral library, slipping with kindness between customers until an exit door led them outside. The balcony was spacious, welcoming a salty breeze. Railings of concrete and marble bound them into a semicircle where a view stretched to the horizon of small edifices, but gave way to a stretch of blue deeper than any he'd ever seen. The Well was to their left, yet still colored the waves with a golden stroke at their crests. The sun now sat directly above and an azure hue coated the underdepth.

"Wow," Kale admired the new sight, "It's huge. I never knew there was so much water…"

"It's amazing. Look over there," She pointed to a spec on the horizon, "It's a barge. They're bringing in foreign cargo. I like to guess what's on them."

His eyes followed the ship as it moved. "I wonder what the other countries are like. My father was from overseas, but I've never been."

"It's the same for me." Astrid brushed her hair back and looked at him. "I was born the day of The Waking, but Father and Mother used to travel a lot."

He leaned against the rails and stared deeply outward. "You said she was Finnish?"

"Yes, Richmond had a research grant for foreign energy studies. That's where they met. He was working at a lab to develop clean and renewable power sources. She was a secretary in his department. She used to tell me how they fell in love. It was his way with words that won her over."

Kale snickered, "sounds about right."

"He's always been that way." The girl rested her chin on a palm, leaning out over the rail. "There's a feeling within him that I've never been able to figure out. When Mother died, something happened. He never laughed, he never smiled, he was deadly serious." She turned and looked him directly in the eye with a serious expression. "But it changed when you arrived. Even after what happened… with… Phoe-" She cleared her throat. "Even after that, I've seen him smile and laugh a few times. I don't know why or how you did it, but something clicked within him. Like he'd found a purpose again."

The words took him aback. "What?" He couldn't think of a reply. "How could I have… I mean, I don't understand. I haven't caused a single good thing to happen."

Astrid looked down. "Maybe you're right, but I noticed it. It's like he's having fun again."

"Fun?"

What is she talking about? Fun? Fun torturing me? Fun sending me to do his dirty work?

"I thought about it last night. I couldn't sleep. I think since the two of you are total opposites, it's given him a reason to keep moving forward. You know, he never wanted to send Phoebe here. Admittedly, I was scared and I could sense hesitations in him. I didn't have the courage to go into such a new place and have to take care of her and if I'm being honest, I don't think he had faith in me. But now you're here and we've been able to build trust, things have taken a turn for the better." She offered a gentle smile. Her eyes were immensely deep with the reflection of the waves swirling along her irises.

How can she say that? Things have gotten better?

"I-I never thought about that…" Black tendrils of hair fell over his face and his feet felt awkward turning away from her.
"It's the truth." The ocean stole her attention once more.
He didn't reply.

After a long and silent gaze out on the translucent waves, they began the trek back. Kale wasn't particularly excited to read, but he welcomed whatever he could do to take his mind off of the mission. He'd have to contact Richmond soon and find a time to sneak him into the city, but that could wait. For now, all he had to worry about was a half day alone with the girl who he was now fascinated by.

Richmond did, however, call them through the neural transponders once they'd arrived at the residence wing.

[Hello you two, how has the day been.]

Astrid was the first to jump at the voice. "It was great! We found several books to read. I can already tell we're going to learn a lot!"

[That's good. Right now, that's all I need you to do. Are you getting used to the city?]

"A little," Kale interjected, "We still haven't explored much."

[I hear the restaurants of the Guiding City are astounding, especially in your district. Supposedly, the food is unlike anything else in the world.]

"It'd be nice if we had any money," he replied sarcastically.
"Oh, Kale," Astrid perked up after removing her suit coat, "we do. Father gave us each $15,000 with our vouchers. The city runs on the old-world standard."
"WHAT?" His heart nearly stopped. "15,000?! When were you gonna tell me that?"
She giggled at his visible disbelief. "I thought you already knew."

[Indeed. The money should be plenty to suffice your stay. In fact, due to the limited economy outside the walls, prices are quite low within the city.]

"Do you realize how much money that is?" Kale took a seat while grasping his head. "That could save people. If we had that kind of money in the slums we wouldn't have had to-"

Richmond was not amused by the accusation.
[I'm aware. Do keep in mind though, once all of this is finished, we will have saved more lives than money ever could.]

He considered the words. "I guess you're right."

[Why don't the two of you take some time to explore the city tonight? Find some *exquisite cuisine*. Appreciate your new life.]

"I have to admit," the girl twirled a strand of hair, "that would be nice."
"Well," the thug reclined, "you won't have to convince me."

[Don't be afraid to enjoy yourselves a bit, you deserve it.]
A beep signaled the end of his call.

"So," Kale spoke to Astrid as she sat on the side of her bed. "What kind of food do you like? I'm sure you've had some variety."

"Since you asked," she thought for a moment. "I'd say I like anything fried."

"Really? Never had it." He sighed.

She frowned at him. "That's sad."

"Yeah," he mocked, "That's what happens out in the slums though. No such *delicacies*."

Her fingers began tapping on her voucher, prompting beeps and lights to flash on her face. "Why don't we get you some?" She showed him the screen which broadcast the facade of Oriental lettering and pictures of golden victuals.

"It's funny." He closely inspected the screen. "Our old hideout is in a shop that looks kinda like that."

"Good." She perked up. "Now we can make it a good memory. The first step in changing you."

He sat for a moment. "I don't know how to feel about that…"

"The only thing you need to feel right now is hunger." She laughed, inspecting her appearance in a mirror. "Are you?"

"Hungry? I guess."

"Good."

The restaurant Astrid had chosen was situated near the town square, but along a different stretch of road than the bar Kale recently attended. It wasn't far, but it would still be a journey back out into the city among the crowds he couldn't stand.

"Why don't we go buy some new clothes too? Something to make us fit in a bit more." She proposed the idea while staring discontentedly at the suit she'd been wearing for days. "I am getting pretty tired of how tight this is." She wiggled her arms, which caused her coat to pull around her back.

Kale was repulsed by the suggestion. "Absolutely not. I'm not about to look like those idiots out there."

"You never know, ya' might find something you like."

But he did find something he liked. After a brief period of rest, they'd gone back into the town square of the commerce district and located an apparel store. The gleaming windows prominently reflected the multicolored lights of mercantile stalls, yet were translucent enough to allow a vast assortment of garments stark visibility.

When they'd entered the store, strange music quietly provided an ambience of calm, but occasionally throughout the repeated song, an irritating beep blasted at sweltering volume.

I don't understand this city at all...

Kale's eyes were fixed on a long black jacket that shared a similar flare to his suit but flowed as sable fog. A long hood hung over its back and the only annoying gold to be found was a pattern of three stripes along the left shoulder.

"Hey, this actually looks pretty cool," he admired.

Astrid found irritation in its design, "It looks like something a criminal would wear."

"Am I not one?" He shrugged.

She sighed and began browsing nearby dresses, "whatever. As long as it makes you happy."

The clothing racks were outfitted with light scanners on their edges to allow the seamless purchasing of items. The clothes themselves, in almost a fashion of magic, wound nanofibers throughout to change their construction according to the wearer. In the Guiding City, such an inconvenience couldn't be allowed.

As he slid the jacket over his shoulders, a comforting shroud of shadow filled him with nostalgia. When he scanned his voucher, a strange message displayed on the screen. *Cyber cloak(sable) adjusted to size(M) Spectral holopaths active. Tap to light your path.*

What's that supposed to mean?

He shrugged and pulled it in tight, hiding the formal wear beneath. Astrid had disappeared into a changing room and Kale found a seating area close to the door. He sank into the darkness of the hood. With the girl momentarily gone, the corners of his lips curled in satisfaction.

Am I... having fun?

Nonsense, how could he? In nearly every moment since he'd entered the city, his brain wallowed in self-pity, but she had a magic about her, the ability to make it disappear, like a quenching rain in a hot desert. Relief from the unshakable shame he felt deep down, the validation he so desperately warred for, he felt a taste of it when he was with her.

She emerged draped in a sapphire wrap dress. The fabrics wound their way like snakes around the meandering curves of her body. In the customary fashion of the Guiding City, gilded streaks crossed around her knees, but it wasn't enough to distract his eyes which stared diligently at her face.

A tinge of shyness withheld her eye contact. "W-What do you think?" She gestured a small half-turn.

The words for his admiration didn't exist. He could only manage, "it's nice."

"You like it? I think it's great." Astrid willed her chin to turn upward, to signal confidence, but her cheeks leaked a blush revealing her truth.

Kale studied his appearance in comparison. "I think you look a bit too good to be with me right now."

She retrieved the pieces to her suit from the fitting room and walked over to where he sat. The dress held tightly to her figure with each step. "Well, I like it. You chose that dark jacket after all."

He felt embarrassed, a dreg in the company of a queen. "Should I find something else?"

Her eyes fell and she frowned. "You like your jacket, I like my dress. It's all good."

As they walked along the busy streets, wind whipped through the alleys and psionic advertisements sought to bring him discomfort, however within the confines of the new jacket, he felt he could block them all out. Astrid didn't seem to mind. The terrible gusts of passing linear railway cars and rummaging shoulders in the crowds couldn't penetrate her newfound confidence in the dress. She strutted ahead as if she wanted to be seen, a contrast to the body language of their first meeting. Kale offered her his eyes. In fact, he couldn't keep them off of her. The neon luminescence of the city appeared to fractalize off of the dress and her hair swirled through the air, snatching his gaze every time he attempted to look away. It didn't matter. He welcomed it.

She had chosen a diner on the corner of the nearest block as their destination for an afternoon meal. Geometrically impressive tables were situated outside, twisting and bending in ways gravity shouldn't allow, yet they appeared to be optimized for the convenience of necessary patrons. If the customer was tall, the table rose to meet their arm level. If the person they ate alongside was short, it drooped to their respective wish without compromising the other. The technology was impressive, he admired it, but greater than all else was the smell. As with the dinner they'd had at *Le Lien*, he could taste the tender sweetness in the air.

The sky had become a deep violet, beautifully contrasting The Well's bright yellow and collections of citizens loitered around. A tune from nearby speaker drones graced the area with the plucking of a lyre. For the first time, among the many faces of indiscriminate contentment, he felt natural. Astrid's face ogled at the sights. The front of the restaurant sprinkled colorful lights onto the street, hovering slightly above the golden tables and winding architecture. The skyscrapers rose higher than the light could reach, tracing a gradient translucence with every rising meter as if the diner occupied a perfect pocket dimension of its own.

"It's beautiful here." She spoke as they arrived at a free table outside the front.

"It is." Kale slouched into his seat and looked at the dishes of others around him. Steaks, steaming vegetables, psychedelic soups, and a plethora of foods he'd never seen before decorated the many plates.

"Everything looks so good. I've never seen food like this before." His face followed the entrees which reached their respective tables via drone.

Astrid sat across from him, folding her legs and brushing a loose strand of blond from her eyes. He felt a lump in his throat and looked down to the table where he located the voucher interface to order food.

The two did not withhold greed when making their selections. The drones carried crisped chicken, oozing pork, bubbling liquids, and multicolored herbs, their rotors spreading heavenly aromas beneath their noses. Awestruck, they stared at their plates, unable to tarnish the displays with their hands.

"Holy…" the girl admired.

Kale let loose a sweet whistle, practically eating it with his eyes.

But before the two could dig in, a hand struck Kale's shoulder. Armored, flaxen fingers demanded his attention as a low voice spoke from behind a Guiding City officer's helmet. "Sir, could you come with me for a moment?"

Baffled, the hungry thug snapped back. "What? Why? I didn't do anything."

"We have reasonable suspicion to question you. Please come with me."

His jaw hung loose. "For what? Tell me what I did!"

A cold steel pressed into his lower back, prompting a chill to spread through his veins. Slowly, Kale rose from his seat, hiding the gun from Astrid's springing view. "I- Okay."

Is this about trespassing in the Sympath territory? Is that even a crime? Is it the map from Skyridge? I should've known! I'm so stupid!

"Kale? What's going on?" Her eyes widened and she began to get up.

The officer interjected, jabbing a finger in her direction. "Stay where you are. If he's innocent, he'll be returned shortly. " Their face was hidden behind a dark visor. The voice was unrecognizable to Kale; subsumed in static to mask its identity, but as he rose to level height with the guard, it whispered, "*I have a message from the captain.*"

"Astrid," he peered down at her distraught face, "I'll be right back." He leaned his head backward, hissing beneath his breath in reply, "*don't let her see the gun!*"

He was led a block away, beneath the shadow of a closed department store. The civilians had long dissipated, like bees fleeing darkness. Mannequins stood as sentries in the windows keeping watch on stragglers and the officer, in uniform alone, shoved Kale against an alley's wall.

"Tomorrow," the masked man spoke slowly, raising his gun to eye level. The silver of its barrel swam like water in the sable darkness.

Kale winced and leered between his disheveled hair. "What about it?"

"You'll bring the man to meet our captain. The southwestern gate, F6, will be opened when you show the captain's sigil. Do you still have it?"

Kale's hands slowly fell into his pockets, rummaging for the strange icon he'd received. A sharp prick to his fingertip located it. "I've got it." He never broke eye contact.

"Good." The gun lowered. "Should you fail to meet us tomorrow, we'll be forced to dispose of you, so I'd recommend you don't."

"Tsk." He snarled at the arrogant lackey. "For a gang that's supposed to care for everyone, you sure are violent."

The golden helm turned to face him in a dead-locked gaze. Only a visor of twinkling interfaces stared back. "We do what we have to. For a better future."

Kale found it difficult to reply. The robotic certainty triggered something within, something he couldn't immediately ascertain. "Do you think the others feel that way? That you're the good guys."

The officer's shoulders straightened. "Maybe they do, maybe they don't, but I don't care. Only the ones who win will ever know who's right or who's wrong."

His brows scrunched at the man. After a short pause, Kale stepped forward out of the officer's intimidation. "I'm going back to my meal."

A clearing of the man's throat signaled his release. "Make sure it isn't your last."

The cloaked thug shot a nasty gaze in reply and without words, walked disconsolately back to the happy diner.

He no longer had an appetite.

Astrid sat impatiently twirling her thumbs above the food. Her foot, beneath the table, bobbed uncontrollably to a sporadic rhythm, but when she saw Kale emerge underneath the diner's lights, she perked up. "What was that? Are you okay?"

Without a word of reply, he sat down, staring intently at the ground.

Should I call Richmond? I have to tell him.

"Kale," she flattened her hands on each side of the table, "talk to me."
"It was nothing. They had the wrong guy," he lied.
Her head tilted, surveying his downcast demeanor. "Doesn't look like nothing."

The words pulled his face upward to meet hers. No matter how much he wanted it, there were still secrets to be kept. He couldn't come clean, not for her sake. She couldn't know about his mission and the dirty business Richmond had thrust him into. "Like I said, they had the wrong guy."

Visible disappointment tainted her expression. "Okay..." The beautiful dress she wore lost its appeal, as did the food.

I'm sick of lying...

There was a toxin spreading in his gut and he felt at any moment, he might vomit, but despite the discomfort, he managed to curl his lips into a half smile. "Well, let's eat."

The food was tasteless. The conversations that accompanied their meal were dry at best and an invisible blockade prevented genuine words from being spoken. The lies he carried felt like a chain around his neck, holding him down from rising to her perfection. If only he could be so blissfully ignorant.

In silence, they strode back to the residence wing, beneath the gloaming sky. Aside from a few necessary remarks to the other, there were little words shared as the night crept on. Kale couldn't bring himself to contact Richmond. Whether it was a mental diversion or cowardice, the only thoughts that lingered before the night's dreams were of dust.

Chapter 11
Echopraxia

The moon and sun both showed early the next morning, battling control of the sky as the hues shifted between fire and ice; Kale stared them down respectively and his breath steamed on the chill air. Donning his new jacket and heavy hood, dew puddles splashed beneath a pair of trainers he'd retrieved from Richmond's old stash. He still couldn't believe the pompous scientist ever wore them.

He'd left Astrid sleeping, going once again behind her back at the jest of the host. Synapses fired wishes to speak with him, triggering a beeping deep within.

[You're up early, what's the matter?]
Richmond's voice fluctuated with morning grogginess.

"I'm sneaking you in, be ready in an hour, southwestern gate F6. You've got a meeting with the Sympath captain."

[Oh? It's not like you to bark orders at me. Newfound confidence?]

He wasn't in the mood for games. "I'm tired of it. Let's get this over with."

To reach the F6 gate, he'd have to trek a new path through the city. The skyscrapers of the commerce square covered alleyways like a spider's web in all directions. The hologram on his voucher indicated that he must take the fourth on his right, a darker, less gold expanse that brought a sense of comfort.

Throwing his hood over his head, a small electric staccato chimed and he looked down at his voucher. *Cybercloak holopaths active, tap to light your path.*

I forgot about that... Guess I'll see what it does.

When the tip of his index finger met the screen, orange light dissipated through the world, lining the street with fractal rectangles. The shapes molded and replicated infinitely until all that remained was a line dead ahead along the road's center.

Woah.

He pocketed the voucher and followed the light.

[Why today? Did you contact them again?]
Richmond queried strongly, finding his usual holier-than-thou tone.

"Yes… Well, technically they contacted me. While Astrid and I were out eating, they held me at gunpoint, but lucky for you, she didn't see it." The muscles in his jaw ached from holding a continuous frown. The shops throughout this particular alley were shrouded by deep shadows. Storeowners didn't beg for his money, enticing him with golden trinkets, jewelry, and freshly aromatic foods, but rather kept to their own, offering only scoffing eyes for the outsider. He enjoyed their displeasure.

[It seems our insider was right about them, a rather frightening bunch. Tell me about this captain.]

"She's a monster, the biggest woman I've ever seen, but I couldn't outsmart her. You may be in for a treat." Kale became increasingly curious as to what might happen when the two met. Would Richmond play his mind games with her? Would his manipulations succeed? The thoughts began to circulate with infinite possibilities.

[Ah, that does interest me. It's been some time since I've spoken with an equal mind. I miss the challenge of being among the studious.]
The host likely didn't mean the words as an insult, simply noting the obvious that among the tenants of *Le Lien*, he WAS the smartest, however, the words irked Kale.

He ignored the comment. The dark alleyway of unwelcoming shops gave way to a vista of mechanics. Large robotic machines twisted and groped among half-completed buildings. Smoke plumed all around as their ends welded metals and golds, fashioning their heated forms to the greater AI will. Drones watched carefully, measuring the exact precision of each architectural placement by emitting a bright, orange scan. There was no cautionary tape to ward off wanderers, but the streets throughout were littered with scrap.

The Vultures would love this…

"What have you been working on anyway? What's your plan on the outside?"

There was a pause, an uncertain air of breaths that Kale heard over the transponder. Something uniquely uncharacteristic of the host. Almost a tinge of… nervousness? He couldn't tell for certain.

> [There is… an uncertainty. The situation in controlling The Well's energy has taken an unexpected turn. You see, I've designed several ley lines to direct power around the slums, however after the flow reaches a distance of fifty yards past its origin point, the power seems to… deviate.]

"What's that mean?" Kale shifted beneath the monolithic structures, doing his best to avoid the sight of meandering drones.

> [The phenomenon is almost as if the energy disobeys the conductor. While the power I currently source within *Le Lien* behaves as standard electricity or heat conduction, at the distance I specified, it is able to pass beyond its wires and travel freely through soil and air. I have yet to determine why.]

Kale didn't fully understand why this had Richmond in such a tizzy, but it mattered little at the moment. The only thing to focus on was slipping him into the Guiding City unnoticed. "I'm almost to the gate. Where are you?"

There was a fallen building to his right, past the machinery. Entangled beams of metal wound like roots underneath a high-standing wall that fell at an acute angle. It appeared nearly impassible, hiding everything beyond. Amid the winding metals, a red banner swung tattered on an edge.

What's that? Is it the entrance to an occupied zone? They told me to come here after all…

He didn't have time to question it. The orange light's path depicted a road that clearly did not exist, yet led directly through the wreckage before him.

> [I'm making my way. I'll arrive shortly. They told you the zone is occupied?]

"Yep. That's what she told me." Though his brain screamed not to, his feet carried him beneath the banner, into the wreckage. "The Sympaths supposedly control both the gate and the surrounding area. I'm about to find out if that's true." As with the primary zone controlled by the Sympaths, what lay behind was a similar expanse of old-world buildings. Windows were busted out of shops, polygonal structures still fashioned with white brick, perhaps a first draft of the modern style the city now bore.

The first signs of habitation came from the whooping whistle of a bullet ricocheting off nearby brick. The sound sent a chill down Kale's spine, but he held his chin high in the air.

"I wouldn't move another inch if I were you!" A voice yelled from a spot unseen. "What's yer business here?" It wielded a countryside accent with the words.

He didn't know where to direct his voice, but hollered back, "The captain sent me. I have proof."

With one hand raised into the air, he reached deep into his pocket and withdrew the icon he'd been given.

A rustling came from ahead as the figure dropped into the dirt street from a nearby window. His feet kicked dust up and a tan poncho plumed with the wind. His face was masked, but one blinded eye commanded attention between matted locks of brown hair. "Let me see that," the man hissed as his hand snatched the object away before Kale could react.

"She told me you'd recognize it and wouldn't interfere."

"Ah," the man slipped a sigh of disappointment, "you aint kiddin'. Headed to the gate, I reckon?"

"Yes, there's someone I have to bring inside."

The masked man relinquished the icon back to the thug and holstered a pistol beneath the poncho. "Hmmm. If it's the captain's orders, there's no time to waste. Let's get movin'." He whistled, waving a hand around the air. At the motion, Kale heard a rustling, and several previously unseen gunmen rose from the shadows around.

He felt his stomach drop.

That many? I barely noticed...

He was escorted through the dilapidated rubble of a once-strong megastructure. The construction would've been pleasant before The Waking, but now reminded him solemnly of home, if he could call the slums 'home.'

Every few yards, more and more gunmen emerged and turned their weapons away. The security around the gate was immeasurably tight. Previously, when told about the unrest in the Guiding City, he'd held many questions about how such a great haven could fall, but after seeing the strength of only *one* of the many factions it became clear.

Are they all this organized? I don't want to imagine what the others are like.

He thought about the rivalry the Sympaths had mentioned, a war with a supposed 'Aeonic Order.'

Kale tried to break the silence with his guide, brushing dirt out of his face that had been kicked up. "The captain mentioned something about the Aeonic Order. What's up with them?"

"Huh?" The man tossed an eye backward. "What'd she tell you?"

"Not much, but they accused me of being a spy. You guys are at war with them?"

The guide's head returned to a strong forward march. "Nah, at least not like you think. It's politics."

"What do they stand for?"

"Ah, they're on some human augmentation crap. Since the Guiding City is closed off, they think it's the perfect opportunity to advance cybernetics and technology. They're in the pocket of that Brianna Sky. She's weird… Ain't even human anymore if you ask me."

He feigned ignorance, remembering the giant face.

"I've heard of her. She's called the 'Machine Goddess?'"

"Right. She thinks she's found the secret to immortality. Cures for everything without needing The Well's light. I guess it's kinda noble, but I just can't stand on top of the graves of all them outside."

Kale found himself sympathizing with the thought. "I see."

"All these different gangs, like ours, are tryin' to elect the next Exegete. We want our cleric to be chosen."

"So, what's that mean?"

"It's about messaging. If we can get more people on our side, then we'll win the election. So we have to show 'em."

He didn't fully grasp what the man was trying to say, but the gate began to come into view. "Why does it matter whose cleric is chosen? What's it mean?"

"What? You don't know?"

"Not really. I'm new here."

"Well, I'm no teacher, but the clerics get to decide what The Well does. Supposedly they make a wish. That's why it matters so much, because they control the future."

Kale stopped in his tracks, stared at the back of the man's head before he took notice, and attempted to hold his jaw in place. "What did you just say?"

The guide's brows furrowed as he turned back at the awestruck thug. "Huh? Why're you so confused?"

"You said the clerics control The Well…"

"Yeah..."

What? How is that possible…

The Sympath turned away and looked upward. "Anyway kid, we're at the gate."

The gilded doors rose high into the sky. Several roughly dressed guards wielding black rifles stared down from above and the guide whistled and similarly waved his hand. "Open 'er up!" He yelled to the men at the top who began to work on a large screen. With screeching sounds of metals coming to life, the doors began to part. After tinkering on the screen, the men readied their rifles and pointed the barrels forward.

"Alright, who's the guest?" The guide asked, hand falling to his hip.

Kale raised a hand to block dirt that flew in from a newly allowed gust. He squinted between his fingers. There were numerous people outside, crawling and scrambling over one another to get through the gate. Yells and screams of begging ripped the air. "LET US IN! LET US IN! PLEASE! MY CHILDREN! WE NEED FOOD! LET US IN!"

Kale felt dirty.

Standing in the middle of the crowd was the finely dressed scientist. His white hair was slicked back and he wore his trademark marigold suit. The hands of the beggars dared not touch him.

"GET THE HELL BACK OR WE'LL SHOOT!" the men up top screamed.

"Hey!" The guide nudged Kale. "Hurry! Who're we letting in?"

Kale pointed dead in the center, "Him! The one in yellow."

The guide withdrew his pistol and marched forward, "Let him in! The dressy one!" He struggled, grabbing Richmond's arm and yanking him through the gate. "Close it!" He hollered after they'd passed.

The screaming came to a deafening silence as the golden mass found its closure. The people were once again locked away.

"Well," he looked up at the host's face and spread his arms toward the trashed cityscape, "welcome to paradise."

"Indeed," Richmond replied. His milky and sharp face scanned the surroundings.

With a sigh of relief, the Sympath guide holstered his weapon and brushed his shoulders. "The guards have been alerted not to fire on you. Just follow the road back." He pulled a cigarette from his pocket and lit its end, blowing a thick cloud toward them. "Hope the captain treats ya' well."

Something isn't right.

"Hey." Kale frowned, "why are you keeping them out?"

Richmond raised an eyebrow at the question.

"Huh?" The guide scrunched his brows.

"If you guys want The Well to be for everyone, why don't you let them in?"

A plume of nicotine was blown in the air. "Ya' want them all to die? If I let those people in, they'll be rounded up and jailed. The few that manage to avoid capture'll spend their days in hiding and they won't get food or water without a voucher. So if we want to help them, we have to do it right."

The words made sense. Even if he could identify with the pleading faces he'd seen, the only way to do them good was to follow orders.

Tsk.

With a thank you, they walked the dirty path to the golden haven. Kale eagerly told Richmond of the guide's earlier words.

"He says the clerics have the power to control The Well. Any idea what that means?"

"Control?" Richmond brought a hand to his chin. "No. Astrid has never shown signs of control over her communion. Those episodes have always been afflictions rather than conversations."

Kale led, his dark cloak flowing like a shadow in his wake. "That's what I thought too. What do you think she'll say about it?"

"She'll likely be as confused as we are. Although, my mind is quite gripped in thought of other matters right now."

"I bet. Are you prepared?"

"Oh, I am always prepared."

Kale passed a glance backward, "you ever been pressured before? Threatened? They'll probably put a gun to your head."

Richmond released a chuckle. "I knew a man once, a poet, award-winning, regarded as the greatest. I knew this man in my days at university. He was an immigrant who fled Venezuela during times of unrest. Unfortunately, before passing safely into the United States he was captured by rogues, a band of outlaws who ransomed them to the authorities. Surprisingly, he came out unscathed. Do you know what he told me? Among everything they threatened him with, their weapons were no match for his words."

"I have to admit, you're pretty good with words."

"Indeed." The host smiled to himself. "I am prepared."

"So then," Kale spoke after the two emerged into the construction yard of mechanical appendages, "will you see her? Astrid I mean."

Richmond scanned the moving parts at work before him, studying their every machination and fully understanding the processes. "Ah," he admired, "They're beautiful, completely autonomous, devoid of human interaction, serving one purpose to its fulfillment. If only I could possess such laborers."

Kale drooped, "Is that supposed to be an insult?"

Richmond stuffed his hands in his pockets and continued his stride behind Kale's guidance, his loafers carefully flattening the ground to avoid staining in the dirt. "To answer your original question, no, I will not see Astrid. She can't know."

"Right…"

The two stepped into the commonwalks of the Guiding City; Richmond began to grow increasingly impressed. His eyes lit like a child's on Christmas morning. Here were the complete works of his vision, technology beyond his imagination, and the power to save humanity, yet NONE of it was his design. The star was but a dirty rag and the Guiding City an invaluable diamond. "In the time I visited this place," he began, "it was but a bud. Untamed, unsure of itself, but I see it has since bloomed; the firstfruits of my vision achieved ten-fold."

"*Your* vision?" Kale didn't understand the scientist's ramblings. His jacket was blown apart by a passing linear railway car and he fixed his hair into shape.

Richmond did not flinch. "Indeed. I envisioned such technology ages ago. Although, no one would know…" There was a crown of sorrow atop his voice.

"Boohoo," Kale mocked, "you didn't get the credit."

The host glared, "I wouldn't expect *you* to understand."

"Anyway," he began to walk towards the city, every step noticeably advancing technology by millennia, "the Sympath headquarters aren't far, we'd better keep moving."

But the pale host couldn't contain his wonder as the highly sophisticated cityscape stretched around them. "I see, purely geometric, exponentially beyond its years." He opened his longing arms to the sight. The many drones of the air stole his view, like comets on a clear night. The gravitational capabilities of the railway cars shook him to his knees, "I had no idea. Manipulating the very waves, hovering on their own density. Kale, I want to bring back samples."

The thug began to grow increasingly irritated by Richmond's childish excitement. "I'm not stealing anything for you."

"Fine." He rose to his feet and stuck his chin forward.

"Business matters first."

It took much longer to reach the southern factory gate than he'd have liked. The fear of the Sympath captain plumed the cortisol through Kale's physiology. He gritted his teeth every time Richmond ran off like a dog without a leash. The golden promontories of the commerce district's square stole the host's attention and he'd attempted to mingle with the shopkeepers, asking them strange questions beyond understanding. The denizens of the Guiding City were equally bewildered at the queries about their vouchers and if the drones operated on an analogous higher order, but before they reached the gate, Kale yanked him aside.

"I'm on a time limit here! They're waiting and if we take too long, I'm the one who's going to pay." His scarred face and hands sucked Richmond back to reality. "I need you to focus."

Richmond sighed.

"Sometimes in a garden, green shoots grow from the dirt, even if they are not the correct lifeform. They often grow much better than one's original plant and when left to run wild, the very soil will become tainted. The only solution is to burn it all to cinders and purify the foundation."

"What're you even talking about?"

The host turned back towards the city, eyes traveling along the gigantic megastructures and gleeful faces of the commoners. "I will have no qualms in leveling this city to dust, but honest human curiosity is something that cannot be easily contained, Kale."

"Whatever. Let's get moving."

To Kale's honest surprise, the voucher he'd been given directed the gate to open. The sun was high in the sky and the activities of the commerce district operated on all cylinders, but this time he had no worries about slipping into the occupied zone. Confidently, he marched forward into the dust with squinted eyes. If the lackeys watching in dark windows along the path saw them, they'd immediately notice the golden keepsake he held out in front. Richmond seemed unfazed at the unseen eyes that trailed them.

"They're watching," Kale cautioned without turning to make eye contact, "don't worry though, they won't engage, not as long as I have this." His breath hung like a dank fog, hot and heavy and he felt a slight quiver in the knees. Despite the outward appearance, as the path progressed, so too did a nervousness. He made sure not to let his hand that held the apparatus waver.

"Are you prepared?" Richmond queried, strolling the desolate path as if it was his own backyard.

"Yes. I'm fine," he lied.

After a brisk walk, time seeming to move without haste in Kale's mind, the captain's right hand, Joyner or so he was called, appeared seated in the dirt, soaking in the rays of the sun. He wore a new white vest, covering armor plating that stretched the length of his arms and legs. Above the gruff attire, the subordinate's boyish face did well to create a feeling of ease in those that challenged the Sympaths; a fine tool for winning mind games. A fallen steel tower provided quaint seating, it seemed, because when the thug let out a discontent call, the Sympath replied with irritation.

"Hey," Kale yelled upon seeing him, "we're here!"

Before rising to greet them, Joyner took a moment to meditate. "'Bout time," he mocked. With a whistle and hand wave identical to the other Sympath guide they'd met earlier, gunmen stirred in the shadows, hiding their rifles. "So this is the man," the right hand observed, scanning the scientist from head to toe.

Richmond placed no stock in the threats, sticking a hand forward and smiling, "it's my pleasure to meet you."

The offering was met with an unimpressed slap. "The captain's ready to see you. I have to admit, I didn't expect you to exist."

"So now you know I wasn't lying," Kale shot back.

Joyner shrugged, keeping his aloof smile through the passive-aggressive words, "People say a lot of things when a gun is pointed at them."

"Tsk." Kale stared at the man, ready to avenge his defeat in the days prior. He recalled the feeling of his knuckles striking him and desired to feel it again.

"Anyways," he threw his hands together, "best not to keep her waiting."

Richmond inspected the sleeves of his suit which had become tarnished by clouds of dust blowing down the road. Disgust appeared on his face. "Indeed."

They were led once again through rubbled memories of a long-forgotten factory. Kale didn't recall the environment, as he'd been unconsciously dragged through the path upon arrival and mentally overloaded during departure. He watched the back of the Sympath's head with ire.

Richmond studied the surroundings, eyeing the mechanical formations. "This is the southern factory district, no?"

"It was," Joyner mumbled, "makes a good fort, don't you think?"

"What was manufactured here?"

"These are the old sentinel factories."

"sentinels?" Kale's interest increased. "Find anything?"

The right hand shifted, raising a hesitant eyebrow, but simultaneously withdrawing an item from his boot, "just this." In the palm of his hand, he showed a disk about the size of a large coin. "Ocular lens." He held it in front of his eye. "Thermal."

"May I see?" Richmond inquired.

It was tossed to the host who studied its intricacies at lightning speed. "Ah, I understand. I'd wager this is outdated." He stared at Kale through the lens, spying his figure in harsh red.

Even the remnants, the inactive dry bones of the machines, chilled Kale's spine.

"Correct," Joyner responded, "The sentinels that were built here were abandoned for the current models. These required a pilot, but the new ones are fully automated, controlled by the Aureate's AI mind."

So it was a machine's decision to randomly destroy Le Lien… It was random…

Kale kept to his cloak as Richmond discussed the history of the dilapidated surroundings with the Sympath right hand. How the host could remain so calm and collected knowing full well of the upcoming interrogation surprised him. He never ceased to be impressed at the apparent perfection.

They passed through the makeshift arena, the world was colored tan in the clouds of dust, and the faces of foot soldiers turned in surprise at the infelicitous arrivals.

"The captain's quarter is right past here." Joyner's aloof smile faded to a professional stare.

At the opposite end of the arena was a barbed door, constructed of twisted metals and rusted spikes. The door was built for a giant, but given the gargantuan nature of the city, it felt relatively small. Fallen beams of rusted iron stuck out of the ground like fingers reaching toward the sky. It was an uncomfortable sight.

She was waiting, contemplating a large paper that covered the expanse of a metal table as they arrived. Her arms broadly gripped the edges, the striations of her massive forearms rippling. "No," she whispered lowly to herself, yet her commanding aura allowed the message to be interpreted by the newcomers, "they won't give it up. Not a chance."

Joyner cleared his throat. "Captain."

Her eyes rose at a snail's pace. They scanned, like a hawk, the man who had been requested. Richmond stood nonchalantly, hands stuffed in his pockets, chin high, and returning an equal gaze. The war between them had already begun and Kale started to sweat.

"Joyner, trespasser, take the back of the room. No words."

The Sympath bowed slightly and retreated to a bench hidden in shadows at the room's entrance. Kale did the same, yet on the opposite side. He wouldn't go near the other man.

"And you are the one." The captain took a seat at the prominent throne, beneath the rising light of The Well. "If what your cohort says is true, then I believe we have much to discuss."

Richmond offered a half smile, squinting his eyes and looking around the expanse which was relatively empty aside from the massive war table, "may I have a seat?"

The captain's face turned upward, she was cloaked in a dark green military vest, with the sleeves removed and thick cargo pants stained with the dust of her zone. Her feet were wide beneath her and the valleys of her cheeks tensed. The inky hair was crossed in a complete braid creating intimidating symbols along her scalp. "I've been told you have some technology that could be useful to me."

The host chose not to immediately respond to the question, but instead walked around the war table, studying the contents of its surface. His feet softly tread towards the captain's throne stopping less than three feet away. He stuck out his hand. "Richmond. Am I supposed to call you 'captain' as well or is there a more formal name you'd like me to refer to?"

Kale glanced at the lackey sitting across from him. Neither dared breathe.

A visible irritation spread along the captain's face. "No, there's no name." The outstretched hand was not met and an awkward silence ensued.

"I see," Richmond slipped backward and rested against the edge of the table. "Very well, I understand business is important. I believe we both know why we're meeting today. We seem to have aligned interests."

"There's a small chance that you could be of use to me. Incredibly small, but a chance nonetheless. I've been told about the technology in your possession. You've created a receptacle for The Well outside the walls of the Guiding City, is that correct?"

"That would be a very demeaning description of the technology I've created."

She peeled her eyes at him, "I'll take that as a yes."

"My star is far beyond your comprehension."

The Sympath captain scowled. "If you're not worth my time, then this discussion is easily concluded." Joyner began to stand, hand falling to his hip.

Richmond clapped his hands together and began to pace. "Right! I've been told about your goals as an organization. The Sympaths are hedging their bets on a cleric, working for a member of the Aureate council. You think that it's as simple as electing the right exegete," he stuck an index finger in the air, "but I'll tell you this, you will fail."

Her chin rose, "What do you mean?"

"Oh, it's quite simple. You're under the impression that an elected official is going to throw away everything they've built, everything that brings them comfort, everything that guarantees their power… Foolishness. Have you met the cleric in person?"

"I have."

"And what did they say their ambitions were?"

"The cleric we've selected to base our strategy behind believes in the cause. When brought to face The Well, they will enact the will of the people. Bringing down the walls of the Guiding City and unleashing the future upon the world."

"And you truly believe that?"

"We do."

"Then that is why you will fail." Richmond stood promptly, staring down the deathly eyes of the captain. "When the time comes and your exegete is selected, you will have no influence. That cleric is wholly bound to the Aureate or at least one member. There will be NOTHING you can do besides hope, and

I'm not a strong believer in hope. No. For you to truly succeed, you need a cleric of your own."

"What you don't realize, outsider, is that there *are* no other clerics than the ones owned by the Aureate. They were snatched as soon as they could speak. We've taken the measures to sneak an agent into the Clerical Dwellings. She's a trusted woman, extremely capable of building a dependence, indoctrinating someone."

He's trying to wager Astrid?!

He turned down his head. "If you have someone so cunning, what makes you think they haven't swindled you?"

The captain rose, squeezing her left hand into a fist. Veins bulged beneath her skin. "You were brought here today to discuss technology. I don't need a lecture on clerics. Tell me about your machine, nothing else."

Richmond hesitated, his lips curled into a frown. "My technology is built to channel The Well's infinite power outside the city. It's a generator of sorts, a source to bring hope to the greater world. Since the Guiding City sees it unfit to share with the slums, I aimed to do it myself."

She grunted. "Talk to me about power sources. You know them well?"

"Indeed. I was elected into a special task force before The Waking. We were assigned to research clean and renewable forms of powering cities overseas. Out of all those appointed, I was the only one to produce results. I was a pioneer in studies of The Well before the Aureate took over."

"And you've managed to understand the properties of The Well? How its light works, how it creates energy, optimizing conduction."

"I have."

"Do you know how to shut it off?"

Richmond furrowed his brow, tracing his chin. "I've made a handful of developments in that area."

"What about electricity?"

"Child's play," he replied proudly.

"Then, if you're so efficient with power sources, I'll need you to craft something for me." The burly woman began turning her eyes down to the large parchment on the table. It was a map, a topographic depiction of the nearby districts. An area was circled to the west, deep into territory that was marked by a black star. "In three days, my men will begin an operation. To the west, beyond our occupied zone, is a contested area between our forces and the Aeonic Order, the shipyards of Skyridge Technologies. We've dealt with skirmishes almost daily, but there are rumors of a treasure there-an old world sentinel, never used by the Aureate. It was the last manufactured before they switched to the autonomous ones."

"I see." Richmond leaned in, his milky eyes narrowing. "So it requires a pilot."

That's what was on the map!

Flashbacks played in Kale's mind of the horrible Skyridge laboratory and Brianna Sky's mechanical face.

"Wait!" Kale jumped to his feet, causing Joyner to do the same, ready to take him down. "That's the sentinel from the Skyridge layout?"

The Sympath second-hand raised his pistol, "You're not supposed to speak!"

The captain waved her servant down and turned her eyes on Kale. "Yes, and thanks to this, we now know its precise location, however, we will still need boots on the ground to confirm."

Richmond queried, "so, where do I come in?"

"I want you to create a diversion. Something to… turn off the lights. You see, the Aeonic Order headquarters lies in the eastern half of the old bay district. Before the last election, foreign ships harbored there every day. The area is perfectly situated to monitor the happenings on the water." She leaned back, crossing her massive arms. "They take advantage of a Skyridge relic. The Aeonic Order can locate every ship and every airborne craft that travels in and around the Guiding City thanks to a powerful transducer. However, this device was not built to run on the energy of The Well and still draws its power from electricity generated by nearby hydroplants. If we can shut down their radar, they'll be forced to withdraw their forces until it's restored. They won't know what to make of the situation."

The two met eyes and an unseen message joined their thoughts as one in a strange echopraxia.

Richmond slouched, contemplating, "you want me to create an EMP powerful enough to reach their base?"

She nodded.

The scientist began to laugh. "Well, that ought to be fun." He turned to the back of the room. The sun had risen high in the sky, bringing light equal to that of The Well through the many cracks and openings in the walls. "What do you say, Kale? Care for a little heist?"

Going back there? Like hell!

He stared at them, confused. He couldn't understand the giddy snicker that adorned Richmond's face. "Do you have any idea what she just said? She's going to steal a sentinel!"

"I understand entirely." He turned back to the captain who couldn't contain a smile of her own. "You don't intend to wait for the election at all... Rather than hope for the people to buy your message, you want to force your way to The Well. If you can bring a cleric in contact with the light, tell me, is that how they awaken their powers? Direct exposure?"

"Oh?" The captain leered her angled face, "for someone who sounded so confident, you don't even know how this works?"

He shrugged, "Testing your knowledge." Kale saw through the lie.

"I'll tell you this. No one besides the Aureate knows exactly how the clerics manipulate The Well, but whenever a new exegete is elected, things change. The light seems to do exactly what they want, or what their political motivations need. So the common belief is that the clerics can control The Well."

"You're taking on quite the gamble then."

She scoffed, "the thing you advised against. Hope."

Richmond pointed at her with a smirk, bouncing his hand up and down like a parent scolding a child. "That's dangerous."

"Then," the captain said, unwavering, "we have a deal."

"I believe we do."

An unpleasant miasma crept through Kale's system, like flies beneath the skin and he spoke up. "Richmond, can I talk to you for a moment? Privately."

The host paused before turning to reply. "Captain," he mocked, "may I?"

The captain took a seat on her throne, crossing her legs without moving her eyes which watched the thug at the back of the room. Her fingers waved towards the door.

When the two were just beyond the entrance to the captain's quarters, Kale began to interrogate the host, clenching his jaw and pacing back and forth. "I thought we were keeping Astrid out of this, you were about to use her!"

Richmond folded his hands and turned his chin upward. "Kale, there are things you have yet to realize. I've thought it over. There is virtually no chance their cleric disobeys the Aureate. All will be for naught."

He scoffed, "So what? She'll be taken... Used... If we let those bastards at the top find out what she is they'll steal her away and you'll never see her again!"

"My policy remains the same. As long as this operation succeeds, we can overthrow the Aureate without sacrificing Astrid's identity." His words rolled off the tongue in a demeaning chord. "Think about it. If the walls come down and thousands of slum dwellers storm the city at once, it will create enough confusion to ensure her safety."

Kale pulled his coat in tight, covering his body in shadow. "Right now, you're talking a lot differently than you were a few days ago. What made you change your tune?"

Richmond brushed his conditioned white locks back out of his view. "I've simply done the math. The people here believe the clerics, upon touching The Well's light, can influence its will. It makes too much sense not to be true, and if it is, then this is no longer a political war, Kale, it's a race. We have the opportunity to bypass the Aureate altogether. Rather than gambling on a whim that this unnamed cleric under the influence of those in power will betray them, we can sneak in one who truly believes. One who we trust wholeheartedly."

He couldn't deny the fact that Richmond's words made sense, but the idea of involving Astrid in the volatile happenings of ragtag gangs made his stomach turn. She hated everything about his past identity and instead of changing for the better, he would be changing her. "I... I don't like it."

As if she was summoned by fate, the transponder in Kale's mind began to beep, undeniably Astrid trying to contact him. "Crap! Hold on." He turned away from the host, sticking a hand backward. "Don't say a word!"

He answered the call.

"Kale?"

"Yeah?" he replied, preparing a million excuses for the anticipated question.

"I've been reading this morning. There's something we need to talk about. The book... There's some crazy stuff written in it."

He breathed a sigh of relief at the fact that she didn't ask his whereabouts. "I should be back in a bit. Can it wait til then?"

"I... I guess."

He gave no reply, but she didn't exit the call.

"I know you told me to trust you, but I'm worried. Where are you?"

He turned back to Richmond, posing a question with his eyes. "You know I can't tell you that."

"Then, can I trust you?"

The two men stared at each other.

"You can trust me."

"Okay."

The call ended.

"We don't need to use her." Kale's hands were clenched.

Richmond matched his motion, frustration written on his brow. "I'll take your opinion into consideration."

"It's more than an opinion."

"You fail to understand the gravity of our situation. I've no time to waste on trivialities."

"You think your own daughter's safety is trivial?" He couldn't believe the host's words. "You're trying to put her in the Sympath's hands. They'll use her however they want and it won't be up to you."

Richmond's forearms pulsated as he jabbed a finger between Kale's eyes. "I told you before and I will tell you again. I must prove that I can topple this city. There is no one above me, no one else who can act in a way that secures our future. Surely, you would've realized it. I *will* become the bringer of salvation to these people and you can't stop me." A resonant anger brewed beneath his words. "I'm done with this discussion. If you're not willing to trust my actions, then you can find someone else to work with. Besides, my use for you is nearing its end." He turned back to the captain's quarters.

To think... That I'd be the one with good intentions.

Kale's eyes glared through the shadow of his figure at the back of the prim and proper marigold suit.

Chapter 12
Communion

After their short squabble, the amount of information he was awarded ran thin. Richmond was ordered to remain in the Sympath's occupied zone and Kale was sent away to await further instruction, only told that he would be a participant in the coming operation. To steal a sentinel... The words chilled his neck. The sun had disappeared as it normally did in the early afternoon, becoming subsumed by The Well's majesty. Everything was gold.

Kale took a moment to collect his thoughts. There was simply too much to process. If he returned to the residence wing, Astrid would have a new mystery to unravel, but he couldn't claim comfort in the city, not among the gleefully inhuman citizens. Surprisingly, he found himself missing *Le Lien*.

Where do I belong?

His brain settled on the former. He couldn't leave Astrid waiting any longer. Along the way back he considered the hostile nature of Richmond's words. Regardless of how he felt, Richmond was dead set on his goal, indifferent to the means. Kale couldn't shake the eerie realization that his plan seemed the most effective.

She was reclined in a leather chair underneath bright chandelier crystals in the lobby of the residence wing when he arrived without notice through the front doors. A checkered button-down shirt was tied around her waist and she slumped casually in an orange top and jeans. In all views, she appeared happy except for the bright red circles around her eyes and crumpled tissues on a small table beside her.

"Have you been crying?"

She jumped slightly at the words. She hadn't noticed his arrival. Her hands quickly shut the book she was reading. "N-No, I just... A little."

Kale found a seat opposite, crossing his legs. "There was business this morning."

"Business?" The book was placed among the tissues with the spine facing him, THE CLERIC WISHGRANTERS: A BRIEF HISTORY OF GIFTED CHILDREN.

He eyed the words. "Yeah, just business. Nothing to worry about."

Astrid's hands ran along her lower eyelashes. "Is he in on it?"

The words stunned him a bit.

How would she know? Did he tell her?

"I've already told you I can't talk about it."

"Why?" Her tone rose slightly. "Does he not want me involved? Aren't I a part of this?"

"Astrid." He tried to keep calm. "Stop."

She matched his confrontational posture, talking with a whisper of authority. "I saw you. Earlier. I went out to the square after I noticed you were gone. I saw you. And I saw him. You went past the gate. So you don't need to tell me… I already know."

What? How? Did he tell her? Did he lie to me?

He managed to maintain his composure, leaning forward on his knees. "You have to trust us."

"Trust? I haven't been told a thing since we got here! You've been going behind my back and I feel… Honestly, I feel betrayed."

"It's just business."

"If it's business, then why can't I know?"

"Because sometimes business gets people hurt and we don't want you to get hurt."

"I don't care if I get hurt. You need to leave that stuff behind! What does he need to do business for? Money? He's never cared about money… How'd he even get in?"

"This is a complicated situation. It's a lot bigger than you or me."

"Then don't you think I should know what you've been sneaking away every day for?"

Kale leaned toward her with a leer, quickly hissing the words to not alert others in the room. "Astrid, if anyone finds out what you are, you'll be taken away by the Aureate and become a slave. You'll never see anyone ever again!"

"I… I know that. This isn't something I chose…" With a labored sigh, she dropped her head to her hands. "I want to be useful."

He slouched back, sinking into the soft leather. "I know, but you have to trust us."

She sniffled slightly, folding her hands over her lap.

"So," Kale attempted to change the conversation, "what's in the book?"

Her face softened and she retrieved it from the table. "It's about the Clerics. So much makes sense. It explains why the communion hurts, why I can feel The Well when I'm this close and…"

"And what?"

"I-" For some reason, she couldn't bring herself to continue.

"What?"

She took a deep and long breath. "It says that the clerics control The Well."

He recalled the words of the captain and the guide. "That they make a wish, right?"

A look of suspicion crossed her brow as if she was surprised that he was unfazed. "That's what the author thinks. I don't know anything about it though."

"Crazy, isn't it?" Kale folded his arms. "I heard the same thing. The people believe the clerics can wish for The Well to obey them, that they can control what its light does. That's why the election is so important. That's why the factions formed and are taking it so seriously. And there we were on the outside… No say in the future..."

"It's sad." She traced her forehead, "the clerics are so controlled. They can't even live like normal people."

"With a power like that, I can see why."

"I skimmed towards the end, it seems like no one knows exactly how it works, but apparently direct contact is the trigger. If a cleric is brought to The Well, they make their wish."

"So it's like a wishing well… That's funny."

"A wishing well?"

He'd forgotten her limited knowledge of the old world. "Back in the day, there used to be wells, big pits where people collected water or ones that spouted water. People would throw coins in and make a wish."

Her eyes lit up. "So it has a price?"

A price?

"I don't know. Find anything about that?"

She looked at the ground, unable to meet his eyes. The action roused suspicion in him. "No… I don't think so."

The front door slid open with an electric hiss and a woman walked in, guiding two smaller children with each hand. She was bent over, scolding one of them with a quick whisper. Astrid eyed them with her lips pursed.

He studied her.

"Kale," she spoke without turning to him, "have you ever thought that Richmond might be wrong?"

"Huh?"

"Like, maybe these people deserve to live here. They *are* people."

"What're you talking about?"

"The people here are happy. They have their own lives and he wants to take that away." There was sadness in her tone.

The words annoyed him.

"Astrid, think about this, for every one person you see here that's happy, that's enjoying the city, that looks healthy, there's ten, even a hundred others outside those walls that are starving, living in dust, and have never felt a soft bed. I lived that horror for most of my life…"

"I know, but…"

Kale stood and walked to the edge of her chair. She dodged sight of him, staring only at her lap. "I'll never forget it. If we have any chance whatsoever to help those people, to give them the opportunities that the citizens of this city take for granted each day, then that's what I'll fight for. Richmond knows that. I expected you to know that too." He couldn't believe his own words.

Why do I care about that all of a sudden? Am I lying? I never cared when I took their money back then… Why should I care now?

He scoffed. "Besides, it's not like Richmond's trying to kill anybody. He just wants to distribute the power back to the people… Right?"

She stood slowly, brushed her hands through her golden hair, and tightened the button down-shirt around her waist. With a deep breath, she picked up her book and clasped her hands around it, holding it tightly to her midriff.

"I want to go sit by the channel," she spoke quietly.

"The channel?"

"Come with me."

He accompanied her in silence, strolling the technocratic streets beneath the towers of gold. Bright vehicles flew like insects in orderly trails above and a green hue decorated the little clouds they could see beyond the vibrant streaks of The Well. A massive neon advertisement lit the sides of tall buildings; a campaign announcement to vote for Damian Shikov in the upcoming election.

Astrid found herself conversing with the citizens, complementing their outlandish outfits and offering friendly jokes to children. Her motivations were clear. She'd seen enough death and destruction.

Kale frowned from a distance, covered in the dark cloak.

This complicates things. She doesn't realize it, but it's not up to her...

He couldn't help but ponder the question; would Richmond really wager her, even if it went against her beliefs? In the end, the wish would be hers alone, if that's really how it worked. He didn't know. He didn't read the book. He'd seen no proof. As far as his knowledge went, they were risking their lives on superstition, and the choice was not his to make.

He watched her silky hair bob with each stride. There was a lean with her walk, a hunch, almost as if she was reaching for something beside her, low to the ground. There was nothing to reach. Her hands fumbled until they returned to holding the book.

He felt sad.

The river's water lapped at concrete shores as the two found a seat on a spindly golden bench. A scent of salt decorated the air. The bench was situated beneath a strip of shops where glassy windows sent multicolored lights out onto the street and various discount sales urged the citizens to visit. There was just enough noise to be tolerable, to give their conversation cover.

"He wants it to be you." Kale spilled the secret.

"Me?" She didn't look at him, instead fixating her eyes on small fish riding the current below.

"The Sympaths, a nearby faction that shares the same belief as us, have their own cleric, apparently, but Richmond doesn't believe they'll be able to wish for the cause."

"So he knows too? He knows what the clerics do?"

"It sure seemed like he did."

"This is all so sudden. I knew deep down there was a purpose to it, but I never imagined it would be so serious."

"If that's true then, Astrid, you can change the world."

She didn't immediately reply, but instead retrieved a flower from the grass beneath them and twirled it between her fingers.

"Do you trust him?" Kale prodded.

"It's always been this way... Science and the cause over everything. He used to be empathetic, but after Mother died, he became totally obsessed."

He frowned, unsure what to make of the words.

"I don't think he ever moved on. I think it broke him."

"You think that's why he's so hyper-fixated? He wants to make sure that never happens again?"

"Yeah."

Kale hung his head, "In four days, I might die."

Her eyes snapped over, the emerald irises glistening in the sunset. "What?"

"I'm being sent on a mission into rival territory, the old bay district, to infiltrate the Aeonic Order and steal the last remaining manual sentinel."

Her jaw fell low, and her eyelids widened as if in the presence of a monster. "You can't be serious!"

In the eastern sky, deep blues trickled upwards like tendrilous envoys of the night. The sable locks of Kale's hair veiled the shadows of his face. There was nothing to feel about the matter. "Boss's orders."

"And you're okay with it? You're just gonna do what he says?"

"What else am I supposed to do?" He began to grow frustrated, biting his lip as he spoke, "I've told you this before, but I have no choice. I'm his little experiment. That day, when Phoebe died, I became a machine, another tool in his collection. I've been trying to think that all of this is somehow my atonement or whatever, but at the end of the day, it's not." His hand fell to his left pocket, feeling a dry square. It was the drawing. The token of her appreciation. He'd kept it safe through everything so far.

"I know he has good intentions."

"Whether or not they're good intentions for the world, it won't be good for me."

A silence followed. With every word, the sky grew darker around The Well and a chill decorated a breeze that rode the waves of the river.

Astrid looked into the water. Her fingers wound together. The checkered shirt tied around her waist blew slightly. "Then, if the clerics really can do what everyone says, there's only one thing to do."

He met her eyes beside him. Something was brewing in the deep pupils which now bore a determination. "What d'you mean?"

She smiled. "I'll do it."

"Astrid, you can't."

"Back then, when we were walking I realized it. I've set my heart on the world that I would have, regardless of my father's designs. Whether he means well or not, I don't think he would act without the purpose of making the world a better place. But I'll make my own decision and we can change the future."

"You mean, you're willing to risk that? You're going to risk becoming a slave to them?"

"If it means doing what I was born to do, then yes. Even for the brief time we've been here, I've observed this city. Maybe he's right about it all. Maybe they're just hoarding the wealth and the knowledge so that the rest of us suffer outside. Or maybe they've realized that if the people here can live their best, then that's worth what's happened to the rest of the world. Either way, I can't accept it. I was so conflicted, watching the families live and love one another. But every time I saw their smiling faces, all I could think about were those hands, reaching out at us as we walked to the gates, begging and crying for even a portion of what's taken for granted here. You were right."

"So, what's the plan?"

"I don't know. I need to think on it."

"I've got four days to think. Then I'll be part of the heist. So, in that time, we need to figure out the right plan of action. It's a race. At least that's what Richmond said. It's a race to get a cleric to The Well before the election. That sentinel is the key. If they get their hands on it, they can steamroll straight there."

A fire lit in her eyes. "What if you were the one to take it?"

"What?"

"What if *you* took the sentinel?"

"You mea-"

At that moment, something changed. Astrid's eyes appeared to gloss over and her brows furrowed. Her hands rose to grasp her head and a panicked aura captured the air between them. Kale grew confused. Her mouth opened to speak, but she couldn't form words. He could see a faint yellow brighten beneath the makeup on her forehead.

"Hey," he reached over, placing a hand on her shoulder, "what's going on?"

"No, no," she turned away, hiding her head in her hands, "not now!"

"The cleric thing? But we're out in public…" He scanned the surrounding area quickly. The population wasn't heavy in the area, but enough eyes were on the river that if things escalated, someone would see.

"Kale," her voice was labored and she spoke through her hands, "I have to get back. I-... They can't see!" There was a raspiness. He could tell she was hurting and if it was anything like the last time, the pain would only get worse.

He began to rise to his feet, noticing the light on her head radiate even brighter. With a groan, he removed his jacket from his shoulders and draped it over her head. "Hang on," he reached out an arm, constantly glancing over his shoulder to tally onlookers. "I'm going to carry you."

"Wha-," her whole body winced with the words and he could hear her breath seethe beneath the cloak.

A slight embarrassment filled Kale as he took her arms, throwing her hip over his shoulder and steadying her behind the knees. The eyes began to turn their way, but he didn't care. As long as they couldn't see the cleric glow, the awkwardness didn't matter. The route back to the residence wing was a considerable distance, one that would pass between numerous civilians, even as the afternoon sun had set.

With a slight jog, careful not to hurt the girl whose face was buried in his back, he skipped along the sidewalks, brushing past confused faces that turned their way.

"MOVE!" he yelled at the clumps of bodies before him, "She's sick!"

This could NOT be worse timing!

"Kale," she mumbled into his shirt as they ran, "it's t-talking."
"Hang on! just a little longer."

With squinted eyes and a pale face, he came upon the final corner to the residence wing. He could see the door and began to run slightly faster, trying his best not to cause further suspicion. With one hand, he removed his voucher from his pocket, but a voice called from behind. "Is everything okay?"

Kale, flinching, turned to see a Guiding City officer stepping out of a polygonal car that was stopped at the sidewalk's edge. It was a woman, he could tell but heavily clad in a golden uniform.

"Yes!" He jumped with the word, "She's sick, but we-"

The officer began to remove her helmet, inching closer. "Sick? I can take you two to a clinic. There's one not far."

"NO!" As the doors began to open, he stepped inside, but he couldn't hide the sweat that had begun to fall from his bangs.

Not now! Leave us alone!

The woman raised an eyebrow. "Let me see her. Are you sure she's alright?"

"Yes, all good, she has seizures. Episodes, you know? I just have to get her to bed and she'll be fine."

"Seizures? But her face is cover-"

"Thanks! I've got it under control!" Kale shouted and slipped inside the wing before she could get another word in. He looked over his shoulder to see the officer poking their head to watch them. Her hand rose and she spoke into her wrist.

I can't deal with this! No more interruptions!

Thankfully, he wasn't pestered any further as he continued to carry Astrid up the elevator and down the hall to their room. He could hear her sniffles and sharp breaths. The communion was still going.

With tired arms, he slid her off his shoulder and onto the soft bed. Removing the jacket from her head, he could see her bright red face, twisted in terrible strain. Her mouth opened to breathe but hissed in fragments.

"Choose," she spoke unclearly, "choose… take, choose."

"What?"

"It's… That's what it's saying…"

"What's that mean?"

"Give, choose…" Her head fell into her hands. The golden strands of her hair wound between her fingers.

Kale nervously sat beside her. He placed a hand on her back, feeling a rapid heartbeat. She was hot to the touch. "Just a bit longer. We made it back."

Several minutes passed before Astrid began to settle down. It felt like an eternity to him. Every sound made him jump as if at any moment an officer would bust through their door and take her away.

I don't think anyone saw the light. I'm being too paranoid…

When she finally regained her senses, the pattern of breaths regulated and she fell backward onto the bed, staring up at the ceiling.

"You okay?" Kale asked, unrelieved.

With a hefty inhale, she cleared her throat. "I think."

"Good. Any pain?"

"It's gone now. It's over."

"I don't think anyone saw-"

Unexpectedly, a chuckle escaped the girl. She broke into a string of laughter, dropping her arms beside her.

"What?"

"What's my luck today, huh?" Astrid grabbed a pillow at the head of the bed and placed it over her face. Her voice was muffled, "that couldn't have been worse timing."

Kale, still deeply pale in the face, questioned her.

"No, it could've been a lot worse. It could've been really bad."

"Bad? They would've taken you!"

She laughed more. Something about her careless reaction irritated him. "I know," she said, "but they didn't see."

"I hope! That officer was suspicious. She knew something was up. I looked like a damn criminal!"

"It's alright. They didn't see. Everything's okay now."

He looked at her with wide eyes, taking a second to reflect. He looked down at his hands which continued to shake nervously. "When they stopped me, I saw her watch us go in and say something. I think they might've-"

"Hey," she rose and took his hands, making them still within her own. "They didn't see."

"How do you know?"

She removed one hand and touched her forehead. A faint glow remained and in the low light of night, he could see it beneath the makeup which had run down her face. "I can feel it. I can feel that everything is okay."

"You can feel that?"

"I can."

He took a deep breath, watching the floor.

"Do you trust me?" She continued gripping his hand.

"I..." He couldn't think of the proper words to say.

Of course, I trust her. But then, why am I so afraid?

He replied with an extensive exhale, "it's myself I worry about."

"It's always been this way for me. Having to live in fear of being seen. I thought it'd be different here, but it's all the same."

"What do you mean?"

"I secretly hoped that when we got into the city, I could finally be my own person."

"You're forced to hide on the inside, while I'm forced to struggle outside."

"But I also have another feeling, more than just things being okay." Astrid stood up, walking directly in front of him. Her stance was wide, feet far apart; determined. "I want to make another promise."

"A promise?" He stared at her.

"Like we did before coming here. The one where we promised to tell the truth. Now, I want us to promise that we'll move past the things we're forced into."

"Too dangerous."

She shook her head and stuck her hand forward, extending the pinky. "I'm tired of living in fear. I've realized that I'm the only one who has the opportunity to change things. Richmond realized it. It can only be me."

Kale held his hand up hesitating. His chin was low. "Is that what it told you?"

"Yes."

So then, it's just me. They've seen the truth and are ready to act. I have to move forward.

Their pinkies locked along with their eyes.

"So," Astrid slinked away, bringing her knees between her arms at the top of the bed. "We have four days?"

"Four days. The operation will be dangerous." He played the oncoming heist in his head. If everything went according to plan and Richmond concocted a means to blackout the zone, then there wouldn't be a conflict, however, Kale knew all too well that things never went to plan.

"But it shouldn't be. They won't know you're there, right?"

"That's what we're counting on."

"And if they do?"

"I don't know."

She stared out the massive window beside her, transfixed on the light of The Well which illuminated the fantastic city outside. "You saved me again today. I knew I could see something in you."

The words warmed him slightly. He slouched against the wall, able to see her eyes which peered over her knees. There was something immensely deep about their emerald shimmer. "I just did what I had to."

"You know, the last time we spoke like this, I said I wanted to be the one to change you, to save you from that part of yourself that you couldn't deny. But here I am again thanking you." She smiled to herself, trying to hide it, but he could see.

He didn't know how to respond.

She continued to talk. "Have you ever loved someone... been in love?"

"There was never time for that. To love someone means to trust them, and back then, I could never trust anyone."

"I never had the chance either."

He remembered back to that night and recalled the feeling of her lips. "Why did you kiss me?"

There was a pause in their conversation. He couldn't tell if it was bashfulness that made her hesitate or something else, but after a minute she spoke. "I wanted to try it."

"Kissing?"

"No, loving someone."

So it wasn't pity?

He couldn't look at her while he spoke. "Then, did you find that you could love me?"

She didn't reply but instead moved from the bed into the shadow where he sat. "Since we arrived here in the city, I've wanted to be someone new. Back in *Le Lien*, I could never find myself. I was only ever what Father wanted me to be. But now, through tragedy, effort, or circumstance, all my ties have been severed. I can choose to be sad, I can choose to be grateful, but either way, now I'm free to be me."

Subsumed in darkness, their lips met again.

For the following days until the operation, they forgot about The Well, Richmond, and the lies.

Chapter 13
Theraphosa

"YOUR UNIT, NEWCOMER, IS REAR RECONNAISSANCE! YOU WILL BE RESPONSIBLE FOR OVERWATCH AND OVERWATCH ALONE!"

The captain's voice boomed through a thick headset he'd been given as several squads of Sympath soldiers lined in perfect order throughout the dusty arena of the faction's headquarters. Richmond had alerted him earlier that morning that everyone present in the coming operation should report to the captain by midday, but even though he'd made sure to arrive early, the captain appeared displeased. She was adorned in heavy armor, black plates of Damascus steel, or so he thought because when she slammed a knife into her chest, oily waves rippled across its surface. Her eyes were lit with a flame of ambition, visibly excited about the coming operation. Richmond stood to her side, watching the sun travel through the sky, but paying Kale little mind.

Kale had been partnered with an athletic man, whose face was gentle, but harbored something beneath. One of his eyes was shut, scarred by a long slash that traveled vertically down his face. He'd offered Kale a pleasant greeting, wishing him luck.

"Desmond." the partner stuck out a calloused hand, "You'll be with me in the recon unit. We've got the easy job." He spoke with a thick African accent.

"Tsk." Kale shook the outstretched offering. "I hope you're right."

"Don't worry so much," The soldier twirled a chain between his fingers. "if things go south, it'll be you that makes it out."

"Me?" Kale gave him a side-eye, "aren't we supposed to be partners?"

Desmond stuck his chin upward, frowning. "I've got a mission of my own. My sister is in there." He flattened his hand, revealing the chain, one that connected silver dog tags with an etched name on the surface; 'Nia.' "She was part of Skyridge before the factions took over, now a hostage by the Order."

"Skyridge..." The name made Kale shiver.

"It was the research laboratory in the Bay District, run by Brianna Sky. That twisted diplomat used her own employees as ransom to buy campaign funding. But nobody's gonna tell you that in the city."

He stayed quiet.

Their conversation was cut short when a man walked over to Kale and slung a roughly shaped vest into his arms. "Here, put it on."

He buckled as he caught the garb, heavy in awkward areas. "Bulletproof?"

"A bit."

"What do you mean a bit?'" He bent his brows at the other who then withdrew a black pistol from his hip.

"Take this too."

Kale took the handle of the gun, an FN Five-Seven with green dot sights.

"Twenty rounds," the man told him. "Don't waste 'em."

He'd handled guns in the past, although in the slums, ammunition was sparse. Bullets were saved for life-or-death situations and if wasted, meant little to no protection from unexpected dangers.

The captain's voice resumed in his headset, "LISTEN CAREFULLY! THIS IS HOW THE NIGHT WILL PLAY OUT: OUR NEWFOUND ALLY HAS CREATED AN ELECTROMAGNETIC EXPLOSIVE, A LITTLE GIFT FOR THE ORDER, THAT WILL BE DETONATED ONE HALF-MILE ABOVE THE DISTRICT'S CENTER. THIS WILL CUT OUT ALL POWER TO THE BAY DISTRICT THAT DOES NOT DIRECTLY RELY ON THE WELL'S ENERGY. THE OUTAGE WILL TERMINATE ALL LARGE BODY TRACKERS IN THE AREA AND IF ALL GOES ACCORDING TO PLAN, THIS WILL RESULT IN A FULL RETREAT OF AEONIC ORDER FORCES. AS YOU ALL KNOW, THERE IS NO SUCH THING AS ABSOLUTE DARKNESS, SO YOU MUST USE THE SHADOWS WELL.

OUR TARGET IS THE LAST REMAINING MANUAL SENTINEL WHICH SITS DORMANT IN THE OLD SKYRIDGE FACTORY. FORTUNATELY, THIS FACTORY IS CLOSER TO US THAN THEIR HEADQUARTERS. UNIT 1 WILL BE RESPONSIBLE FOR PILOTING THE SENTINEL AND DOCKING HERE IN THIS ARENA BEFORE THE TRACKER COMES BACK ONLINE. WE ESTIMATE THREE HOURS OF OUTAGE."

Kale winced at the loud voice, staring forward, but holding his headset away.

There's no reason to be this loud!

"WE WILL NOT DEPART UNTIL AFTER THE BLAST! ONCE WE HAVE CONFIRMATION THAT THE EXPLOSIVE HAS TERMINATED THE TRACKERS, THE FRONTAL UNITS WILL ADVANCE UNSEEN. THE FOUR REAR UNITS WILL WAIT UNTIL A SECOND SIGNAL PROJECTS THAT THE AREA IS CLEAR OF HOSTILES. OUR GOAL IS TO PERFORM THIS HEIST WITHOUT ENGAGEMENT, BUT IF NECESSARY, I GRANT EXECUTE AUTHORITY."

Desmond let out a quiet whistle. "Damn. Seems like the captain isn't playing around. You ever killed somebody, Kale?"

"It's not something I like to think about."

"I don't want a man who can't kill watching my back."

"I didn't say I can't."

Desmond nodded.

"If we're going after this sentinel, why is the Order letting it collect dust? What's stopping them from using it?"

His partner laughed. "Politics. Since the Order is directly run by a member of the Aureate, deploying an unauthorized sentinel would be an act of treason."

"But aren't the Sympaths working with a member too?"

"Technically, we're taking advantage of one, but not directly sponsored. Moriarty Jacobs leaves his business in the city unattended. The captain used that to sneak in an insider."

Kale dodged sight of the captain who had begun walking the lines of soldiers, scanning them from head to toe. She would soon reach him.

"How will you look for your sister?"

The African inspected his weapon, a sleek rifle equipped with laser sighting and a foregrip. "I'll stay after everyone. It's better if I do that solo."

When the captain arrived at the last pair, she stood in front of Kale and his partner, hands crossed behind her back and eyes looming over her chin. He gulped beneath her towering figure.

"I have little hope for you, but your involvement in this mission is necessary. You'll be my failsafe."

"Why do you still need me," he asked, "you've gotten your part of the deal."

She replied with a chuckle. "That scientist is crafty. I need you on the battlefield so he can't pull a fast one on me." She turned a glance backward to the spot Richmond stood in his fancy yellow suit. He was in deep contemplation about something, but his milky eyes were locked on his subordinate. "He doesn't believe my plan will work. He thinks my cleric will betray me. But I can't fully determine what his alternative would be. For every question I ask him, I'm met with a riddle. Perhaps you have some insight into why that is?" Her face fell to his, pupils dilating like a snake stalking prey.

She doesn't know about Astrid? So that's his secret...

"I..." He recoiled from the intense presence. "I can't tell what he's thinking either. I'm sure you can see that."

"Well then," she was in a high mood, twirling her knife between her fingers, "the one thing I did notice about that man is that the thought of you venturing into danger riled him up. There's a fascination there, and even if I can't fully understand it, it works in my favor." She stuck the knife towards him. The blade's edge shimmered as it tickled his nose. "Don't fail me."

"NOW! PREPARE YOURSELVES! WE MOVE WHEN THE SUN SETS!"

After the captain dismissed the gathering, Kale hobbled to Richmond's side. He bit his tongue, thinking about the conversation he'd shared with Astrid. Even if their promise felt impossible, he still would be slithering behind his back, disobeying the ever-present watch of the scientist. His mind was made to be the one to steal the sentinel and things were beginning to work in his favor.

The plan had been playing in his mind ever since Astrid proposed it. When the Sympaths snuck into the Aeonic Order's bay district factories, Kale would slink into the darkness, inching his way past friend and foe, and take the object of their mission before anyone could know. It was his one true pride after all. The shadows were his home.

"Are you prepared?" Richmond spoke the words without taking his eyes off of a device that stood cylindrical next to the captain's quarters. Steel confines wound around a glassy core with multicolored wires twisting in unison beneath.

"As much as I can be."

"Good."

"So that's the bomb?" Kale traced the object with his eyes.

"Indeed. We've constructed a trebuchet of sorts further behind the field. It will be launched directly over the center of the bay district. The blast won't be powerful enough to harm anyone, so they'll have no idea why all electrically operated devices suddenly stop."

"Do you trust the plan? I mean, even if they do find the sentinel, how will they pilot it? They think the Order just left the keys in?"

"It's in the headsets." He tapped the frame that wrapped around Kale's head. "Some Sympath agents hacked the access codes. Once one of the soldiers gets inside, it'll come to life."

"So, you think it'll be that easy?"

Richmond crossed his arms. "I can't speak on the things I haven't seen, but I don't believe she's stupid enough to send her men in on a whim. The problem lies in the Aureate leader of the Order. I've heard nothing but horror stories about Brianna Sky."

"The man I'm partnered with is planning on abandoning the team. His sister's a hostage there. Apparently, all the workers in her labs got ransomed for campaign funding."

"Then the stories are likely true."

I was right not to trust her.

"So what do you think about it?"

The host's eyes peeled backward at Kale. "I think the night will be quite different than the captain anticipates."

The orders to launch the electromagnetic explosive came sooner than Kale expected. Every lackey in the Sympath's ranks watched as the bright metal lit up the gloaming sky. Like a comet, the fog of the sea shimmered in its trail. A terrible whistle erupted in their ears. Kale steeled his nerves. The ionic blast flowered into an array of azure and purple throughout the atmosphere, causing all of their senses to fall into a frenzy.

The mission had begun.

Resounding in their headsets, the captain called the first command, "AVANT-GUARD UNITS, BEGIN MARCH. SECONDARY UNITS, WAIT FOR THE FIRST CLEAR. REAR RECONNAISSANCE, DO NOT ADVANCE UNTIL THE SECOND SIGNAL CLEARS."

With halted breath, the first five duos began a run toward the east. The borders to the bay district's factories were a mile away. Kale estimated fifteen minutes before the first signal would come.

But it was earlier than that. After just eleven minutes, a man's voice broke their anticipation. "First units cleared. The factories appear empty. Beginning sweeps."

"SECONDARY UNITS! ADVANCE!"

Five more units of soldiers began their runs. The now dark arena grew to a chilling silence. Every soldier meditated to themselves. Kale traced his fingers along the gun at his side. Desmond, now outfitted in unrecognizable mechanics, looked down at him. "Don't worry, I'll cover you when we first go in, but after that, you should group with the next unit. Remember, you won't be in the action."

Kale attempted to hide his nervousness, producing a half-smile. "Got it."

Please... Please let it be clear.

Sixteen minutes passed before another voice called statically through their gear, "assets located. Area is clear of hostiles."
"REAR UNITS! ADVANCE!"

Before he had a moment to think, they were off. Desmond broke into a full sprint, kicking dirt in his face. With a gag and spit, Kale followed. It had been a long time since he ran a full mile, and by the midpoint, his calves began to scream. The Sympath's occupied zone gave way to a hazy vista of pipes and fog, lit only by the faint incandescence of The Well. The shadows were immense. Kale found himself slipping into them by instinct but always watching the bobbing dark helmet of his partner.

They came upon the edge of the occupied zone; the edge of safe ground. Desmond raised a hand and Kale stopped. The other rear units slowed their feet, coming to crouches and kneels and wearing the darkness as cloaks.

"Rear reconnaissance in place. Awaiting confirmation to advance. Secondary units, come in."

Silence.

Desmond spoke into his headset, "Any secondary unit, report."

Silence.

"Hey," Kale whipped his head around, "why aren't they saying anything?"

A lackey cursed from behind. "I knew that wasn't going to work. I bet their comms got fried too."

"But they confirmed the area was clear," Kale argued. "It wouldn't have changed since then."

Desmond's eyes locked on the area before them. The old factories sat down below; a hill of fortified gravel and patchy grass crept into dark outlines of warehouses and a maze of shipping containers. If the advance units were down there, they would be impossible to make out. "Since we shut off the lights, we're too far away to give a lookout. We'll have to go down."

A tall soldier stood and walked to get a clear view. "We'd be going against orders. Captain said for us not to get involved. We should report first."

"Right." Desmond cracked his knuckles, pressing a button on his helmet. "Captain, rear reconnaissance reporting. Unable to establish communication with the advance units. Awaiting permission to descend."

The captain's voice was notably calmer in their ears as she responded immediately. "I see. Send a unit down to investigate. Maintain communication at all times. Report everything."

"Yes, captain!" Desmond waved to two men behind Kale. "You two, go down to the edge of the shipyard. Stay where we can see you and talk the entire time."

"Sir!" They stood and began a march down the hill. Kale watched with bated breath as they slid down the gravel. Blue streaks of dusk caused their figures to become silhouettes. The area was pitch black, only allowing trickles of The Well's light in. A taste of iron smoke made him cough.

"We've reached the edge. No sight of the secondary units." The group reported in.

"DAMN!" Desmond let out a curse. "Captain, we're unable to locate the advance units."

The captain ripped a frustrated yell. "HOW? The area was clear! It must be an issue with the comms. I'll send additional groups. We have no choice but to advance further. FIND THE SENTINEL!"

Is this one of Richmond's tricks?

The eyes of all parties were white and vast.

A soldier kicked a rock with a grunt. "You heard her! Let's move."

When they arrived at the edge of the shipyard, the two soldiers who had gone ahead scanned the others.

"What the hell is going on? Where are the other units?"

Desmond readied his rifle and looked around the area. "I don't know. Something's going on. We know the area is clear, so it has to be a technical issue. We'll find them on foot."

A nervous tension decorated the dark air. Rifles clicked into place and Kale found his hand drifting to the pistol on his hip. His finger coiled around the cold handle, shaking intensely. "They can't be far, right? Do we have a map of the area?"

"Negative," Desmond replied. "But from up on the hill we could see the entrance to the old factories. Should be about a half mile north. We'll comb the area, briefly splitting apart, and regrouping every few minutes."

Slowly, Desmond pointed to each of the duos, eyeing them with one direct pupil, and signaling to walk in opposite directions. Everything was silent. There were no footsteps, no words, but most importantly, no gunshots they could hear which meant that no firefights had broken out. Occasionally, a hiss from gas rising between gaps in the wiry pipes caused Kale to jump out of his skin.

Desmond hissed at his partner, "Keep your eyes peeled. Something weird is happening. They should've reported back. Even if the comms weren't working, they would've sent a return party. Prepare yourself for the worst."

He shivered in reply.

A thick fog had begun to build in the area as the temperature rapidly dropped. He could barely see the outline of the man who led through the dark. He also could barely see the two other soldiers who checked in from their left.

"Any luck?" One asked.

The African's head snapped over. "Not a sign."

"What's going on?" Kale gritted his teeth, "Do we know where the sentinel is?"

"Our only option now is to find it and get out of here. What about the others? There should be four more of us."

"Not sure. They broke off to the right."

Desmond tapped his headset. "Rear units, check in."

Silence.

"Rear units. Respond."

Silence.

"They're gone too?"

A panic began to set in throughout the group. "There has to be something out here. If they were just lost, we would've run into someone by now!"

Desmond lowered his head. "All we can do now is assume the area is full of hostiles."

Kale gulped.

"Eyes up, boys."

Everyone readied their weapons out in front. The four men each covered a direction, moving as one through the shifting maze of containers. They couldn't make out color or shape in the deep invisibility, only able to judge direction by placing the glow of The Well to their left. The factory warehouses were north, and to the north, they hobbled.

There was a whistle in the air, a strange whirring, like that of a machine spinning to life. The further they traveled, the more it grew, with beeps and a high-pitched hum rising in audibility.

Kale whispered. "It sounds like some machines are online. Are we too late?"

"I'm not sure," Desmond replied, the barrel of his rifle swaying in front. "Until we see hostile soldiers, we've got time. The sound might be the hydroplants beneath us. They generate electricity deep underwater. The EMP wouldn't have shut those down. All we did was scramble the converters."

"I hope you're right."

For several minutes, they moved in silence. Their feet rolled without lifting along the concrete ground. Occasionally, a pebble would crunch beneath their feet, causing Kale to jump, but he remained stable, watching intently down the neon green sights of his pistol.

Twenty rounds. I can't waste any...

As they began to reach the edge of the field of containers, the haze compounded with sea fog, growing much thicker. If there was an enemy before them, they wouldn't know until it was too late. Kale could tell the others thought similarly, watching their shoulders twitch with every sound.

Then, Desmond stopped, raising a hand to halt the others. None dared breathe. Through the heavy mist, a light appeared, a red wave moving robotically from left to right. It scanned the area with a wide sweep, illuminating every surface.

"What's that?" Kale hissed under his breath.

"Shhhh," the others snapped. "Don't make a sound."

The light disappeared before it reached them. All eyes stared intently at a gap in the containers in front. A sound of tapping and clicking echoed through the area. Something was moving; a perfect march of metal against metal and it was coming closer.

Desmond ordered them to hide behind a wall to their right and everyone slid their backs against the cold surface. Peeking around its edge, the leader watched but snapped his head back as red light filled their view.

"M6 Spider. It's a Skyridge drone. No wonder..."

"Spider?" Kale could feel his knees quiver.

"Combat drones. They're seekers. Quadruped robots with infrared scanners. They're patrolling the area on guard... Must've killed everyone else..."

"Killed?" Another soldier leaned in front of them. "The hell are you talking about? We haven't found any bodies!"

"That's because there aren't any to find."

"What?"

"My sister was involved in the research. They run on The Well's energy, using its light in particle deconstruction. If they hit you, there won't be anything left." Desmond hung his head. "The EMP wouldn't have shut them down."

"Wait," Kale eyed the taller man, mouth agape. "You knew about those things? Why didn't you say something?"

"I never knew they'd been finished. Nia only worked on the concept… We have to get out of here."

"Can they hear?"

"I don't know…"

"Can we kill it?"

"It's full metal. I doubt it."

"So even our guns are useless?"

"Probably."

They could hear the ticking of its mechanics walking nearby.

Kale clenched his hands together, tightening the straps of his vest and holstering his pistol. "How many do you think there are?"

"Enough. If we haven't heard any communication, I estimate at least five in the area."

"Thirty soldiers… You're saying it killed them all?"

"Killed isn't the right word. They no longer exist."

None of the soldiers responded.

"Here's what we'll do before it comes back." Desmond slung his rifle over his back, staring at them through his helmet. "Every man is gonna have to move on their own. If you want to live, I suggest you haul it to the edge of the shipyard. Don't try to be a hero."

"What about you?" A soldier asked.

"I have to stay. I have another reason for being here."

"I'll stay." Kale raised his head, holding a fist to his side. "I'll find the sentinel. That thing won't see me. I'm good at hiding."

Desmond stared at him, analyzing his frame.

I don't have a choice… I have to! Astrid is counting on me…

"You wanna die?"

Kale chuckled nervously, "no. But I'm used to sneaking. It won't catch me."

"Then, on the count of three," The African held his hand in the air. One finger fell. The next fell. Then, with a nod, he closed his hand.

In every direction, they ran, feet flying from under them and carefully avoiding the waves of red light that swam through the fog. Kale found himself separated from the squad, keeping the light of The Well to his left.

To the north. The warehouses are to the north. It'll be there. It has to be!

He ducked and dove from shadow to shadow, keeping watchful eyes and turning his head like an eagle in every direction. He hadn't seen the machines that lurked around the corners, he didn't want to, but the thought of the spider drones caused his hairs to stand on end. He could picture the sharp legs of cold steel that he heard tapping in the air around him. He could feel its red gaze on his neck as if at any moment he'd find his body reduced to atoms. But it was the fear that made him so watchful.

When he reached the edge of the shipping container jungle, a row of four warehouses stood across an empty road where abandoned polygonal cars sat stationary and lifeless. Gigantic lamplights poked above the pale fog, their bulbs offering no visibility. His eyes traced a path across the road, hiding in the deep darkness that obscured the ground. But along that path, they caught sight of something else.

Marching along the road that stood between him and his destination was a vexing contraption. Four triangular appendages tickled the ground beneath it, their points seemingly hovering, puncturing the earth in an orderly step. The legs were armored in silver plating that appeared almost translucent, but determinable by the contrast of thick wiring beneath. Between the tops of the legs, above a central body, a round module spun like clockwork with a singular eye projecting a red scan across the surroundings.

Kale held his breath.

The drone trekked a path in the opposite direction of him, and he began to shift at a crouch across the expanse. Every few seconds, its head would look back, spouting the terrifying light in his direction and he flattened his body beneath the haze.

The fog must block its scan. It's far enough away...

When the light passed, he shifted his shoulders, crawling towards the warehouses and stopping like clockwork when he heard the spider's head turn back.

After a grueling stretch to the warehouse doors, he stood and peered inside. It was pitch black, but by squinting his eyes he could make out boxes strewn throughout. No sign of the sentinel. Surely, something as big as it wouldn't be hard to find.

The spider drone had gone far out of sight to the furthest warehouse, but in this search, he'd have to go towards it. Its robotic order and stationary march almost caused it to seem harmless. It was a deceiving appearance. After all, they had wiped out the advance units, completely erasing them from the world. He couldn't let it happen to him.

The next warehouse was similarly abandoned. Wires hung from the ceiling like vines, disconnected from something that once stood within. But there were two more to check.

The spider had begun to march back towards him, it had reached the edge of its patrol zone, turning back to sweep the road once more. Kale slipped around the edge of the warehouse, finding barricades and piles of scrap to hide behind. It was terrifying. When it drew closer, his eyes poked above his hide at it. A singular lens projected the red light, twisting and staring unlike any living thing. But there was a purpose to it. He could feel the radiating evil of the machine by sight alone; cold, calculated, and indiscriminate.

He managed to avoid detection once more, slithering into the third warehouse. Something was different about this one. The floor was hard to determine because when he entered, his feet found steps. A descent stretched for a while, leading to an immeasurable depth. There was something here, he just couldn't see it completely in the low light. Slowly, he made his way down. There were no sounds, no sights, only the cold air and the feeling of metal beneath his feet to guide him. Kale shivered.

Along the staircase that led to utter darkness was a trail of thick wires. His hand traced their rubbery surface. There was no life in them. He only hoped they led to the last manual sentinel.

Please… Please be here…

When he'd reached the end of their connection, a rigid surface of thick plating greeted his hand. But he couldn't see a thing. On their helmets was a small headlamp, but turning it on would alert anyone in the immediate area.

Surely, if he'd made it this far, there wouldn't be anyone. Still, the thought of light made his hair stand on end, the absence of his comforting darkness.

He turned his lamp on. What stood before him almost made him scream, but he felt a mix of elation, relief, and utter fear all at once. Looking before him was a face of infinite machinery; deep lenses of eyes, multiplicative gears of teeth, and shimmering golden armor that wrapped around a skull of wires. The sentinel stared back.

Instantly, Kale commanded his mind to contact Richmond and the host quickly answered.

"Richmond! I found it! I found the sentinel!"

[You did? Where is it? What's your condition?]

Kale struggled to breathe from the adrenaline that pumped in his veins. "It's in a warehouse, attached to a ton of wires, but it's pretty far down below the ground. Looks like it's in good condition though."

[You... You found it?]

"Yes... But I'm alone..."

[What of the crew? The captain said there were complications.]

"Everyone is... All the advance units were wiped out. These drones were patrolling the area... Some kind of spider... The area wasn't abandoned after all."

[I see. No one in your way... Then there's no time to waste. You have to pilot the sentinel.]

"I-" At that moment, a terrifying sound erupted. A screech of steel ripped Kale from his conversation and red light lit up all surroundings. The drone had entered the warehouse. With a yell, Kale dropped to his knees and scrambled to find cover. The light scanned through the area, attempting to locate the source of the noise.

NO NO NO! This can't be happening!

"Richmond!" Kale yelled, frantically looking around for cover. The red lit his whole body, consuming his vision. "It found me! It's here!"

[What? Get in the sentinel! Do you have any idea of the opportunity in front of us? Take it!"]

"I can't! If I move it'll see me!" He pleaded with his thoughts, making himself as small as possible against a dense tract of wires. It was barely enough to hide him and he noticed the trail of his coat hanging past its edge.

[Kale! Get in it! You know what we came here for! Once you do that, there's nothing that can stop you!]

The red light had grown greater. The spider was inching its way down, clicking its metal legs on each step, and keeping its singular eye locked on his position.
"I can't move! It sees me! If that thing shoots I'll be-"

Richmond assumed a tone that Kale had never heard.
[GET IN THE SENTINEL NOW!]

It chilled him to his bones. A voice of complete authority and command. Richmond didn't care if Kale died. All he cared about was his mission and for that, Kale had to risk his life.
With a determined roar, he flung himself from the spot, completely exposing his terrified face to the red light of the spider. From the eye, a golden light began to emerge. A singular beam shot from the head and Kale watched his entire life flash before his eyes.
But the shot did not reach him. In a split second of coordination, he slid behind the giant head of the sentinel, and the ontological light of death became absorbed by its impenetrable golden armor.
Behind the sentinel's head was a hatch hung slightly open. Immense hinges of tarnished gold bent backward, allowing access to the internal systems.

I guess the captain was right. Whoever was working on it before the EMP blew panicked.

As his head passed through the hatch, systems began whirring to life. Green light illuminated the inside, a menagerie of machinery. He couldn't believe the sight before him. The entire interior of the sentinel's head became a giant screen, a portal to the outside, and even though the warehouse was dark, vibrant outlines traced all surfaces. With the newfound visibility, he could starkly make out the spider drone standing directly in front of him, blasting beams of light into the sentinel's face. Though they couldn't penetrate its sturdy hull, Kale winced with each shot.

He quickly turned and pulled the hatch shut. Even with the assistance of gravity, it took all of his back muscles to pull it closed and fully secure his safety from the machine.

"Richmond, I'm inside. It's online. I did it."

[Good. Good. And the spider?]

"It's trying to shoot me, but the beams aren't working."

[Yes. Its armor is impenetrable. Now, there should be a control mechanism. Tell me what you see.]

"Uhhh." Kale's eyes bounced around the cockpit. There were various levers, buttons, and spheres, none of which bore a functionality he could determine, except a large disc in the center which was labeled: SYNTHESIS MAINFRAME (OFF.) "There's a weird circle. Says synthesis mainframe on it."

[That's the connection. Grasp it and it will integrate with your frame. That's how it moves.]

His hands wrapped around the strange device and instantly a woman's voice began to speak: *Synthesis complete. Autonomy granted. Manual control online.*

"I did it." Withdrawing his hands from the disc, he could hear metal begin to move. With each motion, the noise grew louder. He raised his arms. Looking around the interior, he could see golden appendages rise beside him, mimicking his movements. "Woah…"

The spider, still firing away outside, began to slowly step backward angling its head to watch the sentinel rise. Kale reached forward and a massive hand of flaxen steel did the same. He hovered it above the drone, eyes wide in amazement, before swiftly bringing it down. The sentinel's hand slammed into the floor, sending scraps of metal flying in all directions. The spider was smashed to bits.

This is the power… This is the power that attacked us… But now it's mine…

He could barely believe it. The feeling of overwhelming strength coursed through his veins. "Richmond… I killed it… I crushed the spider."

The host chuckled.
[Ah, you feel it then. *That* is the power of The Well.]

We really did it…

Kale began running calculations. "What about the mission? Does the captain know I found it?" Now that he had accomplished the unthinkable, a choice was to be made. He now had options: return the sentinel to the Sympath headquarters and hand it over to the captain, or betray them and rendezvous with Astrid.

[No. I haven't told her. She's in a panic, all units have gone dark.]

"So, what do you want me to do?"

[We're going to make a little detour.]

"A detour?"

[Further east is the Guiding City's Southern Power Distributary. It's a straight shot down a path of supermassive wires that feed directly into The Well. As I said, this is a race, and now we're going to win it.]

Chapter 14
Esthesia

The feeling inside of the sentinel's head could not be properly articulated. It was a sensation of absolute authority. Here was the greatest weapon ever forged by mankind, and it had become his plaything. Kale relished the feeling.

But with it came a problem, the machine was simply too large to fully realize its capabilities. He found himself bumping against the chamber where it rested, unable to properly climb to ground level. The earth shook each time he smashed the invulnerable metal into a barrier designed to keep it in place. He would have to figure out a means of ascension.

"I've got a problem," he said into the transponder.

[A problem?]

"I'm stuck."

[Resolve this issue.]

"How?" He looked around the control panels. Flickering lights and infinite switches caused him to grow exceedingly frustrated and every time he turned his body, he was met with a deafening screech of metal on metal. His sable jacket constantly caught on prodding levers.

[They wouldn't build a platform it couldn't escape from. The sentinel should be able to crawl its way out. Climb, if you can.]

"Tsk." Kale struggled to move. "That's hard to do when it's trapped."

He began flipping switches tactfully, careful to avoid ones that seemed like they would trigger weaponry. The levers marked with a blue color seemed the most welcoming because of their rounded handles. The first caused a bubbling sound to come from behind, a sort of coolant system he wagered, the second prompted a small hand to emerge from the sentinel's palm, triggering an awful string of memories, and the third activated a bright light that illuminated the entire warehouse.

He began looking around. The room was pyramidical, ever descending towards the sentinel in a staircase fashion. Various thin walkways extended around the machine where workers could access every inch of its height and somehow in the darkness he'd managed to find his way to the right one.

The sentinel was situated on a vast platform, several yards wide of thick concrete. Its feet fit perfectly into deep pockets outlined by yellow and black cautionary paint, but up above were gigantic wires that hung loosely. Using the sentinel's hands, he grabbed them and positioned the robot's feet into giant sockets along the walls. He gave the wire a solid tug, and it didn't budge. He could use it to climb.

The balance of strength required not to rip the roof down was tough to gauge without being able to properly feel what the sentinel touched. The top of the warehouse shook immensely as he motioned for the sentinel to lift itself, but after careful precision and a few drops of sweat down his back, it reached the ground level. Bursts of blue sparks popped and hissed from connections that his cumbersome echopraxia accidentally dislodged.

The warehouse's door was just high enough to duck beneath without destroying the construction, but when he stepped outside and commanded the machine to stand up straight, the sight that was revealed shook him. He could see the entire maze of shipping containers, edge to edge. It was larger than any of the soldiers could have estimated, but something else made his stomach rise to his throat. Illuminated by the bright light of the sentinel, the yard was not a collective of cargo, but rather a hive of spiders. Hundreds of marching quadrupeds scoured the gaps of the maze and at once, after being exposed to the light, looked up uniformly. Their red eyes appeared as stars in a night sky, numerous but serving a singular mind.

It was as though they recognized their inability to fight the sentinel because they did not engage beyond watching. Kale almost didn't know what to do. He stared back at them for a moment, counting the eyes, and realizing the gruesome fate of the other Sympaths. There were so many. He considered squashing them, one by one. He now had the power to do so, but something far more important crossed his mind.

"Richmond? What about the captain? She'll kill you if she finds out I've stolen it."

[Don't worry. She's communicating with the new units, they're beginning their march toward the factories. However, you have to get out of there before they see you. That sentinel will be hard to miss.]

212

A lump formed in his throat. "Has anyone else made it back? Any report from the rear reconnaissance unit?"

[Not that I'm aware of.]

Kale winced.
There was virtually no chance they'd made it back to the lookout without catching the gaze of a spider. He'd been the lucky one, prepared to dodge their eyes. The years of thievery had molded his skillset well, but the others, not versed in the art of invisibility would've easily been erased by the weaponry.

Desmond should still be out there… He wouldn't have gotten caught. He knew about them…

Kale raised a hand to trigger communication in his headset. He wanted to contact Desmond, to make sure his comrade was still alive, but stopped.

No. The captain will intercept the comms… I just have to trust that he made it…

"You said to go east?"

[Yes. The Distributary lies between the Bay District and the Eastern Sea Border. It uses the ocean to stay cool. Vast heatsinks hold the wires in place all the way to The Well. It wasn't built for human traversal, but for a sentinel, it should make a perfect road.]

"How far?"

[Far enough, but you won't miss it.]

"What'll you do? You need to get out of there before the captain realizes what's happened."

Richmond chuckled under his breath.
[Don't worry about me, Kale. I'm always prepared.]
A beeping signaled the end of their call.

There were too many variables.

As Kale began to walk, the strength of the sentinel felt incredible. His mobility within the head was not impeded. He'd take a few steps forward as if he would run into the wall in front of him but mysteriously found himself in the same spot. It was as if he was suspended in air, but still felt the tug of gravity. Kale stared blankly around the interior, glowing with iridescent colors and chirping with technologically advanced sounds. It smelled of oil, but didn't bother him, was bright, but depicted the deep night outside, and though he couldn't understand the mechanics that allowed him control, it was his, it was him, and he had become powerful.

I can do anything now.

A dangerous thought appeared in his head.

Now I... I could give this to The Vultures... There's no doubt now... With this sentinel, I'd instantly win back my favor. Father would accept me...

He looked down at his hands. So did the machine.

These are the hands that crushed Phoebe. These are the devil's hands...

His mind was already made up. The choice of how to use those hands was decided four days ago when Astrid kissed him. He would bring her world into being, the one she'd set her mind upon.
Conjuring her image within his mind, the transponder beeped to life.
"Astrid, I did it. I stole the sentinel!"

Her voice was strange when she responded, labored and in an apparent struggle for breath.
[Y-You did? I'm glad... I knew you could do it... I was so worried.]

As the sentinel's feet stomped eastward, each massive foot crashing into the ground and stirring up shrapnel of concrete, Kale began to grow pale.
"What's wrong? Did something happen?

[It's getting worse, much worse. The Well keeps talking to me... It's like it's calling me. Like it knows something's about to happen.]
She winced with each sentence.

The night sky had grown even darker. Everything was subsumed in shadow and he found it difficult to step. His path now led down a long road that bordered the ocean on one side and a multitude of gigantic cranes on the other. Seafoam sprayed against the bank, sending deep fog over the ground and an eerie feeling grew in Kale's gut as if at any moment he may accidentally step on someone.

"I need you to do something for me. If you're strong enough right now, I need you to take a railway car to the Distributary district. There I can meet you and we'll make a beeline for The Well."

> There was a pause before she replied.
> [He told me you'd say that.]

"That was our plan, remember?"

[But we had a promise…]

Kale stopped his march.
"What're you talking about? This was our promise. I'd steal the sentinel and take you to The Well. Astrid, this is how we change the world."

A storm had begun to brew out among the tall waves of the black ocean. The image of lightning, in a sky dominated by The Well, was strange to behold. It appeared to twist among the golden rays as if the presence of a paracausal light disrupted the flow of its energy. The clouds organized themselves in a sinister swirl, appearing powerless in the sky.

> [I know. But as I'm thinking about it now, it doesn't feel right. All we're doing is playing right into the roles we were assigned. It's all just his plan, even if we think we had a choice.]

"But… You said you trusted him…"

[I do trust him.]

"Then why? Why the sudden change of heart?"

Astrid groaned and Kale could hear the voices of others through the transponder. She was among the citizens.

[It feels like if I go through with this, I'll be betraying something. I think it's a feeling from The Well. Remember when I said it made me feel comfortable when we arrived? It's different now. I-I really can't explain it.]

"So what do you trust more, The Well or the people who believe in you?"

[I don't know... I think there's a reason it's warning me...]

The sounds of the machine's feet striking the ground reverberated through the expanse, shaking the massive hooks and wires that stood like a petrified forest around him. The skyline of the Guiding City had grown distant, even in all its gigantism. Kale couldn't determine what lay ahead, only a faint glow of red emanating on the horizon. It made his hair stand on end.

"I'm too far into this to back down. If I decide to abandon this sentinel now, I... I don't know what'll happen. But think about it. This is the one chance we have. This is the chance we came here for! In the end, it's YOUR wish that gets made, not Richmond's. So even if this somehow plays into his grand plan, he can't stop your wish."

She remained silent for a moment then spoke in a monotone.
[I'm boarding a railway car. Which is the closest stop?]

Kale fumbled through his pockets, causing the sentinel to bash itself and shake until he found his voucher and summoned the holomap to appear. "There's a stop at the Eastern Distributary Energy Stations, but I doubt it's for public access, I'll have to find a way to get you through." He began to march again.

[You mean with the sentinel?]

He cursed. "How else? We don't have much time until the Order finds out that it's gone. When they do it'll be hell that breaks loose."

[Okay... I'll be at the station.]

Everything was dark when he approached the entrance to the Distributary. Massive golden spires stood adjacent to a gate marked with giant glowing letters: GUIDING CITY ENERGY SPECIALISTS ONLY.

There was a clear trigger on the right side of the sentinel's internal control board marked M137 105mm. Kale knew what it was. The sentinels were armed for extreme measures, no doubt, because the gun would evaporate anything in his path. The thought made him sweat. In order to grant Astrid entrance to the zone, he would have to employ those extreme measures.

[I'm here, but Kale... There are guards, a lot of them. They're working.]

"Astrid, listen carefully. I need you to stand away from the gate, as far as you can. Something's about to happen and when it does, I need you to run through... fast."

[What? You don't mean- There are people here!]

"Get ready." He grasped the gun controls. A large cannon sprung forth from the sentinel's shoulder with a screech of steel. Green circles appeared in his view, steadying the cannon's aim. He pointed it towards the golden gate, unsure of what would happen. His hand shook.

The blast rumbled the earth around him and he heard Astrid scream through the transponder. The gate blew open like a smashed fruit, spewing debris in all directions.
"RUN! NOW!"

Sirens began to wail all around as lights blasted from the spires. Drones buzzed from the roof and the area took to maximum security. Yellow bars rose along the ground at entry points.
"Astrid hurry! We have to go now!" he yelled, frantically looking for her within the chaos.
As he turned his gaze toward the destroyed gate, he saw her, like an ant scrambling through the pieces of destroyed gold. Even from the sentinel's massive height, he could see her panicked eyes, desperately staring at the robot. He snatched her, scooping her fragile body into the metal hands. He brought them to the back of its head and commanded the hatch to open. She slipped inside, collapsing on the floor.
Kale turned around to look at her. There was pain on her face, red around her eyes, and though he could see she was wearing makeup, golden light protruded from her forehead. Her arms were bleeding.
"You okay? Did you get hurt?" he asked, hands still shaking.

"I-I'm fine, just my arms, I fell and cut them, but it's not bad." She was pale and struggled to stand. Strands of her hair were stuck to her face and her legs quivered. The entrance hatch closed behind her and the sounds of alarms grew quiet.

"We're heading straight for The Well."

He turned toward the northwest. The Distributary was built like a great canyon. Gigantic silver rectangles emerged at its edges like flying buttresses, designed to channel the heat of The Well's incredible power and exude energy. Even he, as ignorant of thermodynamics and electromagnetism as he was, recognized the insane power on display because at the base of the heatsinks, the sea was boiling. The wire was like the root of a great tree, beyond belief. He couldn't even tell it was round, but it did have ridges that allowed it to bend. How humans constructed it, he couldn't fathom.

The sentinel stood at its edge and began the descent to the wire. Since everything was so large, the sentinel maneuvered as a human in their natural scale. Richmond was right, the wire made for a perfect platform that the sentinel could walk along and if he had told the truth, it would be a simple trek to The Well. It almost seemed too easy.

"Kale, I need to tell you what I'm feeling." Astrid was slouched against the back hatch, clutching her head. She was in her formal attire but stained by the residue of the sentinel's blast and the blood from her arms. Her tie was mostly undone and her suit coat was tied around her waist.

He was walking in place, controlling the sentinel's movement, but did his best to look back at her. "If it's bad news, I don't think I can handle it right now."

"Something is wrong. I know it."

"It's probably stress. Who knows what we've just unleashed… Every force of the Guiding City is gonna be after us." His own words made him sweat. "We've got no choice now."

The sky was black, darker than any night he'd ever seen, but as they drew closer to The Well, its glow failed to make it any brighter. There were several miles to cover, but in the sentinel, it could be done relatively quickly.

What have we done?

Richmond's voice broke into their minds.
[Kale, what's your status?]

"We're together in the sentinel. Not long until we reach The Well." His voice was unstable.

[You'd better hurry. Everything in the city is on high alert. They're coming for you.]

"What are we supposed to do about that?" The sentinel slipped, causing them to fall. Astrid screamed. Thankfully, Kale caught its tumble before it could slip into the sea. "Something's wrong with Astrid too. She has a terrible feeling… She thinks it's from The Well."

An intense sternness coated Richmond's voice.
[There's no room for feelings now. Move forward.]

"What about you? What will you do?"

[That is not your concern right now. Go.]
A beep signaled Richmond's exit from the call.

"Kale…" Astrid tugged on the back of his shirt. Her face was drenched in sweat, her hair catching in her eyes. The insignia of the Clerics was now fully visible through her makeup. "I can't anymore. It's too much. It hurts…"

He hissed between his teeth, beginning to command the sentinel to sprint. "Just a little longer. We're almost there."

He ran, the machine stomping with creaks and metallic whines. They were easily traveling faster than a car and when he checked the map on his voucher, he saw that they would soon reach The Well.

But he could sense something from behind. Red boxes began to flash inside the sentinel's control.
!WARNING!
!WARNING!
!INCOMING PROJECTILE!

BOOM

Something impacted them from behind, throwing the sentinel to the ground. He lost his footing on the inside, slamming into the wall and collapsing.

"What was that?" Kale yelled, recuperating his equilibrium.

He could hear it through the thick metal, an intense buzzing from outside. He ordered the robot to stand and turned toward their rear. Hovering above the wire was a drone, but not like one he'd ever seen. It was easily the size of a helicopter, equipped with four hoops that suspended it. Blue streaks of light crawled along its central body and stationed at its head was a terrifying sight. The face of Brianna Sky stared forward, like a figurehead on the front of the primary module. It was the same otherworldly face that he'd seen in Skyridge's main Laboratory.

A message broadcasted inside the sentinel's screen and her multilayered voice commanded their attention. [Whoever you are, thief, what you've stolen is something classified to even the Aureate themselves. I'll give you one chance to exit the sentinel or I'll rip you from its head.]

Astrid was compromised, balled against the wall of the hull and cradling her head. He couldn't imagine the pain she felt. Kale stuck his jaw forward and gritted his teeth. "Hang on. It's about to get rough."

He gripped the controls to the 105mm cannon and aimed it dead ahead at the drone. His finger squeezed the trigger. When the bullet exited the barrel, the drone whipped out of its path, dodging the warhead with ease.

Another message played inside: [Theft of government property, deployment of unauthorized military weaponry, unauthorized synchronization, attempted murder, assault, vandalism, trespassing, you've just signed your life away.]

"Get out of our way!" He fired another shot that zipped into nothingness. The 105mm cannon was too heavy, he'd have to utilize a lighter caliber.

The drone flew towards him, deploying small rockets that blew up at his feet. He could feel the sentinel rattle, throwing his balance aside. It was difficult to track the drone. It zig-zagged through the air, rotating around him like an annoying bug, but it had a stinger. Small peppered shots ricocheted off the sentinel's armor, doing nothing to harm them, but disorienting his internal screens. He located two other weapon controls: a 55mm machine gun and a makeshift steel hammer that doubled as the machine's counterbalance.

He squeezed the machine gun and followed her drone, firing rounds at incredible speeds. Most of them missed, sailing into the night, but a few dug into the drone's rotors. They were dealing damage, he could tell because the movements slowed and the drone took to greater heights. Missiles rained down from above, impacting the sentinel's armor, but unable to break through. He squinted through the darkness, following the faint streaks of blue with his gun.

The steam from the boiling ocean obscured the sky and it became nearly impossible to judge where the next shot would come from. Kale gasped for air as his adrenaline took over.

Looking up through the haze, he squinted to spy the next glint of missile flare. With a red hue, a sizable projectile burst into his sight and he brought the sentinel's left hand up to intercept. It collided with its fingers, sending sparks and fire along the arm.

A warning alarmed within the cockpit.
!STRUCTURAL INTEGRITY BREACHED!
!ADJUSTING COUNTERBALANCE!
!PRESSURE REGULATION IN PROGRESS!

The fight could not continue without a visual identity on the drone. He'd be peppered to pieces by tracking rockets until he fell into the ocean. There had to be a way to entice the drone to descend. As long as it sat above the boiling sea mist, then it would rain down fury forever. The old model of the sentinel was not equipped with a visual lens that could penetrate the heavy steam and the radiation of the heatsinks scrambled the thermal readings.

Fine then. I'll force you to come down.

He began to sprint along the wire, running toward The Well. Rockets zoomed toward him, but the sentinel's immediate radar allowed him to properly dodge. Now that he knew to expect them, he could throw off their trajectory. The struggle covered immense ground and the haze dissipated the closer they got to The Well. Left, right, behind, around, explosions blasted the terrain. Massive crackles of energy released where the rockets penetrated the power distributary.

Brianna Sky's drone had descended to the ground now, flying along the wire's surface. The hoops were turned almost at 90 degrees for maximum speed and two long poles extended from the drone's nose.

GET AWAY FROM US!!

She was closing in, gaining speed by the second. There was a secret to the poles that had been deployed, but he didn't want to find out. He sprinted even faster, but she kept up, practically tickling the sentinel's back.

Time began to slow as Kale considered his options of combat. There were seconds remaining before it reached them, and he had to act quickly. Then, as soon as they were about to make contact, he jumped. The sentinel spun in the air, grasping the right hoop of the drone and slamming it into the wire. Sparks flew in all directions and electricity arced between its joints. With a roar, he punched down into its primary module, crushing its armor beneath the mechanical strength. He raised it over his head, gripping it tightly, and flung it down into the bubbling water of the sea, then, in quick succession, fired three shots where it submerged. The water exploded, steam filled the air, and shards of blue plating rained from the sky.

Chapter 15
The Final Exegesis

    The architecture surrounding The Well was a fractal contradiction. The light was blinding, and he could feel the sheer power exuding from its incandescence. The wire was one of many, attached to massive dishes that tilted toward the crater where the light sprung from. Surrounding them were vast platforms built from intertwining metals. He couldn't pinpoint the exact material because when his sentinel stepped onto them, golden ripples traveled through the patterns as if the light recognized who was approaching. The blend between life and machine converged at that point. Kale's jaw hung low and when he blinked, the light showed straight through his eyelids. "Wow..." was all he could muster.

    Astrid did not look up.

    The veins in her hands were bulging through her skin and she was gripping her forehead. Almost like a connection between wires, the Cleric insignia shined between her fingers, reaching towards The Well. Perhaps she didn't need her eyes to see it.

    "Astrid," Kale began, excitedly, "we made it. We're here."

    She didn't reply.

    Surprisingly, the area was clear of life. The sentinel's radar did not detect outside projections. If there were security features in place, their arrival had not triggered them. There were no workers monitoring the great wonder, no guards scouting for trespassers, and no birds flying around, not even drones.

    Kale wondered why. Perhaps it was the fact that there were no points of accession. The heat of the wire would've vaporized any human that tried to traverse it. The sentinels were off-limits during the time of governmental unrest. But with the Guiding City on high alert, surely the most precious resource would've been guarded, yet there it was, open and beckoning them.

    He knelt, bringing the sentinel to a mirrored pose. Astrid's shoulders were cold and he could feel her shaky breaths. "Can you stand?"

    "I can't," she said, laboring to bring her emerald eyes to his. "It's like I'm in a body that's not my own. It feels like it's taking me over. It hurts..."

With a few taps of the control board, the rear hatch opened to the outside. Chill air trickled in and blew apart his sable jacket. Kale turned his eyes back to the girl. It was pitiful. A creeping sympathy took him over.

She's fighting for her purpose. I can't even imagine how intense it must be. If I'm a normal person and so captivated by this thing, how much more must she feel it?

"I'll carry you." He wrapped a hand beneath her knees and shoulders, hoisting her into his chest. Her silky hair fell around his arms, but her hands continued to shield her head. The image pained him. She resembled a child hiding from a monster. "Just a little further."

He stared at the light, moving upwards into the sky like a planetary fountain. The Well truly was beyond all comprehension. There was no natural cause for its emergence, no declaration of its arrival, no demands for its existence, and among all the science humanity employed to attempt understanding, it simply was.

"Richmond, we made it."

A whipping sound resounded in the air around them, like the blades of a helicopter descending from the left. Kale snapped his head sideways and held Astrid tightly. From the clouds, a golden vehicle like the polygonal cars of the city drove through the air and found a landing point opposite the sentinel.

NO! Not now! We're so close!

Kale set the girl down, reaching for his hip and finding the pistol from his mission. He clicked the slide, readying a round, and aimed it at the new arrival. "Astrid, get behind the sentinel! Someone's here!"

The green sights shook in his view, and he watched with staggered breath as the side door of the vehicle began to open. He was cold with fear, fighting back the desire to run. They were so close, closer than he could've ever imagined, and he was not going to let anyone stop them now. All he had to do was bring her into the light and everything would be solved. The world would be repaired.

From the door, a brown shoe stepped down, followed by marigold pants and a suit to match. A head of milky hair, sharp cheekbones, and quartz eyes stared at the gun.

"Richmond?" Kale lowered his weapon. "How did you-"

"So then," the host walked toward them with a lowered gaze. "Everything is in place."

A flush of relief radiated through Kale's nerves and he drooped his posture. "You scared me. I thought it was over…"

"The Sympath captain was so preoccupied with her mission that she didn't notice the disappearance of her private aerocar." He pocketed an object that Kale couldn't fully make out. "You're not the only one capable of sneaking about. All that chaos you caused served me well." Richmond's attention turned to the compromised girl who hadn't paid his arrival any mind. "It seems the strain of communion is becoming too much for her, but we have to act fast. Kale, there's an army on its way."

He holstered the gun. "I figured. The entire city must be on alert. But I'm surprised The Well itself is clear." He scanned the area once again to make absolutely sure.

Astrid struggled to raise her head. The blood stains on her arms had spread to her midsection and she'd lost her coat in the battle against the drone. "Father… I… I know what I have to do but… It feels wrong… I can't explain it."

"Now is not the time for feelings, Astrid." The scientist gripped her wrists, pulling her to her feet. She whimpered but obliged and stood on her own. He pointed to The Well, guiding her eyes with a steady hand. "Right there is the salvation of the world. Go. Make your wish. Fulfill your destiny. Do it for Phoebe." His face was stoic, but Kale recognized a signature fire behind the pale eyes, one he'd only seen in their first meeting.

Something irritated him about the interaction, and he postured himself between the father and daughter, offering her a shoulder. "I'll take her."

Astrid sunk her weight into him and turned her face into his chest.

Richmond stood back, crossing his arms and looking forward. "Very well. Go."

With a whisper, she spoke into his ear, out of the range of the host. "Kale… This feeling is real… It's warning me…"

They walked towards The Well, staring at the bright magnificence. It drew closer and closer, offering a haunting warmth, like a fire that could easily spread out of control.

"If it's warning you, then what should we do? We can't turn back now. If we abandon this mission, we'll die. The Guiding City will kill us for what we've done and they'll make you a slave, just like the other Clerics."

"I… I don't know what to do…"

He gritted his teeth. "You're the only one who can make a difference now! Remember our promise? This was OUR choice, no one else's. You are free. You don't have to hide anymore; you can face what you are!"

Tears began to fall along her cheeks, and a great sadness filled her green eyes. "You... You don't understand... There's something I didn't tell you. Kale, I need to tell you the truth."

"The truth?"

Her face was almost entirely consumed by the golden light, but he could see the remnants of her comforting appearance. "Do you remember that night? When we made our promise..."

"Of course I do."

"I lied to you."

"You lied?"

"I just couldn't... I couldn't tell you..."

"Tsk." He cursed and grabbed her shoulders, turning her to meet his eyes. "That doesn't matter now... I lied to you too. I lied so much! But we can't! We can't stop now. Whatever it is that's going on it has to wait until after. Make your wish, Astrid, then we can figure it out from there. Even if everything you told me, about wanting to love and about forgiveness was all a lie, none of that matters. It's okay."

There was no room for confessions. At that moment, love was an afterthought. The fear of incoming armies, and the uncertainty of what was to come far outweighed his emotion.

Her eyes fell, defeated. "Fine... I'll make my wish."

The edge of the light was within arm's reach and they came to a stop. It appeared solid like a wall of gold, but with motion and radiance. Kale was mystified, entranced by the shimmer, and reached forward, extending a hand to touch it.

"Wait!" Astrid caught his hand. She was hunched over, straining with every ounce of her strength to stop him. "You can't... Right now, it's angry."

His fingers could feel the extreme imminence of The Well's power, but he retracted his hand.

Astrid forced herself to stand straight, chin fixated on what stood before her. Her jaw was sharp and though the edges of her eyes were red and puffy, she looked like a goddess, illuminated by the brilliance of her insignia. Her hands held one another, grasping her left thumb with her right. The light was inches away.

Kale looked at her feet. The platform they stood on continued for several yards into the light and he wondered what might happen if he were to step into it.

"You know," She began, not turning to meet his eyes, "these past few days have been some of my favorites. My whole life I had Phoebe to turn to... She... She forced me to grow up, having to shield her from the dangerous world outside. Richmond was there to protect us, but he always pestered me about destiny, my purpose, and my role as a Cleric. I knew all along. Ever since the first day, I knew I would never get to do things normal people do like go to a school, go eat at restaurants, or even fall in love."

Kale looked at her face, eyes widening.

She turned to him, smiling. "I didn't lie about loving you. You gave me everything I could never have, whether you knew it or not. I could tell deep down that you deserved to be forgiven. I didn't care where you came from, or what you were before you arrived at *Le Lien*, none of that mattered. I was simply thrilled to meet someone who didn't treat me like a precious thing."

Kale held her shoulders. "Why are you talking like that? We've got the whole world ahead of us! All you have to do is wish for it!"

She grabbed his face with cold fingers and pulled him in, meeting his lips with her own. She was trembling, and he began to feel a terrible sense of dread. The kiss lasted for a minute until she let go and turned back towards the light.

"My lie to you was that I knew I could never be free."

He stared at her. He didn't know what to do, how to feel, or what to say.

Astrid stepped into the light of The Well, casting her eyes over her shoulder. "Now, I'll make my wish." Her entire form began to glow, her skin, her clothes, and her shadow being consumed by gold. Her voice became harmonic, like those of many speaking at once. "My wish for the worl-"

The transponders beeped to life and Richmond's voice filled their minds.

[Raze it all to the ground! Destroy this city and all its citizens.]

Astrid's eyes grew wide and she opened her mouth to speak, turning back towards them in the light but he could no longer hear her.

Her golden figure reached for her head.

Kale turned around, to see Richmond's pale eyes boring into her, an untold fury on his face.

An intense rumbling began around them.

Something was stirring within The Well, a vitriolic reaction.

The wires, massive beyond imagination, started to ripple. Staggering pieces of the platforms cracked and fell into the crater of The Well's light.

Both men buckled under the quaking and struggled to stand upright.

"HEY!" Kale yelled, staring deep into the light. "WHAT'S HAPPENING?"

A hand stole Kale's shoulder.

"It's done." Richmond yanked him backward, sending him away from the light.

More pieces began to fall, opening sinkholes that led far into the earth.

Richmond turned away from The Well, searching for a means of escape and locating the sentinel some distance behind them. "If you don't want to die, come with me!"

"But... She's still in there!" A massive beam of light broke through the ground beside them, evaporating the metal around it. He yelled, rolling out of the way of newly formed cracks. The light was becoming volatile and sporadic. The Well pulsed with a newfound frenzy.

Richmond was fast at work restoring power to the sentinel which still kneeled offline. Sounds of systems whirring to life broke through the air and the sentinel's heavy metal clanged together. "The wish is made, Kale! It's over!"

"What are you talking about?!" He scrambled to gain a view of the girl within The Well. New bolts of destruction spouted around, one singing the edges off of his jacket and burning his skin. He clutched the injury and continued to look within. "We can't leave her!"

"She's a cleric! This was meant to happen!" The sentinel now stood promptly, synchronized to Richmond's movements. It reached a hand out toward the boy.

No... This isn't right! She never completed her wish... This isn't what she wanted... Did the transponder break her thoughts?

The sentinel marched over to where Kale stood and knelt beside him, exposing the inner hatch and Richmond behind the controls.

"You!" Kale's face grew infinitely pale. His black hair blew aside from the golden wind. "You caused this! When you spoke in the transponder, you made her wish for destruction!"

A terrible sight became apparent at the words.

A wild smile of teeth spread across Richmond's face and he began to snicker. "We won."

This… This can't be happening!

"No…" Kale stammered back, falling to his knees. "You knew she couldn't do it! That was your plan the whole time! You knew you could put that thought in her head when she made the wish!"

The scientist tilted his chin upward, staring down at Kale with disgust unlike any he'd seen before. "Why are you acting so pathetic now? I told you. I am ALWAYS prepared! I told you the day I met you what my vision for this world was and yet… here you are surprised that I brought it into being."

He looked, face agape at the twisted scientist before him. "That's not what she wanted! You mean you didn't trust her?!"

"I don't play games of trust!" Richmond slapped his chest, "I told you, I am the ONLY ONE who could topple this city and offer The Well's power to the world. Not you! Not Astrid! And *certainly* not a ragtag faction of delinquents."

Kale hesitated, almost being blown aside by the sheer power of The Well. "Are you really going to leave her?"

Richmond did not react to the statement. "Astrid's purpose is fulfilled."

Fear clenched his stomach. It was unbelievable. Here he was caught between two powers, the sinister revelation of the scientist's mind and the awesome strength of The Well and at that moment, he couldn't tell which was more dangerous.

The host continued to speak, rearing the sentinel to a position of readiness as the light of The Well expanded further. It would soon reach them. "You played your part well. Far better than I'd imagined for the price I paid. When we get out of here, I'll relay a message to your father. I'll inform him of the deal we had and I'm sure he'd take you back into the flock."

Kale couldn't tolerate the words he was hearing. He couldn't respond to them. He couldn't even rise to his feet. He glanced over his shoulder back to The Well, desperately trying to locate Astrid within the light.

He couldn't.

But without commanding his body to do so, he instinctively found himself reaching for his hip, gripping his pistol, and turning it to the marigold man before him.

Richmond's eyes stared down the green sights of the gun, unwavering and unflinching.

The words echoed in his mind:
You are the fledgling and I am the parent. If I die, you die. Our twin souls are eternally bound. Isn't that charming?

"I'm not leaving without her!"
Richmond scowled, staring down the threat. "How foolish you are."

Kale squeezed the trigger.

He braced himself, preparing for the recoil, but there was no blast. Instead, his body became paralyzed. A terrible pain erupted through his ribs. Lightning traveled through his veins like his blood had become fire and he found himself face down, tasting the dust of the ground. The pain was immeasurable, far greater than the first time he'd felt it. It was horrible like he'd been dropped into a pool of acid. He tried to scream, unable to even move his eyes. A ringing blasted his ears at a volume unbearable and as he began to lose consciousness, he felt cold steel grip his body and fleeting weightlessness as if he was flying.

The world that stretched out before him when he finally came to was one he recognized all too well but had never seen. Clouds of dust and dirt billowed all around. Hills of rolling soot rose and fell as far as the eye could see. There were no golden towers, no pellucid signs of advertisements, no webs of neon, and no entangled railways in the sky, but the light of The Well still dominated it all. It was different, however, the calm glow that he was accustomed to seeing every time he looked up now raged with pulsating agony. Between the golden rays, he noticed darker greys hiding in its depth. It didn't climb perfectly upward, but rather crackled in crooked offshoots like a tree that had been dead for many years.
"The world will now fall to chaos for a time."
Kale looked up. He found himself sitting in a dirty pile of rubble, a great distance from The Well. He was leaned against the greasy metal of the sentinel's foot and Richmond sat in the palm of its hand which had been lowered to an appropriate height for a human. There was a freezing breeze in the air and the host was holding a cigarette in his mouth, blowing puffs of smoke that caught on the current of the wind transporting the smell of nicotine into Kale's nose. His eyes stared dead ahead over the desolate wasteland.
Kale wrapped his arms around his knees. "I didn't know you smoked."

"Only in times of extreme distress." Richmond blew another cloud.

"Distress?" Kale could hardly temper the thought. "You won. You got everything you wanted. The Guiding City's in ruins. There are no more walls to keep people out."

Richmond took a deep inhale before responding. "My daughter is gone."

Kale felt his heart sink to his stomach.

There was an initial desire to lash out in rage. A quick, emotional irk to attack the inhumane scientist, to catch him in his hands and strangle his neck, to beat him with his fists, but when Kale stared at his own dirty hands, the feeling left and only dread remained.

"Why didn't you save her? We could have taken her with us…" The voice that left his mouth was hoarse and he could feel water building in his eyes.

Richmond leaned back into the sentinel's palm, staring up at the sky. "Kale, I solved the mysteries of The Well long ago. Once Astrid's clerical abilities were discovered I devoted myself entirely to understanding the properties of its light. The galvanic nature of its power was easy to unravel, it simply is infinite, end of story. But when I delved into the secrets of its interaction with life, the mysteries began to present themselves. You see, there is not a thing in this world that comes from nothing and so I proposed the question, 'why would this paracausal power grant so much to our world and ask nothing in return?' It was beyond my understanding. That was until I heard from my insider about the common understanding of Clerics. They give themselves to The Well's light, wishing for it to obey their desires. I realized the dark truth that I could never reveal to Astrid, that The Well is a well of souls and that a soul is the price of a wish."

"So you knew!? You knew that she would die and you lied… You killed her." He felt his lips tremble as the events connected in his mind.

The scientist turned to Kale, fury written in his eyes. "I thought you would understand by now. Men like us… Men of action… Men who have a higher calling for the world… We do not get to enjoy the luxuries of ordinary life. We *act* so that others can. You walked the path of ruin before you met me, swindling and stealing your way to profits, but I gave you absolution."

"Absolution? This sure looks a lot like hell."

"I fashioned you into something better. Now, you can look back on your actions with gratitude! You served the world."

All emotion left Kale when he heard the words. "That night, when I snuck into your lab, I told you I didn't want to serve the world. The world was nothing but cruel to me."

Richmond scoffed, muttering a curse beneath his breath. "Don't tell me you don't see it!" He waved his hands toward the desolate hellscape that remained in place of the Guiding City. Thousands upon thousands of slumdwellers were running towards The Well, bringing with them scraps of belongings on their backs. Kale could see the wicked smiles on their faces, the revelation that they could finally partake in The Well's blessings. Children and families ran together, and caravans of refugees congregated around the golden light. "Look at these people! What we've created here is a garden. We have tilled the soil, a foundation where the green shoots of hope may soon grow."

He scooped a handful of ash and dirt, letting it fall between his fingers. "I met good people while I was there. The Sympaths, Desmond, the guys from the rear reconnaissance unit, even an officer that was kind to me. Are they just… gone?"

The words did not penetrate the host's stoic expression. "The dead are raw materials. For a garden to thrive, the soil must be purified. That's all there is to it."

Kale pulled the hood of his coat over his head and sank into the shadow. "Was all this just an elaborate plot to get your revenge? I killed Phoebe… Now you've broken my heart…"

The host chuckled between exhales of smoke. "Revenge, eh..? I'd hardly considered it."

"You're a liar…"

Richmond leaned forward, tossing the cigarette from his hand into the ashy ground. "As I said, the world will now fall into a state of chaos. Millions will converge upon The Well to claim its power and advance humanity on a global scale. There will be wars, but a new future will blossom. There will be scientific breakthroughs. There will be new life, but there will never be a monopoly on this precious gift that was granted to our world. The Well will now be a beacon for all of humanity and if such an atrocity as the Guiding City emerges, then I will be there to wish for its destruction once again."

Printed in Great Britain
by Amazon